A THOUSAND PARDONS

a novel

Jonathan Dee

"That rare thing: a genuine literary thriller, with a trenchant, hilarious portrait of our collective longing for authenticity."
—Jennifer Egan, Pulitzer Prize–winning author of *A Visit from the Goon Squad*

PRAISE FOR *A Thousand Pardons*

"Graceful prose and such a sharp understanding of human weakness
that you'll wince as you laugh."   —*People*

"Dee is adept at meshing the complexities of marriage and family life
with the paradoxes of the zeitgeist. In his sixth meticulously lathed and
magnetizing novel, he riffs on the practice of crisis management. . . .
[and] nets the absurdities of a society geared to communicate in a
thousan[d]   er can
barely m   *Booklist*

"Propulsi[   ]illions

PRAISE FO

"Dee is   riously
funny. . .   bserved
dystopia[n   ]ty."
                                                             Review

"In the tr[   ]h with
greater k[   ]deeply
flawed ([a   ]ut. In
pitch-pe[r   ]t given
up on re[   ]entially
unfettere[   ]ly middle age,   lympus
itself an[d   ]on.
Dee has   but the
new Am[e   ]fe. *The
Privilege[s   ]twenty-

first century. Adam and Cynthia Morey finally resemble no one so much as ourselves."
—*Chicago Tribune*

"Savage satire . . . Dee is admirably relentless." —*The New Yorker*

"Scintillating . . . Dee is a remarkably skilled portraitist with a rare talent for rendering his characters' points of view with deep empathy."
—*The Washington Post*

"[A] transfixing account of the rise and rise of a 'charmed couple.' . . . Composed in Dee's typically elegant style—gorgeous, winding sentences."
—*Los Angeles Times*

"Dee's luminous prose never falters; he's a master."
—*Entertainment Weekly*

"[An] intelligent, glossy, moving depiction of the American superrich . . . extraordinarily beautiful." —*Financial Times*

"Invitingly told . . . Dee illustrates why indirection in this new-money morality tale can be so much more effective than a heavy hand. . . . [The characters] ought to be living out one of the bleak narrative prophecies of Richard Yates, whose piercingly astute writing Mr. Dee's own work has long resembled. . . . Big, busy and highly entertaining."
—*The New York Times*

"Dee has a great eye for detail, physical and emotional, and invites us to watch with eyes wide open as the Morey family sails past disaster into a future most people—until they read about such matters in novels as good as this—would think they would like to inhabit."
—Alan Cheuse, NPR

"Lucidly written and with a pitch-perfect ear for contemporary mores and dialogue, *The Privileges* is entertaining—and morally ambiguous." —*The Economist*

"Blends social commentary with psychological exploration . . . Dee has a gifted essayist's way with a phrase." —*The Seattle Times*

"Dee is a seamless writer . . . [He] never mocks his characters or subverts their charms. It's the [characters'] complexity that separates *The Privileges* from other novels that mine the same shimmering urban terrain." —*The Philadelphia Inquirer*

"Dee is a writer of skill and emotional depth . . . *The Privileges* should catapult him to darling status—deservedly . . . An electric, funny, tragic, loving tale." —*Time Out New York*

"Striking the right note for our times, Dee precisely captures the unethical world of a Manhattan hedge-fund manager, his disaffected daughter, and the glittering dangers of success." —*The Daily Beast*

"Dee notably spurns flat portraits of greed, instead letting the characters' self-awareness and self-forgetfulness stand on their own to create an appealing portrait of a world won by risk." —*Publishers Weekly*

"The novel goes down like a perfectly chilled glass of champagne—crisp, sparkling and delicious." —*Bookforum*

"Buoyant . . . thoughtful and bracingly unpredictable." —*Kirkus Reviews*

"Dee's achievement in *The Privileges* is the way he adeptly penetrates the mindset of these relentlessly narcissistic characters, giving us insight into what drives them in their need to acquire and dominate. It's hard to imagine anyone liking, or even sympathizing with, Adam and Cynthia, and yet Dee's discerning portrayal of their inner lives keeps the pages turning."   —*BookPage*

"Captivating [and] shrewdly realistic."   —Salon

"Dee breaks fresh artistic ground with the sheer beauty and quiet poignancy of his prose . . . A suspenseful, melancholy, and acidly funny tale about self, family, entitlement, and life's mysteries and inevitabilities."   —*Booklist*

"*The Privileges* is verbally brilliant, intellectually astute, and intricately knowing. It is also very funny and a great, great pleasure to read. Jonathan Dee is a wonderful writer."   —Richard Ford

"The subjects of money and class are seldom tackled head-on by our best literary minds, which is one of the reasons that Jonathan Dee's *The Privileges* is such an important and compelling work. *The Privileges* is a pitch-perfect evocation of a particular stratum of New York society as well as a moving meditation on family and romantic love. The tour de force first chapter alone is worth the price of admission."
—Jay McInerney

"*The Privileges* is an intimate portrait of a wealthy family that gradually becomes an indictment of an entire social class and historical moment, while also providing a window onto some recent, and peculiarly American, forms of decadence. Jonathan Dee is at once an acerbic social critic, an elegant stylist, and a shrewd observer of the human comedy."   —Tom Perrotta

"Mr. Dee has given us a cunning, seductive novel about the people we thought we'd all agreed to hate. His case study of American megawealth is delicious page by page and masterly in its balancing of sympathy and critical distance."   —Jonathan Franzen

"Here is an incredibly readable, intelligent, incisive portrait of a particular kind of American family. Dee takes us inside the world of what desire for wealth can do, and cannot do, for the self, the soul, and the family. The story is told with admirable conciseness and yet with great breadth, and the reader is swept along, watching the complications of such desire unfold."   —Elizabeth Strout

BY JONATHAN DEE

A Thousand Pardons
The Privileges
Palladio
St. Famous
The Liberty Campaign
The Lover of History

A THOUSAND PARDONS

Jonathan Dee

A THOUSAND PARDONS

A NOVEL

 RANDOM HOUSE TRADE PAPERBACKS | NEW YORK

2013 Random House Trade Paperback Edition

Published in the United States by Random House Trade Paperbacks, an imprint of The Random House Publishing Group, a division of Random House, Inc., New York.

RANDOM HOUSE and the HOUSE colophon are registered trademarks of Random House, Inc.

RANDOM HOUSE READER'S CIRCLE & Design is a registered trademark of Random House, Inc.

Originally published in hardcover in the United States by Random House, an imprint of The Random House Publishing Group, a division of Random House, Inc., in 2013.

The author gratefully acknowledges the assistance of the Guggenheim Foundation.

LIBRARY OF CONGRESS CATALOGING-IN-PUBLICATION DATA

Dee, Jonathan.
A thousand pardons : a novel / Jonathan Dee.
p.   cm.
ISBN 978-0-8129-8338-8
EBook ISBN 978-0-679-64500-9
1. Divorced women—Fiction. 2. Business women—Fiction.
3. Man-woman relationships—Fiction. 4. Corporations—Corrupt practices—Fiction. 5. Political corruption—Fiction. I. Title.
PS3554.E355T57 2012
813'.54—DC23   2012018513

Printed in the United States of America on acid-free paper

www.randomhousereaderscircle.com

9 8 7 6 5 4 3 2 1

Book design by Carole Lowenstein

A THOUSAND PARDONS

1

HELEN TRIED NOT TO LOOK AT HER WATCH, because looking at your watch never changed anything, but it was already a quarter to seven and her husband's headlights had yet to appear at the top of the hill. Evening had darkened to the point where she had to press her forehead to the kitchen window and frame her eyes with her hands just to see outside. Meadow Close was a dead end street, and so even if she couldn't make out the car itself, the moment she saw headlights of any kind cresting the hill there was a one in six chance they were Ben's. More like one in three, actually, because by turning her face a bit in the bowl of her hands she could see the Hugheses' car parked in their driveway, and the Griffins', and that obscene yellow Hummer that belonged to Dr. Parnell—

"Mom!" Sara yelled from the living room. "Can I have some more seltzer?"

Twelve was old enough to get your own fanny out of the chair and pour your own third glass of seltzer. But it was Tuesday, and on Tuesday evening guilt always ruled, which was why Sara was eating dinner in front of the TV in the first place, and so Helen said only, pointedly, "Please?"

"Please," Sara answered.

She couldn't help stealing a look at the kitchen clock as she closed the refrigerator door. Six-fifty. Mr. Passive Aggressive strikes again, she thought. She wasn't always confident she understood that expression correctly   passive aggressive—but she referred to it instinctively whenever Ben failed to do something he had promised her he would do.

Sara was sitting on the couch with her plate on her lap and her feet on the coffee table, watching some horrific show about rich girls; she still wore her shin guards but at least she'd remembered to take her cleats off. Helen placed the seltzer bottle on the table at a safe distance from her daughter's right foot.

"Thank you?" she said.

"Thank you," Sara repeated.

Then they both turned to watch a beam of light finish raking the kitchen, and a few seconds later Helen heard the lazy thump of a car door. Instead of relaxing, she grew more agitated. She hated to be late for things, and he knew that about her, or should have. Ben walked through the front door, wearing his slate-gray suit with an open collar and no tie. When he was preoccupied, which was his word for depressed, he had a habit of pulling off his tie in the car and then forgetting it there; last Sunday Helen, passing his Audi in the garage, had glanced through the window and seen three or four neckties slithering around on the passenger seat. It had sent a little shudder through her, though she didn't know why. His eyes moved indifferently from Sara to her dinner plate to the TV as he trudged past them toward the hallway, but his expression didn't change; he was sunk too deep in whatever he was sunk in even to make the effort to convey his disapproval. Helen followed him into their bedroom. He finished emptying his pockets onto the dresser and then turned toward her without a trace of engagement, as if she were trying to talk to a photo of him.

"We're late," she said.

He shrugged, but did not so much as consult the watch right there on his wrist. "So let's go," he said.

"You're not going to change?"

"What for?"

She rolled her eyes. "It's Date Night?" she said.

He scowled and started taking off his pants. Really, it was like having two adolescents in the house sometimes. So that he wouldn't lose focus—he was perfectly capable, these days, of sitting on the bed in his shorts with his lips moving silently for half an hour or more—she stood there and watched him pull on a clean sweater and a pair of pressed jeans. His hair still looked like he'd been driving with the top down, but whatever. That kind of detail Sara was very unlikely to notice. When he was done they marched back out through the living room and Helen grabbed her bag and kissed Sara on the top of her head.

"You can call either cell," she said. "We'll be back by eight thirty. You know the drill."

On the television a girl and her father appeared to be auditioning a group of male strippers. "Happy Date Night," Sara said in a deep voice meant to sound hickish or retarded, and with one finger she mimed inducing herself to vomit.

They took Ben's car because it was still in the driveway. Helen tossed his necktie onto the back seat. He drove too fast, but only because he always drove too fast, and they were ten minutes late for Dr. Becket. Not that Becket seemed to care. Why would she? She got paid for the hour either way. So if she doesn't mind, Helen thought as they took their seats at the threadbare arms of the couch, and Ben doesn't mind, then why am I the only one who minds? What is the matter with me?

"So how was your week?" Becket said. She wore her hair in a tight gray braid whose teardrop-shaped bottom was nearly white. The office was in the rear section of an old carriage house that had long ago been converted for commercial use by a real estate broker, who operated out of the half of the house that faced the road and rented out the back. Fourteen years ago, when they were trying to make themselves look stabler and more prosperous for the insanely superficial Chinese adoption agencies, Helen and Ben had bought the Meadow Close house from that very broker. Now it was night and the only light on in the house was Dr. Becket's. Where was her husband? What did her kids do when she worked nights? Helen didn't always feel that certain about her, but unless you wanted to drive all the way to White Plains and back, Dr. Becket was the only game in town.

"Maybe a little better," Helen answered, when it became apparent Ben wasn't going to say anything. It was a lie, but in the atmosphere of this sorry room the truth was generally something you had to work up to. "We tried some of the things you suggested last time. We tried to at least sit down for meals together, even though that's difficult with Ben working past seven most nights."

"I know a number of couples," Becket said, "find that it works well to set aside one night a week for spending that kind of time together, make it part of the schedule rather than subject to the schedule, if you see what I mean. Like a Date Night." They both snorted, and it gave Helen a little nostalgic pang, honestly, just for the two of them to laugh at the same thing, at the same time. Becket raised her eyebrows, with her typical maddening dispassion.

"We can't really use that one," Helen explained. "We've been telling Sara that we're on Date Night every week when we come here."

"Maybe we can tell her that Thursday is our night to date other people," Ben said.

"That's not really that funny," Helen said, but it was too late, Becket was leaning forward, sinking her teeth into it like she did into any stupid, spontaneous thing either of them might ever blurt out. "I'm curious why you say that, Ben," she purred. "Is that something you'd like to do? See other people?"

Helen closed her eyes. Dr. Becket was just confirming every stereotype Ben held of her, every complaint he went through on the drive home every week about how she was a huckster, a charlatan, who didn't do anything except repeat whatever you said to her and then ask you what it meant. Why are we even doing this? he would ask. What is the point? Because you had to do something: she had no better answer than that, which was why she usually delivered it silently. You had to try something, even something as wasteful and frustrating and demeaning as this weekly hour in the back of the carriage house, because to do nothing was to find it acceptable that you were in a marriage where you hardly spoke to or touched each other, where your husband was so depressed he was like the walking dead and yet the solipsism of his depression only made you feel cheated and angry, and your daughter was old enough now that none of this was lost on her whether she knew it yet or not.

But now thirty seconds had gone by and Helen hadn't heard him say anything or even make some kind of immature, derisive sighing sound, as he usually did; and when she opened her eyes again and looked at him, what she saw, to her astonishment, was her husband wiping his eyes with the back of his hand like a child.

"Yes," he said. "Yes. I mean Jesus. I would love to see other people."

Which could only be followed by a momentous silence; but since silence was anathema to Dr. Becket, on the grounds that silence might belong to anyone but vapid professional jargon was something that could bear her own distinctive stamp, she said to him, "Stay with that."

"Not anybody in particular," he went on. "In fact, a stranger would be best. I would like to wake up tomorrow next to someone who has no idea who I am. I would like to look out the window and not recognize anything. I would like to look in the fucking *mirror*," he said with a truly inappropriate laugh, "and see other people. I mean, I cannot be the only person who feels that way. Are you seriously telling me that you don't feel that way too?"

It wasn't clear which of them he was speaking to; he was staring at the carpet, tears hanging from his nose, and stressing certain words with a kind of karate-chop motion of his hands.

"Helen, what are you feeling right now?" Dr. Becket said.

Ben was right, she thought; it was all an act, the gray-haired old fake maintained an air of smug control even though she had no better idea what the hell was happening in front of her than either of her patients did. "A lot of things," Helen said, trying to laugh. "I guess mostly that that is the longest I have heard him talk at one stretch in like a month."

"Because it's all so *unsurprising*," Ben said, very much as if he hadn't heard anyone else's voice. "I'm scared of it. I'm scared of every single element of my day. Every meal I eat, every client I see, every time I get into or out of the car. It all frightens the shit out of me. Have you ever been so bored by yourself that you are literally terrified? That is what it's like for me every day. That is what it's like for me sitting here, right now, right this second. It's like a fucking death sentence, coming back to that house every night. I mean, no offense."

"No *offense*?" Helen said.

"It's not that Helen herself is especially boring, I don't mean that, or that some other woman might be more or less boring. It's the situation. It's the setup. It's not you per se."

"Oh, thank you so much," Helen said, her heart pounding.

"Every day is a day wasted, and you know you only get so many of them and no more, and if anybody uses the phrase 'midlife crisis' right now I swear to God I am coming back here with a gun and shooting this place up like Columbine. It is an existential crisis. Every day is unique and zero-sum and when it is over you will never get it back, and in spite of that, *in spite of that*, when every day begins I know for a fact that I have lived it before, I have lived the day to come already. And yet I'm scared of dying. What kind of fucking sense does that make? I don't think I am too good for it all, by the way. In fact I am probably not good enough for it, if you want to think of it like that. I am bored to near panic by my home and my work and my wife and my daughter. Think that makes me feel superior? But once you see how rote and lifeless it all is, you can't just unsee it, that's the thing. I even got Parnell across the street to write me a prescription for Lexapro, did you know that?" He finally looked up at Helen, whose hand was over her mouth, as if miming for him what she wanted him to do, to stop talking, to turn back. "Of course you didn't know that, how would you know that. Anyway, I took it for two months, and you know what? It didn't make the slightest fucking difference in how I feel about anything. And I'm glad."

Helen stole a glance at Becket, who was sitting forward with her fingers steepled under her weak chin. She could not have looked more pleased with herself.

"Something's got to give," Ben said. He sounded tired all of a sudden, as if the act of denouncing his wife and child and the whole life they had led together had taken a lot out of him. Poor baby, Helen thought hatefully. "Something's got to *happen*. It is hard to get outside yourself. It's hard to get outside the boundaries of who you are. Why is that so hard? But the pressure just builds up until there's some kind of combustion, I guess, and if it doesn't kill you then maybe it throws you clear of everything, of who you are. Well, either way. I suppose that's how it works."

He sat back into the couch, the same couch where his wife sat, and within half a minute he had disappeared again, his face had resolved into the same zombie cast Helen had been looking at for a year now, two years maybe, without ever really guessing what was going on behind it.

"I know it may seem painful," Becket said, "but I think we have really, really given ourselves something to build on here tonight."

He drove them back home, because it was his car, even though she was newly afraid he would just run them into a tree or a lamppost if he saw the opportunity. In fact, she kind of wondered why he didn't. When they reached the top of the hill and came in view of their house, where every light was burning, he broke the silence by saying gently, "Can we at least agree that we are never going back to that heinous cunt's little office again?"

"Absolutely," Helen said. The end of Date Night.

The darkness made the thin ranks of trees at the end of their property line—this early in the spring, you could still see right through them to the back of the water treatment plant—look deep as a forest. He walked ahead of her through the vestibule and turned left into the kitchen to pull the cork out of the bourbon. Sara was in her room with the door closed; her light was still on and the tapping of her keyboard faintly audible, which meant either that she was doing homework or that she was not. Helen wanted to go in but knew she probably couldn't look into her daughter's face just then without crying; so she stood there in the hallway, her shoulder against the wall beside the door, and listened to the inscrutable tap of the keys. Back in the living room, she heard the television click on.

She knew what the right thing to do was. Dismantle it together: help him find a new place, work out the money, sign whatever needed to be signed, put on a united front for poor Sara, who'd already had two parents abandon her, after all. But for once in her life Helen didn't want to do it. Why should she make even this easy for him? She'd made everything easy for him for eighteen years, and he repaid her by making an explosive, weepy public display of his horror at the very sight of her. Screw the right thing. If he hated her so much, if life with her was such a death sentence, then let's see him be a man about it, for once, and devise his own escape.

SHE DIDN'T HAVE TO WAIT LONG. Every June, a new crop of summer associates arrived at Ben's law firm in the city for their strange audition. They were given a modicum of real work, though everyone knew and even joked about the fact that this was an extended bait and switch and that if they were lucky enough to be hired full-time they would then be worked as remorselessly as rented mules. It was really an audition for the lifestyle, for their receptivity to perks. They came from Harvard and Michigan and Stanford; they were young and obedient and performed simple tasks in a sportsmanlike way and were then sent out into the night with free passes and the account number of a car service and a sense of coming into their inheritance as dauphins of privilege.

They were at the very bloom of everything for which they felt destined and everything that others would begrudge them, at the very instant of life that a certain type of old hedonist would look back on and wish could have been arrested forever, and one of them, a short, blond, gregarious, almost comically well-built second-year from Duke named Cornelia Hewitt, attracted Ben's attention. He asked to have her assigned to a simple probate case he was working on—it was customary for junior partners to request summer associates based on nothing more than could be gleaned about them from seeing them walk past one's open office door—and by the Fourth of July he had lost his composure to the point where one or two of his fellow partners took him aside, not in any official capacity of course, and advised him to cool it. He could not have cared less; or, to the extent that he did care about potential risk to himself or to the firm, such concerns were powerless against what was driving him. He took Cornelia out to lunch almost every day; he even called her in to work on weekends, which was unprecedented, but in order to be near her there was nothing at Ben's disposal he was unwilling to use. He had a photocopy of her personnel file hidden under the driver's seat of his car.

Cornelia was uncertain how to play it. There had to be an advantage in exciting this kind of intense personal interest from a partner, even if she wasn't sure what sort of advantage; the specifics were hazy, but there was something elemental about it that seemed as though it should be quite clear. She was smart enough to know that the woman tended to get blamed in the end, in these types of situations, if things went too far. She was always searching for a line in her dealings with him, a line where propriety met savvy, both when others were in the room and when they weren't. For Ben's part, watching her struggle to find that line, to figure out in this new adult context what consequences of her own allure she was or wasn't in control of—struggle with woman-hood, in a way—was intoxicating. He began texting her, and calling her on her cell if she didn't respond to the texts, and when the summer was half over, when he began to sense that this whole infatuation was like his life in miniature in that the opportunity to act transcendently was now drifting away from him, he told her that he had fallen in love with her.

Actually, what he told her was that if he didn't have sex with her very soon he was going to die. The rest was implicit. Once he declared himself, once he had renounced for good any claim to ambiguity, legal or otherwise, Cornelia felt the power in the relationship, which up to that point had seemed fluid, shift decisively onto her side, and that was when she really grew interested—if not in taking things to any sort of next level with this old married man, then at least in the potential of his agonizing status quo. By now most of her fellow associates had stopped speaking to her. She grew curious about the limits of what she, in her apparent irresistibility, could get this man—forty-five, previously digni-fied, successful in precisely the way she planned to be, an emotional slave to his lust for her—to do, and in what that might let slip about her future in her chosen field.

She stopped evading his casual touches, stopped hanging up on him when his descriptions of specific longings went past the point of self-restraint. She was not sure whether his complete loss of decorum meant that she would be hired by the firm for sure or that there was no chance in hell they would let her back in the building once her sum-mer contract expired; but by now it had all become an experiment for its own sake, a sustaining of certain emotional inequities in the pursuit of knowledge about the way the world worked and where the best available seat in it might be. A woman of her gifts, she reassured herself, would get hired somewhere. Oddly, Ben realized at a certain point, without the realization slowing him down at all, that while he was irredeemably in love with her, he didn't really like her all that much. But he seemed to have decided that the only way to go out was to go out as a fool, an antagonist, exciting the crowd's derision, because having your cock in the mouth of a gorgeous young girl was the only tolerable state of being he could imagine anymore, and was worth anything the cowardly circle of his peers could throw at him.

Helen had no inkling of any of it, but it would be unjust to conclude that she was stupid or oblivious or in some sort of denial. She didn't miss the signs, because from her perspective—seeing her husband only in the half hour before he slipped out the door in the morning, or in the hour between his arrival at home at night and his climbing into bed after three bourbons and turning out the light—there were no signs to miss. All was as it had been for some time. If he seemed a little more euphoric in the mornings, in a little more of a hurry to drink his coffee and knot his tie and get into the car and drive away from there, she read that only as a reflection of his feelings toward her: he was driving away from something, that is, not toward something else. Conversely, the long drive home up the Saw Mill at night seemed to drain all the dark exuberance right out of him, and when he came through the door there was nothing about his blank face and flat voice that was in any way unfamiliar. What weighed on her most was how poor a father Ben had become. The crazy bored rictus of a smile he wore whenever Sara talked to him was something Sara herself must surely have noticed, or felt. This made Helen sadder than anything else. She couldn't really remember anymore, except in a sort of evidentiary sense, a time when things had been better between herself and her husband, but she remembered piercingly how good they used to be between father and child.

For five days running, in August, Ben rented a room at the Hudson Hotel in the hopes that he could talk Cornelia into going there with him. He had not seen it. All week, each time they were alone, he would remind her that the room waited there, empty and expensive, just for them, and would continue to wait there until she said yes to him.

On Friday, in a sort of invocation of Zeno's paradox, she concluded that she could say yes to him without breaking, either explicitly or in her heart, her vow not to let him have sex with her. At four o'clock he called the car service and the two of them rode in air-conditioned silence up to West Fifty-eighth Street. Ben was shivering. The people who flowed around the windows at every red light passed by as silently and impotently as ghosts; though in another way, Ben thought, he himself was the ghost, for they searched malevolently for him from their side of the smoked glass but still could not see his face. In the elevator at the Hudson he stood gallantly behind her and silently checked out the smooth skin rounding her shoulders, the patch of neck beneath her upswept hair, the incomparable, exaggerated heart of her ass, the legs in high heels that still brought her head up only to the level of his chin. The room was not the nicest in the hotel; it had, in full accord with his imaginings, a vast bed in it, and a shuttered window, and very little else. He sat in its one chair and stared at Cornelia as she stood in the narrow space between the foot of the bed and her own reflection in the dark screen of the television.

"We are not going to have sex, Ben," she said.

"All right," Ben said. He continued to stare, not in an effort to demean or unsettle her but almost as if he believed she did not even know he was there. After half a minute, the impatience of youth got the best of her, as he had guessed it would.

"Well then why did we come here?" she said. "What did you imagine would happen? Did you get what you wanted?"

"Take off your clothes," he said.

"What?"

"Take off all of your clothes, and just stand there and let me look at you. That will be enough." Who knows, he thought, maybe it will be enough. Probably not, though.

"Like hell," Cornelia said. "You'll jump me."

"I promise you I will not."

"I may be small but I can defend myself."

"It's the furthest thing from my mind."

"You'd just sit there in that chair and not get up?"

"I will. You there, me here."

"For how long?"

He considered it. "I don't know," he said. "Until whatever happens next happens, I guess."

She tried to think of it from every angle. If she couldn't come up with some good reason not to take him at his word, she was in danger of becoming a little aroused by the idea. Just the sight of her. Just the sight of her would be enough for him. No harm, no foul. She had always enjoyed the sensation of being admired, and though opportunities to let men admire her had never been in short supply, something about the sight of Ben, sitting patiently in the stiff-backed hotel chair in his tan summer suit, impressed on her that it would not be this way forever.

"You're not going to pull your dick out and start masturbating?" she said.

"Please," he said. "Who do you think I am?"

She stepped out of her heels, and when she straightened up again she was three inches closer to the floor. She had a boyfriend, a large, servile, sullen former lacrosse captain whom she'd dated since college, when she was a sophomore and he was a senior. Over the past two years they had seen little of each other, mostly on weekends when one or the other of them could afford to travel, because she'd been in Durham; but when she came for her summer in New York, where he was already living while working as a junior analyst at Bank of America, it seemed only logical, not to mention kindly optimistic, for the two of them to share his apartment in Fort Greene. It had not gone all that well, in her mind at least, but that didn't mean she was going to cheat on him. He knew all, or most, about the texts and the cellphone calls from her boss. It would matter to Cornelia that standing frankly in the nude in a hotel room for ten minutes or half an hour, while one of the junior partners looked at her with actual tears running down his face, emphatically did not fall into the category of having sex with, or even being touched by, another man. She unzipped her dress, not slowly or provocatively, and when it fell to the floor she picked it up and laid it carefully along the foot of the bed, smoothing it with her hands. Her bra left red lines under her breasts and along the smooth skin below her arms; Ben stared at those lines as they faded away to nothing and felt as if he had triumphed over time. The bounty of her seemed endless. She took off her simple panties, and he saw that she had shaved her pubic hair, not completely but down to a small strip, as they all seemed to do these days, because it was beautiful that way. What a wonderful world, he thought, where women will do something so difficult and intimate and utterly pointless just for the sake of beauty. What a blessing to be a man in it.

"Okay?" Cornelia said finally, resisting the urge to fold her arms over her breasts.

He tried to speak but could not, so instead he nodded and smiled. It was a sad folly, he knew, to assume that even this feeling, the most powerful he could remember, wouldn't weaken in time just like every other feeling; but for the moment he was so suffused with gratitude for living that he could not imagine ever feeling any other way.

When she was dressed again he stood and opened the door for her, and there on the threshold—in no way out of breath, but rather as if he had been standing there for quite some time—was Cornelia's boyfriend. Ben heard Cornelia gasp before he actually saw the boy (he was looking at her ass again, and thinking about the difference between imagining what it looked like unclothed and remembering it) and he lifted his head just in time to receive the first blow right on the mouth. It was like being kicked by a horse. He couldn't believe how much force was behind it. He intuited what was happening, mostly from the quality of Cornelia's screams—she was trying to control the young man rather than plead with him—even though he'd had no idea there was any sort of boyfriend in the picture at all. He didn't appear in Cornelia's personnel file. His name, evidently, was Andy. Ben dropped to his knees and then felt a kind of splintering in the area of his nose before everything went white. The blows were all just one blow for a while, and then they had stopped. "No police," he mumbled in a voice that didn't sound like his own voice at all, and he opened one eye and saw that there was no one there to hear him anyway; the corridor he viewed sideways from his prone position on the carpeted floor was empty, and both Cornelia and his young assailant were gone.

His first thought, naturally, was to go back into the room, which was paid for. But the key card was not in his pocket. It was entirely possible that he had forgotten it on the dresser, or even that he had left it there on purpose since he'd thought they were checking out. It seemed too long ago to remember now. Avoiding all mirrors, he rode down to the lobby, bulled his way through the horrified stares of strangers and bellhops in the lobby, and ordered the doorman to get him a cab.

"Sir?" was all the doorman was able to say.

Ben gave up and barged past him, head down, into the back seat of the first cab he saw. "Thirty-eighth and Tenth," he said. The cabbie was one of those who spent his whole shift talking incomprehensibly into a hands-free cellphone. He might have had Bigfoot in his back seat for all he knew or cared. Ben smiled, and immediately wished he hadn't. Something was broken in there, or if not broken, then way too loose.

The parking garage attendant at Thirty-eighth and Tenth was someone Ben had spoken to five afternoons a week for the last four years, and so the quality of the man's reaction gave Ben a little bit better idea just how bad he must have looked. His lapels and shirtfront were brown with blood, that much he could see, but his new face was still a mystery to him. The attendant—Ben had tipped him a hundred bucks last Christmas but was suddenly unable to remember his name—stood there like a statue, pale and terrified, even though Ben's mere presence should have made the fact that he wanted his car crystal clear without any further instruction. But the man's fear of him brought home to Ben that his spectacularly fallen condition, paradoxically, lent him a certain fleeting authority, a license to say anything, and that gave him an idea. He pulled out his wallet and gave the attendant—Boris! that was the name—two fifties.

"Boris, my man, go across the street," he said as clearly and haughtily as he could, pointing to the liquor store directly across Tenth Avenue from the garage, "and buy me a liter bottle of Knob Creek bourbon. If they don't have the Knob Creek, then Maker's Mark."

And Boris did it, if only to get away from the bloodstained arm around his shoulders. When he returned, Ben took the bag from him and made an extravagant gesture of impatience, as if to say, And where the fuck is my car? Once that was accomplished, Ben climbed in and shut the door, stuck the bottle between his thighs and uncorked it, and began, for the very last time, his nightly commute home to Rensselaer Valley.

He never made it, though he did get as far as County Route 55 just four and a half miles from his house, which under the circumstances was an impressive enough achievement. The trip from West Thirty-eighth Street to Meadow Close should have taken two hours at most; the extra hours were something Ben was completely unable to account for, and no one else ever came forward to do so either. Possibly he was just driving and drinking. The police, called by Helen after she was called by the senior partner at Ben's firm, were not the first to find him; an early-morning cyclist came across Ben's Audi just after dawn, lights on, windows down, having drifted to a stop half in the roadway and half on the shoulder. The fuel gauge was well below E. Ben's breathing was shallow and rapid, and he was lying on his right side across the front seat. He did not respond when spoken to, or when shaken squeamishly by the ankle. The cyclist pulled out his cellphone and dialed 911. He thought he probably ought to wait for the police or the ambulance to arrive, just in case anybody had any questions. He lifted his chin and turned his head, but he heard no sirens, only a light wind moving the leaves. Then he held up his phone again and took some pictures with it.

Ben's unresponsive state was the work more of the bourbon than of his head injuries, though the swelling caused by the latter made things difficult for the paramedics at first. But though it was touch and go in the hours after he was found, in less than a week Ben had stabilized to the point where he was cleared to return home, pending arraignment. For by then criminal charges had been brought against him, and not just a DWI, which by itself might have been felonious enough to threaten his career. Instead, two detectives drove up from Manhattan to stand beside his hospital bed and arrest him for attempted sexual assault. He was so surprised he thought maybe it was just the morphine, but when he asked one of the floor nurses the next day if all that had really happened, she tightened her lips and nodded. Cornelia, Cornelia, he thought. Maybe she really was that ruthless about getting where she was going; or maybe she was that scared of the psychotic boy-giant who apparently considered her his own. Either way, he realized, he was now out in the open water, and he had gone all that way for her sake without ever having the first clue who she was.

Helen didn't even want to let him come home from the hospital, but he was so weak and in so much pain—these days hospitals turned you out pretty much the moment they felt they could do so without killing you—that she caved. Still, she couldn't believe how little sympathy she felt for him. Eighteen years. At night she left the Vicodin and a glass of water by his bedside and went to the living room to sleep on the couch. Sara came out of her room only for meals; school started in less than two weeks. Their phones were all turned off. By the middle of each afternoon Helen longed frantically to get out of the house and just be somewhere else, even for an hour, but she was scared to leave Sara alone with her father and more scared to leave Ben alone by himself. She sat in the kitchen and watched for strange cars through the blinds.

Any old-fashioned hope that this was the sort of indiscretion powerful men might cause to disappear was undone by the camera-phone photos, which were all over the Web in a day, and in the newspapers the day after that. A letter of resignation, which Ben signed, had been brought to him in the hospital. His former partners then let him know, via registered letter, that, in an effort to send the message that they did not condone his behavior, they had filed disbarment proceedings against him as well; they had no real grounds to do so, but just knowing they considered their reputation damaged enough to care about the symbolism of filing was chilling to him. He had a few acquaintances who were litigators at rival firms, but even those who returned his phone calls wouldn't take his case. With a bail hearing imminent, it didn't seem like a great idea to represent himself. In the end he had to settle for a lawyer right there in Rensselaer Valley—the only one in town, in fact—who insisted on a large cash retainer because, as he said to Ben and Helen while drinking a cup of take-out coffee in his second-floor office above the hardware store, he wasn't at all sure that when everything was said and done they would have a cent left to pay him.

"If it's as hopeless as all that," Helen asked the lawyer, whose name was Joe Bonifacio, "then what do you suggest we do?"

"Two things," said Bonifacio. He must have been around the same age as Helen and Ben, sallow and sharp-eyed, and dressed as if for yard work; though he was polite and engaged, she couldn't help feeling there was something obligatory, something ginned up, about his interest in them. You'd have thought he saw a case like this every day. He had apparently spent his whole life, apart from college and law school, right there in Rensselaer Valley, which made it remarkable that Helen couldn't remember ever seeing him before. "One, Ben, we have to start to lay the groundwork for the idea that you are not responsible for your actions, that they were committed in an altered state. You admit nothing, you apologize for nothing. Let me ask you this: had you been under any particular stress in the weeks or months leading up to the incident in question?"

"No," said Ben.

"Yes," said Helen, looking at her husband in amazement. "Yes, he was. He was emotionally unstable. We have a doctor who will surely testify to that. Well, not a doctor, really, but close enough."

"Stop it," Ben said coolly to her. "I don't want to be a coward now. Let it fall on me. If I'm going out, I don't want to go out as one of those guys claiming he's not responsible for his actions."

Which Helen actually found somewhat moving, insofar as she could be moved by anything to do with Ben these days; but when she looked over at Bonifacio, he wore a smirk like he was enjoying a bad TV show. How he must have hated guys like Ben, Helen thought—lawyers who rode off to Manhattan every morning while he climbed the stairs beside the hardware store and tried to act outraged over whatever sad grievance one of the locals might bring in.

"Here's the thing to remember, though, Ben," he said. "It doesn't all fall on you. If you want to go the noble route, while you're off in jail writing your memoirs or whatever, your wife and your daughter will be put out of their house, and any money you have anywhere will be taken away from them faster than you can say 'mea maxima culpa,' all right? Now I am sure you would like to avoid their having to suffer for your sins any more than absolutely necessary, and if you want to avoid that, or at least negotiate it, the only way to do so is to find a way to contest the idea of your guilt."

Ben's response was an acquiescent sigh. His usual practice was trusts and estates, but at bottom, Helen saw, both men were lawyers, and shared an acceptance of the immutable truth of what Bonifacio was saying.

"So here's what we do. Ben will be voluntarily committed to an institution in Danbury called Stages, maybe you've heard of it, where he will be treated for his chronic depression, bipolar syndrome, attention deficit disorder, panic attacks, alcoholism —"

"I don't really have a drinking problem," Ben said.

"Did I ask you if you did?" said Bonifacio, not unkindly. "You'll recall I said there are two things you need to do, and that's number one. Now, as to the rape charge." Helen winced but did not correct him. "It's my opinion that they know there's no there there, in terms of evidence, and that their plan is to withdraw the charge before trial no matter what. They just threw it because they know that you'll never get the stink of it off you. And the reason that's smart, as I'm sure Ben has figured out, is that it softens the ground for the civil case, which in my opinion is where this whole flaming bag of poo has been aimed from the beginning. We have to start insulating you against that judgment as best we can, and we have to start today. So forgive me if I seem to overstep my bounds here, but thing two, Helen, is that you file for divorce immediately, on grounds of infidelity. Ben will not contest it."

Ben frowned. "Does it have to be infidelity, though?" he said. "Because, not to get all Talmudic about it, but, as Helen knows, I was not actually, literally unfaithful to her."

"As Helen knows?" Helen said. "What the hell do I know about anything? I only know what you say."

"It's the truth," Ben said. "No reason to lie anymore."

"If I may," Bonifacio said, tossing his Starbucks cup in the waste-basket behind his chair. "The two of you are straying down a path which, while of course I understand and sympathize, is not really con-structive to our purpose. You're getting worked up about how to know the difference between what appears true versus what is true. You might as well forget about all that for a while. Everything you say or do now, no matter how intimate, is being performed for an audience, namely the jury pool here in town and in the rest of the circuit. It would be good for you to get used to that as quickly as possible."

"Look," Ben said weakly; Helen could see he was tiring. "I know this isn't a very lawyerly thing to propose, but just in terms of, as you say, softening the ground, I think if you could just get me in a room with her—"

Bonifacio was already shaking his head. "If what you want is to let everyone know how sorry you are," he said, "then good luck, God bless, and get yourself a new lawyer. But I'll tell you what I will do. Since you seem to need to get it out of your system like that, why don't you say you're sorry right now?"

"Right now?" said Ben.

"Right here and now. And then never again."

Ben looked down at the floor, and then, with great difficulty, at his wife. He did seem changed, Helen thought, but only in a kind of ani-mal way, wounded and in pain and without his usual instincts. "Please believe me," he said to her. "Even though I don't necessarily under-stand everything I've done, I take total responsibility for it. You and Sara don't deserve any of this. I am so sorry."

"I don't know why," Helen said quickly. "You got what you wanted. It's all destroyed now. I don't know why you don't go back to the house and put up a big Mission Accomplished banner."

"Feel better now?" said Bonifacio. "I didn't think so. Still, if you get the urge again, you can repeat as necessary. Just as long as it's always in this office, and always in front of me."

Helen drove home (Ben's license was now suspended) faster than she liked; she wanted to beat the school bus and be home when Sara arrived, and also to minimize the time spent near him. Ben asked to speak to Sara alone when she got home, and Helen almost agreed to it, just to spare herself the guilt and agony of seeing her daughter's face at the climactic moment of their betrayal of her, a betrayal the girl might have seen coming years ago if she hadn't been so young, too young to anticipate or even, very likely, to imagine it. But it had to be borne, for her sake. Sara didn't cry; instead she withdrew solemnly, deep inside herself, nodding at all the appropriate times, her face a mask, never once contradicting or mocking them, as she would have done in almost any other sort of conversation. Then she went into her room and closed the door and played music (nothing sad or angry, just the same pop music she always played) while Ben packed his suitcase to check in to Stages, and Helen sat in the kitchen and her anger gave way to a meditation on her own role in having failed to prevent the end of life as they had all known it up to now.

For the next few weeks, everywhere she went—which, she realized with the sad, clear vision brought on by misfortune, wasn't really that many places (the Starbucks, the Price Chopper, the middle school, the dry cleaner, the dump)—her neighbors and casual friends pretended not to see her, or to be busily on their way elsewhere across the street, not because they condemned or looked down on her but because the level of disgrace she'd been subjected to was so epic that they weren't even sure how to acknowledge it and thus how to talk to her in the way that they used to. Only her closest friends made a show of everything being just as it was before, which was worse, in a way. There was now an element of performance to their friendship, even when no one else was around to see or be upbraided by their example, which brought home to Helen that it was really themselves these friends were performing for—burnishing their estimation of themselves as people who would not abandon an unjustly scandalized friend.

And in truth it was that notion of herself as a victim that put Helen off too, that made her come up with excuses when friends called to invite her forcefully to lunch or to ostentatiously offer her a ride to the next Parents' Coffee at school. She had genuinely no idea of the depths to which her husband had been descending over that summer, but did that exonerate her—having no idea? It had been well over a decade since she'd had any job other than to maintain a happy home and family environment for their only child, and she had failed at that job rather decisively. So spectacular was her failure that the mushroom cloud over her happy home environment was featured in the newspaper every day for a week, not just at home in Rensselaer Valley, where there was never much going on, but even in Manhattan, where the destruction of some rich Brahmin at the hands of his own perverse compulsions was always a tabloid chestnut.

Every day was a limbo, in which the house—a white, weathered, green-shuttered ranch with a finished basement, which everyone always said was more spacious inside than it looked from the outside—served as both prison and fortress. Ben had not contacted his wife and daughter since passing through the doors of Stages—quite likely he was forbidden to, for a while anyway, according to some twelve-step protocol—and Helen made no attempt to contact him. Though they'd never discussed it, or even said goodbye, it would not have surprised her terribly if she never saw him again. When eighth grade began for Sara a week or so after his departure, it was still much too soon for anyone there to have forgotten anything; at the end of the first day Helen asked her how it had gone, seeing her classmates again, and Sara gave the worst, most distressing answer possible, which was that she didn't want to talk about it.

Then there was the question of money. It hadn't disappeared, exactly, but it was hard to trust that the seventy-five thousand posted for bail would ever grace their account again; and then a Manhattan judge, at the request of Cornelia's lawyers, had taken the extraordinary step of freezing all of Ben's assets, including the house, which prevented them from selling it, for financial or any other reasons. The lawyers argued that Helen and Ben's pending divorce action was nothing more than a cynical attempt to shield themselves from future civil liability, and the judge, without deigning to ask Helen or anyone who knew her whether she was the sort of person who would break up her child's home as a legal maneuver, agreed. Stages cost $850 a day, and there was no timetable for Ben's discharge. Bonifacio's retainer was sixty-two thousand dollars. Helen had a checking account with about eight grand left in it. Her life was such that her only expenses were food and gas, but still.

She would have to go back to work, and she had to do it somewhere other than Rensselaer Valley, because there were no jobs there outside the service industries and because they needed a fresh start anyway, out from under the dark umbrella Ben's madness had opened up above their lives. They needed to begin again. It was just the two of them now. Helen thought about returning to Manhattan after fourteen years and permitted herself to get a little excited, despite the fact that her previous, and really only, job experience had been as a sales manager at Ralph Lauren, a job she'd quit during her second pregnancy when a doctor had consigned her to bed. She had little sense of how employable she might now be in the city (or anywhere else, really), and so she decided to set up a few exploratory interviews. On a Monday morning in mid-September she dropped her daughter, sad and stoic, outside the front doors of the junior high school, then sped home, changed into a suit, and drove herself to the train station.

It had been a long time since she'd held a salaried job. Not that she'd been idle all these years; on the contrary, being a young, bright housewife of means in a community like Rensselaer Valley meant that your commitments gradually expanded to fill your days and then some. People found you; they called you up and invited themselves over on behalf of an array of local organizations: the elementary school, the library, the pool club, the book club, the Democratic Town Committee. She'd even written some stories for the local weekly. All that, of course, was shot to hell now, less by scandal than by the toxicity of pity. Helen had four interviews lined up for today and high hopes for none of them. She was forty-three and had had to go online to learn how to put together a decent-looking CV. No one to help her with that stuff now, and only herself to help Sara with it when the time came. Helen took a deep breath and shook herself to ward off the pessimism she felt settling over her. The train, after all, was full, even though it was past the start of the workday. All these people were headed to the city, yet none of them, or very few, could have had the pretext of a nine-to-five job there. So she wasn't alone. There were plenty of others in the same position which now seemed so marginal to her, even if none of them had gotten there quite the way she had.

The first interview was at Condé Nast. She'd subscribed to some website that listed an editorial assistant's job at *Condé Nast Traveler*, but apparently all the job openings at all the Condé Nast magazines funneled down into one big slough of HR despond that didn't differentiate between one magazine and another. Too bad, because work at a travel magazine sounded attractive to Helen, but it scarcely mattered in the end because it seemed she had grossly misunderstood the nature of an editorial assistant's job in the first place. She thought it had to do with assisting in the editing of the magazine, a notion of which the HR person disabused her with the exaggerated patience usually reserved for dealing with the very old. The second interview was for a fundraiser's job with the Mercantile Library. It seemed to go well enough. At least there was no condescension or hostility involved, not on a visible level anyway. She did notice a sort of quizzical cock of the head when she answered the interviewer's question about the size of the average donation she'd solicited in her work for the town library in Rensselaer Valley. Still, asking for money was asking for money: how different could it be?

She ate lunch at a Chipotle—horrible, but she didn't want to go anywhere nicer and ask for a table for one. Her dignity had taken enough hits as it was. Nervously she checked her cell to make sure there was no emergency call from Sara or from Sara's school. The way her life had been going lately, it would figure that such a call might come on the one day she was two hours from home and didn't want anybody to know about it. Her third interview was in the neighborhood of the Empire State Building, in a shabby little office building with a lobby about as wide as a walk-in closet. Judging from the framed directory she perused as she waited a minute and a half for the one elevator, it seemed mostly full of accountants and tax preparers; she was headed, though, for Harvey Aaron Public Relations. They had advertised, in the *Times*, for an entry-level position as junior vice president, which was confusing, though less so after she walked in and saw that the office consisted of two rooms of identical size, one of which belonged to Harvey Aaron and the other to everyone else—three desks, two of which were occupied by bored-looking young Latina women reading magazines. The third desk, presumably that of the junior vice president, had a pair of running shoes on it.

When Harvey stood up to greet her as she entered, he was still holding a plastic fork and a container of some sort of pasta salad. "Come in, sit down, excuse me," he said, looking around for something suitable on which to wipe his fingers, eventually just giving up and waving her into the room's only other chair. He was older than Helen, maybe sixty or a dissipated fifty-five, and she was comforted by that, since her other stops that day had contributed to the sense that no one worked aboveground in Manhattan who was over the age of forty. He wore a beige suit and a blue tie, a rather stylish one (though it had a new oil stain on it), which suggested the attentions of a Mrs. Aaron. He seemed a little nervous just to see her walk in, as if she weren't the kind of person who normally came around during the day, and maybe for that reason she felt like she could relax a little in front of him.

"Sorry to interrupt your lunch," she said.

"Well, you weren't. I mean you sort of were, but as Mona out there will tell you, I don't really have a set lunchtime, I'm just kind of picking at food all day. Helps me think. Mona?" he said suddenly, much louder. "Any napkins out there, by any chance?" Mona didn't appear, not then or for the remainder of the interview. "So where do we begin? I never know where to begin these things. I know I have your résumé on the computer somewhere." He tapped a few keys and sat back hopefully. "No," he said. He typed something else and hit Return with a flourish. "Son of a bitch," he muttered, and then flinched guiltily. Helen unsnapped her bag and slid him another copy of her CV.

He looked it over. "Computer skills are obviously a big requirement around here," he said. "Just kidding. Anyway, I don't see any sort of public relations background here, and for this job, even though it could technically be an entry-level thing, I am kind of hoping for someone with some experience in the field. Of course I may not get that. You have no experience at all in the field?"

"Not in public relations per se," Helen said gamely.

"Not per se? What do you mean? You have experience that's whatever is the opposite of per se? Per don't say?"

Helen laughed. There was something very unassuming about him, both cheerful and apologetic, even as he was in the process of brushing her off just like everyone else had. "Well, I guess what I mean," she said, "is that I'm actually not entirely sure what it is you do."

He raised his eyebrows. " 'You' meaning me, or 'you' meaning what the hell does 'public relations' mean in general?"

"Both," she said, surprising herself with her bravery. If this had happened at Condé Nast, she would have smoothed out her skirt and left by now.

He pursed his lips. "Rensselaer Valley," he said, surprisingly. "Nice town. I have a house in New Paltz myself. May I—I hope you won't think I'm presumptuous if I ask you something?"

"Not at all."

"There is a certain thinness to this résumé," he said, quite kindly, "a certain, um, provincial quality, that suggests to me that you have a life—a married life, a family life—in which circumstances have maybe changed recently?"

Helen colored, and nodded. She had meant for the CV to cover that up, not reveal it.

"And you have children?" he went on. "Because this is the résumé of someone who has spent the last ten or fifteen years raising a family—"

"One child," Helen said. "Yes."

Harvey beamed at her, as if she would want to share in his professional pride at having guessed these embarrassing facts about her. "Then you already know what we do," he said, tilting his chair backwards. "We tell stories. We tell stories to the public, because stories are what people pay attention to, what they remember. Why? Because when they were little, they had devoted, beautiful mothers like you, who told them stories, and stories are how they first learned to make sense out of the whole big, confusing world."

"Stories," Helen said indulgently, though the truth was that his mere invocation of Sara, whom he did not know, whose existence was no more than generic to him, had caused a little tightness in her throat that kept her from wanting to risk saying anything more. That kind of thing had happened to her a lot these last few weeks.

"Now, because our services cost money, the protagonists of these stories tend to be people who are rich, or famous, or better yet rich and famous. But the stories themselves are everyman stories, familiar. Archetypal. Am I pronouncing that right? We put these figures in stories whose outcomes we're already familiar with from childhood, so that way we know how the audience will judge them when we finish telling them. The stories lead the people to the judgment we want. Is all this making sense?"

"Don't they ever object?" Helen asked.

"Who?"

"The celebrities, the rich people. Do they ever resist being put into these everyman stories?"

Harvey smiled, a little condescendingly, Helen thought. "They're used to it. They live in publicity, it's like their atmosphere, so they already know they'll get judged, and it's just a question of influencing how. Unlike the rest of us, they don't really have the option of assuming there's no one watching. Anyway, it's what they pay us for. We don't go to them, you understand; they come to us. Do you know any celebrities yourself?"

Helen was, naturally, thinking of her husband, who had not long ago been on the front page of the *New York Post*, and whose name a man like Harvey would surely recognize in an instant. In Harvey's world this association with the public realm might even have advanced Helen's case; still, she just didn't feel like getting into it with him. She shook her head.

"Not at present," she said.

"Not at present?" He laughed. "I like you. What about at past, then?"

Helen smiled shyly. "Well, if you want to go back a ways, I actually went to junior high with Hamilton Barth."

She was worried he would laugh at her, at the pathetic tenuousness of this connection, but he did not. Any point of contact with someone as famous as Hamilton Barth was worth cultivating, and respecting. His eyes grew wide. "No kidding," he said. "Where was this?"

"In a little town in northern New York," said Helen, "where we both grew up." "Little town" didn't begin to describe it. They sat in the same Catholic school classroom every year from kindergarten through the eighth grade; Helen's family moved from Malloy to Watertown the following year, but Hamilton made it through only two and a half years of high school anyway before dropping out and heading south to the city, and then west to L.A., to become an actor. Was there any hint, back then, of the deep, tortured, mercurially tempered, disarmingly handsome movie star he would later become? No, there was not, unless you counted the fact that he was short, as the great male movie stars tended to be for some reason, distilled and without excess, like bonsai trees. They weren't close friends back then, but they knew a lot about each other, because you knew a lot about everybody your age in a town that small; and if you wanted to get technical, it had gone a little further than that. The two of them were once paired off in a game of Seven Minutes in Heaven, one Saturday night in the vacant apartment over Erin White's parents' garage. Even though Helen had to bend her knees slightly to kiss him, Hamilton was—and she probably would have remembered this just as vividly even had he not gone on to become a brooding object of desire all over the world—a fantastic kisser, relaxed and confident and patient, and she remembered her shock and curiosity about whom he'd been practicing with, even during the kiss itself. He tried to get under her skirt, just as they all did, but she only had to knock his hand away one time, which struck her as gentlemanly, almost romantic. "You have nice lips" was what he had said to her after; again, not much, except when considered in relation to the soulless things other eighth-grade boys usually had to say to you after you pushed their hands out from under your skirt. She and Hamilton were never alone together after that night, though, and four months later Helen's father announced that they were moving. She'd stayed in touch for a few years with a couple of the old Malloy girls who were still in touch with Hamilton when he started to get famous, but she'd never laid eyes on him again, at least not without buying a ticket like everybody else. She'd made out with Hamilton Barth: it was a story Helen told only her closest friends, not because it was so private but because she worried how lame it would make her sound, this seven-minute brush with greatness from a quarter of a century ago. She certainly wasn't going to trot it out for Harvey, whom she'd known for all of half an hour.

"How about that," Harvey said softly. "Are you still friends with him?"

"No," Helen said. "I mean, it's not that we're not friends, or that we stopped being friends. I hope he'd still remember me fondly, if he ever even thinks about the old days at all, but we haven't been in contact for a very long time."

Harvey's ardor cooled visibly. "Well, in all honesty, he'd be kind of a big fish for a little operation like ours anyway. So, Helen, here's the skinny, as we used to say around here. I've really enjoyed meeting you, and in all honesty I think you could learn to do this job just fine over time; but I have two more people coming in today who actually know how to do the job already. One of them used to be at Rogers and Cowan, for Pete's sake. So I really wish I could help you, but honestly, at this moment it doesn't look too good."

"I understand," said Helen as she rose, and in fact she did understand. She saw how she looked—earnest, naïve, unremarkable—to this sweet older man, and to the whole world of prospective employers at large. He edged around his desk and escorted her to the door, still brushing at crumbs on his torso. "Thank you for your time," Helen said. "That's a sharp tie, by the way. A present from your wife?"

He looked down at it, as if he'd forgotten he had it on, and smiled. "Yes it was," he said. "That was our last birthday together. Of mine, I mean. She passed away that summer."

Here she was feeling so comfortable around him, Helen reflected two hours later on the train home, that she'd forgotten the cardinal virtue of knowing when to keep one's idiot mouth shut. He still wore the ring, though, which was interesting, and excused her mistake a little bit, but did not excuse her opening up a subject like that when she knew nothing at all about him. No wonder the professional world seemed so closed to someone like her. The fourth interview had been so mortifying she was already having trouble remembering it. She was back in the house and in casual clothes ten minutes before Sara got home from school.

The two of them ate dinner together, at opposite ends of the table. A chicken breast with a ham-and-cheese roll-up under the skin, some yellow rice and string beans. Sara had always hated eating dinner with her parents, and took no pains to disguise it. Like all of her contemporaries, she was restless when not doing at least two things at once, and the thought of eating—just eating, without the TV or her iPod on, without a phone in hand, without a book to read—struck her as not just wasteful but sentimental. She talked to her mother easily enough when the atmosphere was more relaxed and spontaneous, but at the table it felt quaint and enforced, all the more so now that the conceit that they were a Normal Family, one that Sat Down To Dinner Together, had been debunked forever. Nothing provoked a teenager like the whiff of hypocrisy.

"What did you do today?" Helen asked tentatively.

Sara shrugged. "Same old," she said. "Class, lunch, class, soccer."

"Weren't you going to Sophia's house after, to study?" Sara shrugged, which could have meant any number of things, but some of those things were so potentially heartbreaking—when seventh grade had ended, and everything was still outwardly normal, Sophia was Sara's best friend—that Helen didn't have the heart to pursue it any further. "How was soccer?" she said instead.

Sara scowled. "The coach is so unfair," she said.

She was developing an acne problem already, just a few months after turning thirteen. One of the many revelations of adoption: whatever had happened to you at the age your daughter was now, good or bad, whatever changes you went through, early or late—it was irrelevant, it was of no value to anyone. Even the fact that Sara and her mother were of different races somehow hadn't prepared Helen for the shock of her own uselessness in that regard. There were no genetic predictors. You were as surprised by what she became as she was.

On Thursday Helen was filling out some parental-consent forms for school and watching CNN with the sound down, in case anything major happened somewhere in the world, when the phone rang. "Helen, it's Harvey Aaron," she heard. "Listen, I am very pleased to tell you that for various reasons those two other guys didn't work out and so I'd like to offer you the job here, if you're still available, that is. Probably rude of me just to assume that you're still available. I'm sorry for that. So are you?"

"Yes," said Helen, amazed, hearing her own voice while watching the anchorwoman's lips move silently on the TV. "I am available."

Harvey asked if she could start as soon as Monday, and she almost said no, but then she realized that there was nothing other than fear of the unknown that would prevent her starting two hours from right now, if it came to that. She hung up and, after a few moments, whooped with laughter. What the hell had she just done? Harvey himself seemed so chaotic, and the office so moribund, that it wouldn't have surprised her if the whole operation went under before she cashed her first paycheck; she had to remind herself that the place had somehow stayed in business for thirty years. It was the first instance of good timing her life had seen in quite a while. She finished off the endless school forms—liability waivers, most of them—with a much lighter heart. That night at dinner, she told Sara what had happened, and what to expect in terms of the change in their routines.

"They hired *you*? Really? A PR firm? No offense," Sara said. "Well, it's a good thing, I guess. I mean I've been wondering if we were just going to go broke or what."

"We're not going to go broke," Helen said quickly. "But it's true, we do need some money coming in while your father's not working." It was so much more dire than that, but Helen was constitutionally averse to talking about money with her child. Besides, she didn't really want to find out how much Sara already knew. "And now we'll have it. So that's great."

Sara looked thoughtful. "What time will you get home?" she said.

"Six," Helen said, though in truth she and Harvey hadn't discussed it. She hadn't even thought to ask him. "But you've got soccer until five most days anyway, and you can go to friends' houses if you don't want to be here alone, and you've got the cellphone if you need anything and the neighbors—"

"Yeah, I think I can survive here for an hour or two all by myself," Sara said acidly. "But I mean—"

"What?" Helen said.

"What about just moving to the city?"

Helen blanched. It was something she had planned to wait at least a month before bringing up as a possibility, on the grounds that there was only so much change a child should be asked to accommodate in one shot. But Sara's whole life was founded on upheaval. It was Helen, really, who had a limit on how much of a chance she was willing to take that life might improve if they just tried their luck somewhere else.

"First things first," she said. "Let's bank a few paychecks and then see where we are. But that's something you'd be willing to consider?"

Sara snorted. "Consider? Try dream of," she said. "These people are hicks. And now they all think they're better than us. Plus I'm not saying I want to forget about Dad or anything but it would be kind of a relief to be able to look at something, or someone, that doesn't remind me he's not here. Is there dessert?"

On Monday Helen took the earlier, more crowded train, full of tense faces and clubby nods of recognition, and showed up at work so far ahead of schedule she had to wait in the hallway for ten minutes until Mona arrived with a key to let her in. She expected some kind of formal orientation, but instead Mona just showed her how to set up Google news alerts for all nine of the business's current clients, as well as twelve other names Harvey had identified as potential clients. When that was done, it was just a matter of waiting for these alerts to show up in her inbox; in the meantime she was handed a stack of gossip magazines and asked to scan them thoroughly for any mention of those same twenty-one names. Harvey came in around eleven; he looked surprised to see Helen sitting there at her desk but then nodded quickly in embarrassment, went into his office without a word to her and shut the door.

Mona and the other employee there, whose name was Nevaeh, spoke all day long to each other but never once to Helen, unless it was to answer some question they couldn't pretend not to know the answer to, like where the ladies' room was. At four forty-five they reapplied their makeup and left without a word to the boss or to Helen. The whole first week was like that. She didn't mind the idleness, or the feeling of being ignored—this wasn't some journey of personal growth or something, she was just looking to keep herself and her child out of the poorhouse—but so little happened around there that she didn't see how any of their jobs could possibly last. She was relieved when Mona handed her her first paycheck and then relieved all over again when it cleared. When she mentioned to Harvey that she didn't feel like she had that much to do, he looked embarrassed and said, "Hurry up and wait, as they used to tell us in the Army," and went back into his office with a bag full of Chinese food and shut the door.

"The guy who used to have your job quit to go back to school," Mona finally told her. "He didn't have nothing to do either. But if Harvey doesn't hire someone to take his place, that's like admitting that the business is shrinking."

Then one morning Harvey came in on time for once and called all three women into his office. "I think we may have something here," he said. "I went out to Brooklyn last night to have dinner with my son, and the two of us ordered out for some Chinese. Any of you ever heard of Peking Grill?"

Mona and Nevaeh nodded sagely. "There's one up in the Heights," Nevaeh said.

"Right," Harvey said, "there's like eight of them. Anyway, we call and ask for a delivery, and they say no. No? They say no, we can't, because our delivery guys are on strike. But you're still open? I say. Sure. So Michael and I walk three blocks to Peking Grill, and we have to cross a god damn *picket* line to get in, and inside it's empty except for one guy who's sitting alone at a table and *crying*, for Pete's sake. Sobbing. He's the owner."

"Disgusting," Mona said.

Harvey glanced at her curiously but then went on. "So someone is apparently trying to unionize the deliverymen at all the Peking Grills, which I would think would be difficult because pretty much everyone who works there is illegal, but nevertheless. They are picketing the owner not only for a wage hike but for back wages for all the years they say they were underpaid. I ask him if he's had any calls from the papers, and he says yes, just that day, from somebody at the *Post*. He hasn't returned it yet."

He sat back in his chair. "So I sense an opening here," he said. "For us. For us to intervene."

Mona and Nevaeh just went on nodding, but Helen, who couldn't help herself, said, "On which side?"

The two women shot her an angry look, and all of a sudden Helen understood that they weren't really following any of what Harvey said either but had just settled on nodding as the quickest way to get through these enthusiasms of his and back to their desks. Harvey, though, looked delighted and indulgently thoughtful, as if he were only pretending to think through a question for a student's benefit, even though someone of his intelligence would have known the answer instinctively. "Well," he said, "the deliverymen don't really have much of a public image problem, do they? I mean, they risked their lives to get here, they're being paid about two dollars an hour, they're sleeping Christ knows where. Everybody already sympathizes with them. In New York, they do, at least. If we were somewhere in flyover country, they'd have a posse out for these guys, but hey, this is Manhattan. Whereas this owner, who came here in exactly the same circumstances but then had the temerity to actually succeed, to make himself a millionaire—his name is Chin, by the way—he's being portrayed as the villain, he's the one with the story that needs to get out. He's the one in need of our expert services. Which is what I convinced him of last night while we ate some very delicious chow fun."

Helen Googled Chin and, sure enough, most of the references to him were scathing. She was printing out a few of them—Harvey disliked having links sent to him—when he opened his door and tried to beckon her into his office without the other two women noticing. "Mr. Chin and I are having lunch today at the Peking Grill up on Seventy-eighth Street," he said when she came in. "I'd love it if you'd come along. You don't have to do anything but take notes. But I think it would be useful if he saw that we're, you know, an operation here, that he wouldn't just be putting his business in the hands of one old Jew who likes Chinese food."

They arrived at 11:30, which seemed early for lunch but was probably scheduled with an eye toward minimizing the presence of picketers; indeed there was only one sullen young Chinese man sitting cross-legged on the sidewalk who lifted his head and glared at them as they walked past him and the row of locked, scarred bikes.

"Mr. Chin," Harvey said. Chin sat by himself at the table closest to the kitchen, his hands in his lap. "My associate, Helen Armstead," Harvey said as he sat down and looked around hopefully for a waiter with a menu.

"You say you help me," Chin said without looking up. "How you help this? Nobody come. Nobody call for delivery. Sixty percent of our weekday business, delivery."

"Well, it is a little early for the lunch trade," Harvey said encouragingly. "Though I confess I didn't have much breakfast myself."

"Fucking liberal Upper West Siders," Chin said abruptly. "They get hard-on for anybody say they oppressed. Guess what? I was oppressed too! I came here with nothing. Same province as all these guys. Only difference between me and them is that I work hard instead of complain and I make something of myself. What you supposed to do here, right? But do they congratulate me, respect me? No. I'm the bad guy now. Some fat bitch with a stroller call me a fascist."

"Well, that's a term that gets thrown around a lot," Harvey said. Chin looked up at him then; his lips began to quiver, and he put his napkin to his face and started to cry again. "Here's the thing," Harvey went on, his calm voice at odds with the panicked darting of his eyes back and forth between his weeping client and Helen, as if expecting her to know, by virtue of being a woman, how to comfort this wounded man whose hardships and resentments she could not possibly guess at. "What you just told us? You've got to get that story out there. You've got to tell people who you are. This isn't just some management-labor dispute. You are an authentic American success story. You need to let us fight back, take the moral high ground from these jealous, petty, self-entitled people who would cut you down, and correct the injustice of the way you've been portrayed by the other side. Right, Helen?"

"No," said Helen.

Harvey fell silent and stared at her in wonder, and, a moment later, Chin lifted his eyes and did the same. Helen had stunned herself as much as them. She hadn't planned to say a thing. She felt what she was about to say coming over her, moving in her, before she understood what it was, and with an air of total conviction she began saying it so that she could hear it too.

"What is the goal here, Mr. Chin?" she said.

He looked at her confusedly.

"To get people back at these tables?" she prompted him.

"Yes," he said. "To get people back into the restaurant."

"Then here's what we do. We apologize."

"For what?" Mr. Chin said, bristling a little.

"America is the greatest country in the world," Helen said. "When there is an honest dispute between worker and boss, you humbly put your trust in the wisdom of the courts, which are the people's instrument. I mean, that's what's going to happen anyway, right? The whole thing is probably on its way to court already, and you'll have no choice but to abide by that decision. So you might as well make it seem like your idea. In the meantime, you only want to be fair. You only want to be a good American and give your countrymen the same opportunity you had, the opportunity to earn what you yourself have earned. We will put you on the front page of the *Post* and the *News* and on local TV."

"What will I say?" Chin asked.

"You will say that you are sorry," Helen said. "You will not defend yourself. You will not contest any particular charge, because contesting it is what allows people to keep talking about it. Without getting into specifics, you will apologize, and ask your customers and the people of New York for their forgiveness. And they will give it to you. They want to. People are quick to judge, Mr. Chin, they are quick to condemn, but that's mostly because their ultimate desire is to forgive."

Chin and Harvey regarded each other submissively. Able neither to agree with her nor to challenge her in front of a client, Harvey pretended somewhat absurdly that this speech had brought the meeting to a satisfying end, and ten minutes later he and Helen were riding back downtown in shocked silence. She had no idea anymore what had come over her. She wondered if she had done the seemingly impossible and gotten herself fired from a job where no one expected her to do any work at all. Harvey, who hadn't even gotten any food out of the meeting, wouldn't so much as make eye contact with her, though in truth he seemed less angry than disoriented and embarrassed, as if he had climbed into the back of the cab only to find a stranger already sitting there. He went straight into his office and ordered out for lunch, and Helen borrowed Mona's old Rolodex and started working the phones. The story was still fresh enough that she found takers everywhere she called. At four o'clock, staring at Harvey's half-closed door, she called three different Peking Grills until she found Mr. Chin again and ran down the list of every media outlet that wanted to hear what he had to say. Over the next two days she sat in his eye line at every interview, just out of camera range but close enough to remind him of his commitment to repent. That weekend the picket lines were still active, but business was up to about two-thirds of what it had been before the lawsuit; customers asked so often if Mr. Chin himself was there that he took to traveling to all eight of his locations every night, just to shake hands with the diners and have his picture taken with them and thank them for coming back. Two weeks later the lawyers for the deliverymen settled out of court for $38,000 with no admission of liability. In return for a raise, they waived their demand to unionize. Mr. Chin celebrated the return of delivery service by going back to 1991 prices for a night, 1991 being the year he arrived in America. Business was so enthusiastic the deliverymen made more in tips that night than they had ever seen before.

Though Helen's own name was naturally left out of the newspapers, Harvey's was mentioned once or twice, and a few of his old colleagues called to congratulate him. One even used the phrase "teachable moment," with which Harvey was very taken. Over the next three weeks they picked up four new clients, a bonanza by Harvey's standards. When Peking Grill threw itself a twentieth anniversary party at their first location, in Murray Hill, Helen spent the day pitching the event to various papers and freelance photographers and then put on a dress and accompanied Harvey to the restaurant. Chin made a special toast to the two of them, in the midst of which he began crying again.

Harvey, after a carafe of complimentary white wine, began to talk himself up a little too. "I must say," he told Helen, "I haven't lost my touch. Not a lot of people would have hired you, you know. But I know people. I can spot talent. And now we are reaping the benefits. You have brought new life to the whole enterprise."

"To your genius," Helen said with a laugh, clinking glasses with him.

"You have brought new life to me too, actually," Harvey went on. "Because after all, I am the enterprise. The enterprise, c'est moi. What I am saying, in part, is that you look quite stunning all dressed up like that."

She laughed again, then stopped. "Harvey?" she said. "Are you coming on to me?"

"It's been a long time," he said, "but I think so, yes. I have a friend who keeps a suite at the Roosevelt. You probably shouldn't be driving home to Westchester, after all."

She put her glass of wine, which was only her second, down on the nearest table and stared at him, flattered and amazed, but mostly disappointed. "You'd do that, Harvey?" she said. "After everything you just said, you'd risk the business by sleeping with an employee?"

He waved grandly. "Business, life, life, business," he said. "I have no use for people who draw the distinction. It is all one. It should all be one. No?"

There was no real danger in the air. Laying her hand gently on his forearm, she leaned over and kissed him on the cheek. "You've revitalized my enterprise too," she said. "But come on. Let's not be kids about it. You don't need to get laid to celebrate every good thing that happens. Anyway, I have a daughter at home, and it's a school night. Just promise me you'll go to that suite at the Roosevelt and have a good night's sleep and I will see you at work tomorrow."

He took her hand and kissed it. "I shall," he said. "But if you think this is all just about horniness or euphoria or whatever, it's not. You are a remarkable, remarkable woman. Joanie would have agreed with me." Helen, though she hadn't heard the name before, did not need to ask who Joanie was. Harvey said his farewells to Mr. Chin and his wife and went outside to hail a taxi on Third Avenue to take him up to the Roosevelt. In the cab, though, with the windows rolled all the way down, he was feeling so good, so awake, that he redirected the driver west, toward his office. He picked up his car from the attendant at the underground garage across the street from the Empire State Building and headed out of town toward the house in New Paltz, even though he'd turned off the oil burner and drained the pipes three weeks ago; Joanie had never minded the cold, but since her death he'd closed it up for the winter a little earlier every year. He crossed the Henry Hudson Bridge and left the city. He drove with his window down, listening to the crickets at the stoplights, feeling the invigorating change in the air. On the Taconic he fell asleep and the car sped straight through a turn and down a short embankment, turning over once and landing upright on its tires. He was killed instantly.

2

THE FOREMAN ON HIS RANCH had called a meeting, just to grab the opportunity to update him on a few things while he was actually there: fencing problems, impending visits from the state D of A and from Immigration, a boundary dispute with the rancher to their south which was complete bullshit but would require hiring a surveyor to make go away. Nothing too far out of the ordinary, just himself and the foreman and two hands whose names he didn't know, and it had all taken place very informally right there on the hacienda after breakfast. The whole thing couldn't have lasted more than forty minutes. Still, it left a bad feeling in him, a rebellious or claustrophobic feeling, which only seemed to tighten its hold inside him as the otherwise empty day went on; he could tell it was the kind of upset that wasn't going to go away on its own, that he was going to have to take some step to snuff it out. A meeting! On the ranch! What had he bought this place for, if not to get away from the world of meetings? He tried some yoga, and he tried reading some Basho translations his new small press was going to publish, but his concentration was shot, and when the afternoon was half done he got in the truck and raised some dust driving down the long, straight road to the front gate. Something mutinous rose up in him at the thought of the security cameras whose lenses took him in as he approached that gate, even though at some earlier meeting he had signed off on their installation. Near the fencing along the berm, he passed the foreman, whose name, impossibly, was Colt; tall and straight in the saddle, Colt looked down at the truck and touched his hat, and it was possible to be contemptuous and jealous of him at the same time.

Five hundred yards beyond the gate was the crossroads; instead of turning left, toward town and the airstrip, he turned right, where he never went, where he imagined it was all but unmapped and a man could be alone with himself and clear his head. And it was like a moon-scape for a while, just the cracked road and the scrub and the mountains, but after about ten miles he saw a sign for a bar; frowning, he decelerated onto the gravel and parked. As it turned out, it was truly a great bar—dark, no TV, nothing but ranch hands and day workers, silent except for the pool table—and he might have settled in for longer, but he hadn't gotten halfway through the beer that followed his third shot before somebody recognized him. The dumb fucking hick leaned one elbow on the bar and stared right at his face like he was staring at a face on a billboard. "Holy shit," the hick said. He gave the guy a smile that was like slapping a book shut, threw a twenty on the bar, and got into the truck again. There was still a ways to drive, apparently, in order to get outside of where he was.

With the windows down, the noise and the heat were tremendous, but still he saw and felt his cellphone convulsing across the front seat beside him. He hadn't even realized he'd brought it along. He thought for a moment about throwing it out the window, but then somebody would find it and figure out who it belonged to, and then that was a shitstorm of a whole other sort. He tucked the phone in his shirt pocket so he wouldn't have to see it anymore.

In the next bar it started vibrating again, right over his heart. He took it out and flipped it open and looked at the text on the screen: Hamilton? Where R U? It was from someone named Katie, which didn't ring a bell. He asked the bartender to pour another shot and leave the bottle. They actually still did that out here. They did it in L.A. too, but then at the end of the night some guy came up to you and handed you a bill for a thousand dollars. When the phone went off again—the bar was so quiet you could hear it buzz in his pocket—he answered.

"Hamilton? This is Katie Marcus from Event Horizon—we're handling the PR for A Time of Mourning? I don't know if you remember, but we met on the set at one point?"

"Of course I remember," Hamilton said. Hollywood was carpeted with young, borderline-attractive, overeager, callow young women like he imagined this Katie to be—on the set, at the studio, in your agent's office, working at the club or in the restaurant or any other business of any description that you might have reason to go into—and he could not tell one of them from another. But that didn't mean you shouldn't conduct yourself like a gentleman.

"Really?" Katie said. "Wow. Well, I'm calling just to remind you that you have that interview with *The New York Times* this afternoon. You got our reminders about that, right?"

She had such a young voice. They got younger and younger. "Remind me again?" Hamilton said.

"The *Times* wanted to talk to you for a profile they're doing of Kevin." Kevin Ortiz was the director of the last film Hamilton had shot. A movie was over, to him, on the day shooting wrapped and he could fly out to the ranch and slowly slip out of character; it was always a surprise to him when a few months or a year later the whole thing came back to life in the form of something strangers could buy tickets to see, and everyone wanted to talk about it all over again, expecting him to remember it, never knowing how much had gone into the effort to leave it behind in the first place. But Kevin he remembered. Kevin was a brilliant young artist, and a great running buddy. He would not have been at all out of place in this bar. "We told the *Times* they could have just five minutes on the phone with you, just to talk about what it was like to work with him. I don't know if you remember, but we cleared this all with you, and you said it was okay, which we really appreciate. It should really help the film out a lot. But if you've changed your mind about it, we can—"

"No, Katie, that's fine." The bartender was walking toward him. "What time does it start?"

"It actually was scheduled for an hour ago? But we can work around whatever you want to do."

"I'm sorry about that, Katie," Hamilton said. The bartender stopped in front of him. "Just have the guy call me any time."

"Well, we don't do it that way, because we try hard not to give out your cell number. So we left it that you would call him. Do you have a pen?"

"Do you have a pen?" Hamilton asked the scowling bartender, who handed him a pencil. He wrote down the New York phone number on his shirtsleeve, hung up, and smiled apologetically as he handed the pencil back.

"We don't allow those conversations in here," the bartender said, pointing to Hamilton's phone. The man's ring finger was bent at a bizarre angle; Hamilton had seen an injury like that on a football player once. His skin was cracked like leather. Beautiful, Hamilton thought. To wear your life like that.

"I'm very sorry," he said. "I didn't see the sign."

"Ain't no sign," said the bartender.

So Hamilton decided he'd better do the interview itself in the truck. Two more shots first: just to show there were no hard feelings, he shared a third one with the bartender, who drank it solemnly and did not so much as touch his hat. Hamilton could feel himself imitating the man's slow gait as he squinted against the brutal sunlight in the parking lot. He got the truck up to speed, looked down at his sleeve, and dialed the number.

"Hamilton!" the nasal East Coast voice said. "So glad to catch you. Thank you so much for taking the time. First of all, I loved the film, I thought you were amazing in it. Where are you right now?"

Hamilton looked out the window. He didn't really know. He'd never driven this far north of the ranch; also, that last drink with the bartender had opened a door, and he felt his mood shifting. Suddenly he had an idea. "I'm in upstate New York," he said. "Visiting family."

"Really? That's cool. Are you—can I ask you—are you in a car right now? Because I'm having a little trouble hearing you."

"Oh, right," Hamilton said. "Hold on a second." He rolled up the driver's-side window, then leaned across the cab to roll up the other one, which didn't quite necessitate letting go of the wheel but did mean that there were a few seconds when he was stretched too low across the seat to see over the dashboard. He felt and then heard the tires drift off the macadam, but he straightened up and steered back onto the road. Nothing out here but scrub anyway. No other cars. You might drift off the road and go for half a mile before you hit anything tall enough to break your axle. "Better?" Hamilton said. His voice sounded way too loud, now that the cab was quiet.

"Much," said the voice. "So I don't actually need to take up a lot of your time—I just wanted to ask a question or two about what it was like working with Kevin Ortiz. It's his first film, he's a good deal younger than you. Did you ever sense any—"

"Kevin is a fucking genius," Hamilton said.

The voice laughed. "No doubt," it said. "But in the beginning, were there maybe—"

"Why did you laugh, man?" Hamilton said.

"Sorry?"

"When I said he was a genius. Why did you laugh at that?"

Sometimes Hamilton hated who he was to other people, but other times there was a kind of mercenary advantage in it; and he could tell that the change in the tone of his own voice had put the fear into this pasty, smug fuck from *The New York Times*, who had never taken a risk, who had never put himself on the line to try to birth something true into this world. "I apologize," the voice said quietly. "I—well, truth be told, I laughed because I guess I thought you were kidding. I misunderstood."

"Why would I kid about something like that? About genius. About art. Do you think these things are a joke to me?" The sun was just singeing the top of the range; light pooled all along the uneven horizon. In another few minutes it would start to get dark and the temperature would fall faster than a stranger to this landscape might think possible.

"No, Hamilton, I don't. That's certainly not your reputation. Again, I apologize. It was nervous laughter, really, because I was nervous about getting to talk to you at all. What do you say we just hit reset, so to speak, and start over?"

"Maybe these things are a joke to you," Hamilton said. There were no lights out here, no cars coming in either direction. On some level he'd known all along—ever since that meeting with the ranch foreman, anyway—that today would end like this; still, he was bathed in shame, so much so that he heard a little catch in his own voice. "Kevin is a rare soul, man. An old soul. Still, he's just a kid, and it kills me to think of what's going to happen to him, people like you, all the pressure on him, pressure if the movie is a flop but even more pressure if it's a hit, you know? He is totally faithful to the moment, to the process, he gave me everything, every single thing I needed to be who I needed to be when I was in that particular space. You follow what I'm saying?"

"Not all of it," the voice said, "but you know what? Really all I needed was one usable quote, and I'm sure I've got that, so—"

"Nobody understands a guy like Kevin. Nobody understands what's required. You are so vulnerable when you put yourself in the hands of a director. You never know what you're buying into. You have this place you need to get to, like I was talking about, a place that's both inside yourself and somewhere far away from yourself, and you need his help to do it, but he could be anybody, you know? You hold hands and jump off this cliff together, and only after you've jumped, only when you're plummeting through the air, do you get to turn and look at this guy you're holding hands with and say, 'Hey, not for nothing, but who the fuck *are* you?'"

The truck had slowed way down, so much so that he thought maybe he was out of gas, but no, there was still a quarter of a tank. He had to close one eye to read the gauge. That last shot with the bartender—he thought it was one; he remembered one—that was the E-ticket shot, the one there was no coming back from until probably tomorrow. That bartender hated him. It was right there on his face. Maybe Hamilton should have punched him in that face instead of buying him a drink, even if it meant getting his ass kicked. Sometimes it was worth it to get your ass kicked. *Ain't no sign.* Didn't that hayseed, Marlboro Man–looking motherfucker even know who he was?

He drifted to a stop on the side of the road. His foot just wasn't applying any pressure anymore. He cut the engine but left the headlights on; he couldn't see one foot past them. He lowered his window and listened to the dark desert. It sounded like a riot.

"Hamilton?" the voice was saying. "Hamilton? You still there?"

And just then—it was as perfect as if he'd scripted it—a coyote split the darkness wide open with a long, soulful howl.

"Jesus Christ!" said the voice. "Are you okay? I thought you said you were in upstate New York!"

Hamilton smiled and snapped the phone shut. His consciousness was separating like the stages of a rocket, and he saw that he was probably not going to remember any of this tomorrow, not how lucid and how reborn he felt right now, not even how he got here; he often blacked out when he drank like this. What a shame. Not being able to recall it meant he would only have to go off in search of it again. He lay down across the front seat; it was cold now, but the air was so amazing there was no question of rolling up the windows. Besides, somebody would come looking for him. They were probably out looking for him already.

SHE'D LAID EYES ON MICHAEL AARON for the first time four days ago, at Harvey's funeral: scruff-bearded, balding, a little doughier than a young man his age should have been—in most respects, she had to admit, a considerably less charismatic figure than his proud father had led her to expect—but her heart went out to him anyway because of the way he had to carry the burden of mourning all by himself. Harvey had no other family, save for a sister with Alzheimer's who was in a home and had forgotten her brother's face many years ago. And Michael had no wife, no girlfriend, no partner if he was gay, which he might have been for all Helen knew. He was the Aaron family. He shook every hand, accepted every kiss, listened to every story, and Helen's stomach clenched whenever the crowd around him parted enough to let her see the panic in his face, the fear of making some religious or social gaffe or not recognizing some name the speaker would have expected him to know. All, presumably, while trying to make sense of the loss of his father, and of his own new status as an orphan. One day that will be Sara, Helen caught herself thinking; she had a kind of guilty oversensitivity to the lot of the only child. All that afternoon she had wanted to cross the synagogue, and then the reception room in the basement of the synagogue, to talk to him, to try to help him out in some unobtrusively kind way, but she couldn't bring herself to do it.

Because she was the one who had killed Harvey. She knew it was ridiculous, which was why she'd never said it out loud to anyone, but the fact remained that he had offered himself to her and she had rejected him and patted him condescendingly on his drunken head and sent him off to his death. She'd watched through the Peking Grill window to make sure he got into a cab, it was true, but what consolation was it to know that you'd done the minimum, when there was something more that you might have done, only you didn't do it? She could have called his cellphone to make sure he'd checked in to the Roosevelt, or she could have called the hotel itself. She could, for that matter, just have had sex with him, and then waited thirty seconds until he fell asleep and taken the train back to Rensselaer Valley an hour late and told Sara some lie to explain it and Harvey would still be alive now. Was she too good for that, did she imagine? It would have been the first sex she'd had in at least a year, probably longer. Maybe it was the last such proposition she'd ever get. If so, it would serve her right. With her haughtiness and her rectitude and her timidity, she had sent that sweet man on the road to die. She was too afraid even to tell his son that she was sorry for his loss, for fear that he would see right through her civilities to all she knew.

But now a second chance had come her way to speak to Michael, and if she thought the first one was potentially awkward, it had little on what awaited her this afternoon. Harvey didn't have a regular accountant, it seemed, but he did have a lawyer, and she and Michael had been summoned to the lawyer's office at 2:30. Helen had spoken on the phone to this charmless gentleman, whose last name was Scapelli, for a couple of hours already, and so she knew what to expect from this meeting, though Michael did not. Scapelli's office had no waiting room or reception area, so Helen sat and waited in a chair about two feet from his desk as he unself-consciously took phone calls about other matters. The recessed shelves above and behind him, where she might have expected to see diplomas or family photos, were given over to a large collection of mounted, autographed baseballs. When Michael got off the elevator at about 2:45, though she remembered him vividly she was astonished to see him as he apparently dressed every day, even for a meeting such as this: a short-sleeved Roots t-shirt worn over a long-sleeved one, torn jeans, and black Converse sneakers of the type (if not the color) that was popular when Helen herself was a kid. Michael, she had reason to know, was thirty-two years old. He was a musician and a DJ, which, Harvey had once explained to her, were really the same thing in this day and age. Harvey had left him everything, which consisted of the house in New Paltz, the now-totaled car, and the business.

"Have a seat, Michael," Scapelli said absently, even though Michael had not waited for the invitation. He slumped in the tattered armchair beside Helen's and nodded to her, a little hesitantly, as if he wasn't sure the two of them were there for the same meeting.

"Helen Armstead," she said to him. "I worked for your dad."

"What's up," Michael said.

"So we are technically here for the reading of your father's will," Scapelli said, "though it's kind of a formality in this case because you both already know what's in it and it's only about five lines long anyway. We've already talked about the house—have you changed your mind about any of that?"

"Nope," Michael said. "Sell that puppy."

Neither man's face betrayed a hint of the surprise Helen felt at this bit of unsentimentality. What business of hers was it, though? Still, she couldn't help feeling a kind of empathetic sting on behalf of the young man's mother. Michael glanced at her, suddenly embarrassed.

"I mean, lots of good memories there and whatnot," he said. "But New Paltz? Professionally it's just not possible for me. Plus the fact is I really need the money."

"Of course," Helen said. "I mean, it's entirely up to you."

"Plus who wants to be that guy? The guy living in his dead parents' house?"

"Which brings us to the business at hand," Scapelli said. "Your father didn't keep the most meticulous records, but we've spent the last few days doing some forensic work—"

"Say what?" Michael said.

"Some forensic accounting work, that's just the term for it, and, in a nutshell, your father's estate right now consists mostly of debt. The big issue is income tax, on which he was apparently a little behind. Now don't worry, you're not legally responsible for that debt just because he willed his estate to you. We can just declare Harvey Aaron Public Relations a bankrupt entity and shut it down, and, from your point of view, that's that. But there are other ways to go as well, which is why Ms. Armstead is here with us today." He nodded meaningfully at Helen to let her know, as if they had rehearsed all this, that here was her cue.

Helen looked at Michael's boyish face—his boyish expression, actually; the face itself was no longer in that range—as he struggled to overcome his own seeming fatigue enough not to lose the thread of what was going on. "I don't know how much you and your dad talked about his agency," she said, "but the tragic—one of the tragic things about his death was that it came just at the time when, after a long slump, it was really starting to turn around again. He had that great, very public success with Peking Grill, I'm sure he told you about that—"

Michael raised his eyebrows as if she were speaking some other language.

"And in the wake of that," she went on desperately, "a number of new clients signed on, more than he'd had in many years." She was just improvising that last flourish, in an effort to say something that would cause some emotion to register on Harvey's son's face; but she assumed it was true, and Scapelli didn't say or do anything to contradict her. "He was such a decent man, your father, and everyone feels so terrible that just when people were recognizing his basic, his basic—"

"So what we are proposing," Scapelli prompted her, with a kind of gentlemanly impatience.

"So what we are proposing, is that we keep the business open for a while, indefinitely really, because if we just finish up the work we've already been hired to do, the fees due on those existing contracts will cancel out the debt that your father was in, and if things keep going the way they've been going, after let's say nine months or a year there should even be a little bit of a legacy for you, an inheritance, not a ton of money but definitely, definitely the way your father would have wanted it. I know he loved you very, very much." How she knew that, she could not have said, but she felt the truth of it, and anyway he didn't seem to disagree.

Michael lowered his eyes for a few seconds, then looked back at her. "You're not asking me to take over the business?" he said.

"Not at all. Just to delay shutting it down, via bankruptcy or any other way."

"Then who *is* taking over the business?"

Helen colored. "His staff," she said. "All of us. I mean, you could also look at it as a good deed in that you wouldn't be putting people out of work."

"And—no disrespect or anything, it's just I don't know—who are you? I mean were you his assistant or something?"

She swallowed. "I'm the junior vice president," she said.

Scapelli had begun discreetly looking at his watch. He was no older than she was, and there had to be some story behind his ending up in this one-man practice with its water-stained ceiling and mismatched furniture, but she didn't imagine she'd ever learn it. "In a nutshell, you're being asked to do nothing," he said to Michael. "Do you have any problem with that?"

"Nosirree," said Michael.

"Terrific. On my end I will basically be going into stall mode with the IRS and the agency's other creditors, which is a lot easier to do now that your father, so to speak, has the ultimate waiver. Anything that helps them collect, they'll be open to. As for you, you're not at any personal risk if things don't go as well as Helen here seems to think they will, not for several months anyway. At the first whiff of trouble, we can just file Chapter Eleven and case closed. Any further questions, Michael?"

"No," Michael said gratefully; like Scapelli, he seemed in a hurry to be done with this meeting, in fact to be done thinking about it, despite the momentous nature, to Helen's mind, of everything that was being discussed. It would have been easy to read Michael's almost panicky dismissal of his father's life's work as ungrateful or unfeeling, she thought, but she saw in it nothing worse than a desire to get used to his new circumstances as quickly as possible, to look only forward, the way you were advised to stare, on a tightrope or a bridge or some other precariously high place, straight ahead rather than down.

The two men were standing and shaking hands, and then Scapelli was putting his lifeless hand in hers to signal that their appointment was over. "I imagine there will be some paperwork to fill out?" Helen said genially, not entirely sure what she was talking about.

"Not really," Scapelli said.

There was only one elevator, and so Helen and Michael rode down together in uncomfortable silence. There wasn't even an attendant in the lobby, if it was fair to describe the half-lit rectangle between the elevator and the front door as a lobby in the first place. The building's main security system seemed to be its own essential undesirability, which left it all but invisible. Helen felt a sudden affinity for buildings like this one and the tentative, marginal enterprises they housed, much like the building that housed Harvey Aaron Public Relations, the marginal enterprise of which she had apparently just put herself in charge. Still, she did not feel as scared as she figured common sense would probably dictate. On the street it was unseasonably warm for the beginning of November. "Which way are you going?" she said to Michael.

"Which way are *you* going?" was his answer.

She pointed north with her thumb. "I think I'll walk back," she said. "Take the air."

"I'm getting on the F," he said in a relieved tone that suggested the F was in the opposite direction. But then he did not move in that direction right away. "So," he said. "I mean, is there any reason for us to be in touch?"

She felt as if she was going to cry. "I think it would be a good idea," she said. "Just from time to time. Of course you have the number there. And you could come by, too, any time. I mean, you're the boss. Literally."

He laughed at that, a little. "You know," he said, "I have to admit, all these years I never really got what it was my dad did all day."

"I didn't at first either," she said. "That was what we talked about the very first time we met. His explanation was lovely, actually. I've used it myself many times since then."

But Michael wasn't listening closely enough to take the bait. "I mean I used to Google him, for God's sake, and nothing came up. Do you even know how impossible that is?" He frowned. "Not to mention that you guys don't even have a website, which is like insane in this day and age."

"That's right, we don't," Helen said. "We really should. Is that something you'd know how to set up?"

He rolled his eyes to indicate the childish level of expertise required. But she could see the smile he was trying to suppress too. Really, even though he may have been too old to pull off the look and accompanying career path that he seemed determined to pull off, emotionally he still read as a little boy.

"Why don't you come by in the next day or two," she said, feeling triumphant, "and help us out with that? Whenever is good for you. Just come by."

He nodded, and they shook hands and set off in opposite directions, Michael to the F, Helen to the forlorn little office to tell Mona and Nevaeh that they still had jobs. That was a moment to look forward to. Neither woman seemed to have much love for the work itself, but a job was a job, and insurance was insurance, and they were all mothers.

BACK AT THE AGENCY the three women whooped and threw up their hands and even exchanged hugs, something that would have been unthinkable not that many weeks ago; and Helen was full of optimism for the business, based, as she readily admitted to herself later on the train home, less on any sort of practical sense of how to run things or plan for the future than on the loud, unembarrassed, supportive sororal energy that now suffused the small office, where before there had been mostly sullen time marking and an excessive emphasis on personal privacy. Mona and Nevaeh thanked her tearfully for saving their jobs, held her hand, and told her sentimentally that this was just how Harvey would have wanted it and that he would be proud of her. Then, two weeks later, Nevaeh stood up calmly from her desk on a Friday afternoon and announced to Helen that today would be her last day.

Helen could not believe her ears. It was plain from the studiously passive look on Mona's face that she had known this was in the works for some time and had shown where her loyalties lay by choosing not to mention it.

"But I thought—" Helen said and then couldn't finish the sentence. She didn't know anymore what she'd thought. Nevaeh, standing in front of her desk, looked down at her with a kind of curtailed pity.

"My aunt got me a job down at the Department of Housing," she said. "I wish the best for y'all here, but that's a city job, and city jobs ain't going anywhere. This here, I can't live with the uncertainty."

Helen was very sensitive to any assumption that she was the boss of this place; true, her title had been senior to theirs (even if titles had always had an element of whimsical inflation around there), and from the day of Harvey's death they had looked expectantly to her not because they thought she knew better but because they just didn't have the interest or commitment to it that she did. But race, she often felt, made the whole dynamic too complicated. She felt that way right now. The three of them were still crowded into the one outer room: no one would have stopped her if she'd moved her few things onto Harvey's desk, but she still hadn't done it.

"Isn't it customary to give two weeks' notice?" Helen said.

Nevaeh shrugged genially.

Helen must have looked especially discouraged after Nevaeh walked out, because Mona actually broke character and tried to cheer her up. "One less salary to come up with every week," she said, cocking her head. "That keeps us going that much longer. There wasn't that much for her to do anyway."

"You're right," Helen said, her eyes stinging. "Of course you're right. Why can't I just think of it that way?"

"Course, I'm looking around myself," Mona said, turning back to her computer screen. Maybe she meant she was looking right now, Helen thought. "You should be, too. I mean it's fine to hope, but when you're responsible for others, you got to make sure they're covered by something besides just hope, you know what I'm talking about?" Helen actually thought for a moment that Mona was talking about herself, that she meant to say that Helen was now responsible for her; but no, of course not, she was referring to Sara, who in Mona's eyes, even though the two women spent eight hours a day together, was the single most real thing about her.

They were not overly taxed by the amount of work they had left to do. It was simple stuff, even though Mona had to explain to Helen a lot of the nuts and bolts of it: how to get out a press release for a nightclub that was applying for a license on a residential block in the West Village and needed some positive coverage; how to gratify a Korean merchants' association out in Flushing that wanted some publicity for its modest charity work; how to talk patiently to a man in Floral Park who had bought up the trademarks for various boomer junk foods, such as Screaming Yellow Zonkers, and was convinced he could make a killing by reviving them. Mona and Helen took the train all the way out to Queens to meet that guy, at his pompous insistence, and then it turned out he was living and working in his married sister's basement. But somehow, miraculously, his checks kept clearing. That contract had another four months to run. Each of these little short-term contracts expired in the same way: with a handshake from the client, a rueful "So tragic about Harvey," and then done. No talk of renewal. Helen split each fee between payroll and the skeletal office expenses and Scapelli the lawyer, who emailed irregular updates on Harvey's shrinking posthumous debt. That was satisfying, as was the thought of actually handing Michael a check when all was said and done. Still, there was something inescapably gloomy about winding the business down like this. It was like Harvey's death all over again, only with a bedside vigil this time. Helen would have lowered her own salary for Michael's sake, but there was just no way she could afford it. Mona spent about a third of every workday looking at online listings for other jobs; Helen knew she should be doing the same but somehow couldn't rouse herself, those days, to think more than one step ahead.

At around four o'clock one Thursday afternoon, Michael showed up at the office, unannounced. He seemed shaken by the look of surprise on Helen's face. "I thought maybe that website idea we talked about," he said waveringly. "Of course," Helen said, ignoring Mona's indiscreetly raised eyebrows, and she showed him to the computer terminal on his father's desk.

"He's designing a webpage for the agency," she whispered to Mona as she sat down again. "It's something we really should have."

"Why?" Mona said and then waved her hands in front of her as if to erase her own question. "What does he expect to be paid for his time?"

Helen made a zero with her thumb and forefinger.

"Like father, like son," Mona said. "Well, I am leaving here at five either way."

"Me too," said Helen, "but he'll be fine here, we'll give him a key," and then she had a brainstorm.

"Michael?" she said, leaning against the doorjamb between the offices. "I just had a thought. One of our last remaining clients is a nightclub that's opening downtown. That's a business I know absolutely nothing about. How would you feel about handling that account with me? Figuring out what past problems have been with license applications, how to avoid them, how to put the owners in the best possible light?"

Michael had been scowling at his father's computer, which was less than state of the art, for most of this pitch. He blinked up at her. "What's the name of the club?"

"Repentance," Helen said.

He sighed. "That would be pretty awkward for me," he said. "I know those guys. So no." He began typing again, and Helen went back to her desk, more crestfallen than ever, not entirely sure what it was she'd been trying to make happen anyway.

She got home on time that night—there was nothing to keep her at work late, nor was there any real reason to take work home on the train—and when she rolled down the car window to pull the day's mail out of the box at the top of the driveway, she found a plump, oversize manila envelope from the office of Joe Bonifacio. It had no stamp on it: he must have driven it over himself, to save the postage. Inside the dark garage she turned the engine off and opened the envelope, and there she found her divorce papers, ready for her signature.

"There is nothing to eat in this place" was how Sara greeted her when she walked into the vestibule. "And I did not think it was even possible to get sick of pizza but I cannot eat pizza again, like ever."

Helen got back in the car and drove to the IGA for a chicken, thinking that they couldn't really afford to be ordering out all the time anyway; on her way home she stopped at the liquor store and bought a bottle of Gewürztraminer, which she hadn't had for years because Ben was a wine snob and couldn't bear even the smell of it. She cooked dinner, and cleaned the broiler, and did the dishes, and then when Sara was in bed she took the Gewürztraminer out of the refrigerator and filled one of the big wineglasses to about a quarter inch from the top. She pulled the divorce papers out of her purse and told herself that she would set aside for reminiscence only the time it took her to get to the end of that glass of wine: when it was empty, she would sign and be done with it. At this point looking at her own past felt to her like standing with your heels on the edge of a subway platform: losing your balance was obviously a bad idea, but if you thought about it too hard you'd go over anyway.

She knew she'd fallen for all the wrong things in Ben—his confidence, his ease in social situations, the way she'd catch him staring at her, the life free from want that seemed like a lock in the company of the kind of man who knew exactly where he was headed. He was so smart. His mind was always going. He treated her more gently than any man, in her admittedly thin experience, had ever treated her. She used to *ask* him to tell her what to read, what to wear, what to order; if, later in life, she found this same sort of input from him invasive or condescending, that wasn't really his fault—the change was in her. She had come to the city after college with the money left to her by her father when he passed away her senior year, money that would not last long, no matter how frugal she was with it. He was in his third year of law school, with a job offer already in hand, and she was working for Ralph Lauren. It seemed as decent a job as any other. She was not a shallow person by any means, but she had no sense of a calling. He was in the city for the weekend, and a friend of Helen's fixed them up. The friend had been out with Ben once herself. "You will love him," she said. "Personally I like them a little more malleable." Helen did love him, and he found her worth loving too, and as clear and shameful as it seemed in retrospect that what had drawn them together was his self-regard and her naïveté, still, even on that foundation, they had been happy for many years.

They had even stayed happy, and boundlessly supportive, through the sad struggle to conceive a child, the three miscarriages, the last of which changed the tone of her doctor's voice dramatically. She had never been told that she was barren—no woman under sixty was ever told that nowadays, it seemed—but faced with the obstacles involved, the drugs and the nine months lying in bed and the long odds against ending up anywhere other than where they had ended up three times already, they decided to adopt. That way they could still be parents at what seemed like a reasonable age. Thirteen months and two trips to China and a move to the suburbs and a lot of Ben's money later, they brought home Sara, eleven months old, the best day of all their lives. One child seemed like such a blessing at that point that two was something they had never even discussed.

She stopped working, while Ben of course still put in long days in the city, and somewhere in those years, static though they seemed in every respect other than the growth of Sara herself, the great drift took place. His life and her life were shaped like parentheses that came closest to touching at the very beginning and the very end of every day. Sex, when they had it, became for Helen a form of denial, the way some couples will point to their children's good report cards as evidence that everything at home is actually okay. They didn't fight about anything—it wasn't really their nature; instead she just watched her husband's face turn slowly blank, and decided to attribute it to the demands of his job. He made partner, and Sara grew into a child with no hidden developmental surprises other than an extraordinary gift for sports, and Helen, at some point, forgot to find anything else to want from life, and this had turned her into a boring person, a burden, a part of the upkeep, and she might have floated along mindlessly like that forever, or at least until Sara went off to college, were it not for the fact that her lack of inner resources had driven her husband insane. She drank off the last of her wine, signed her name to the divorce papers, stuffed them back into her purse, and walked unsteadily down the hall to bed.

The next morning she found a message on her office desk, left there the night before by Michael: "A Congressman called," it said. That didn't seem right, particularly when accompanied by a 718 phone number. Helen dialed it. "Councilman Bratkowski's office," a woman's voice answered. Councilman, congressman, whatever, Helen laughed to herself as she sat on hold; but something about the name rang a bell. Holding the phone with her shoulder, she Googled his name and hit Return, and she saw what it was just at the moment the councilman's voice boomed over the line.

"So you *are* still in business?" he said jovially. "The guy I talked to last night told me Harvey Aaron was dead, which my condolences. You're the folks who handled the Peking Grill strike, right?"

An hour later, Helen was on the subway out to Elmhurst, a ride long enough to give her time to read through that day's *Post* and *Daily News*, much of which was devoted to the reason she'd been called. Doug Bratkowski, a two-term councilman with a wife and three teen-age children, had been caught on a building surveillance camera in the Bronx, beating a young woman purported to be his mistress. Helen had seen the silent, fifteen-second clip online as she pulled her coat on: first an empty hallway, then a large figure in an overcoat pulling a much smaller woman into the frame by her long hair; she pushes away from him, hits him weakly in the chest, and then he punches her in the face. Prodding her down the stairs ahead of him, he turns to scan the hallway behind them, and at that point his face, though bloated with anger, is clearly identifiable.

"Please have a seat," the councilman said, closing the door behind them. His office might have belonged to a storefront lawyer, with fake white paneling and a breakfront that looked like it was made of particleboard. On his desk, facing outward, were framed photos of his family, and one of himself shaking hands with Mayor Bloomberg, both men facing the camera rather than each other.

"Will anyone else be joining us?" Helen asked.

Even his smile was like a hand on her shoulder. "Best to keep the loop as small as possible in times like these, I think. Here is where we stand. The young woman in question is not pressing any charges. She has been publicly named, though, and I'm sure the tabloids have all got their checkbooks out. At some point she may crack, I don't know. So what I need is to figure out how to limit my exposure, not legally, but . . . well, you're the pro, you must know what I'm talking about."

He was a bear of a man, red-faced even when calm, with the tracks of a comb clearly visible in his hair. Helen fought down her fear of him. "Were you having an affair with this woman, Councilman?" she asked.

He affected surprise and smiled again. "Call me Doug," he said. "Is that strictly relevant to what you need to do?"

She wasn't sure it was. But she found herself needing to know it anyway. "Think of me as you would think of a lawyer," Helen said. "I cannot be in a position where I am taken by surprise by information the other side has and I don't."

He nodded. "Well then, yes," he said. "Assuming we have the seal of the confessional here, I was, and am, having an affair with the young woman on the tape. For about two years now. My wife, who is currently not speaking to me, did not know about it until the day before yesterday. There's no love child or anything like that. I never spent any public money on her, I never hired her for any phony campaign job. She is," he said, "just this smoking hot Latina chick I have been banging on the side, just like millions of people do all over the world every day. Does that give you everything you need to work with?"

She recrossed her legs and resmoothed her skirt, just to give herself a few seconds. Then, with great effort, she stared back right into his eyes. "The way I see it, there's really only one way for you to go," she said. "You tell the woman who answers the phone out there that all media inquiries are to be forwarded to me. I will announce that you'll be delivering a statement tonight at, let's say, eight-thirty, plenty of time for the late news and for tomorrow's papers. I don't know what your home looks like, but if the optics are right, we can do it there—outside, not inside—and if not, we can do it here, I suppose. Little cramped, though."

"And what will I be saying?" the councilman asked evenly.

"You will admit to everything. You will apologize to this young woman, by name, for your violent behavior. You will not use any phrases like 'moment of weakness' or 'regrettable incident.' You will apologize to your wife, and to your children, and to your parents if they are still alive, and to your constituents whether they voted for you or not, and to women everywhere. Basically, you will get up in front of the cameras and make an offering of yourself."

Some of the redness drained from his face as she spoke; she could feel, as she'd felt before, the power her words gave her over him. "You really think that's the play?" he said.

"That is the only play. To ask forgiveness. If you hold back in any way, the story lives. Let me ask you this: presumably you are a man with ambitions. What do you want to happen now? What is the outcome that will put those ambitions back on the track that your own mistakes threw them off of?"

He tipped back noiselessly in his chair. "I want to stay in office," he said. "I want to be reelected. This was a stupid thing for me to have done, but it does not define me. It was a one-time thing, and I want to get away from it."

"You will never get away from it," Helen said. "But you can incorporate it into the narrative. You have to be sincere. You have to be completely abject, and not attempt to defend yourself or your behavior in any way. No 'I was drunk,' no 'she hit me first.' You have to take, and answer, every question. You have to hold your temper when people try to get you to lose it. Do you think you can do that?"

"Should my wife be there?" he said.

Helen considered it. She was sure just from talking to him that, for better or worse, he could make it happen. "Depends," she said. "Depends on the look on her face."

His eyes drifted off to one side for a few seconds. "Okay, probably not, then," he said. "Listen, don't take this the wrong way, but this had better work. It's not really my nature to get up in front of a bunch of cameras and show my ass like that."

"It's not about your nature, it's about everybody else's. And it will work. This way and no other."

He stood and lifted Helen's coat off the chair beside her, holding it as she turned her back to him and inserted her shaking hands. "You know," he said, "for what it's worth, this was the first time I ever raised my hand to her."

"That," she said, "is exactly the kind of thing I don't ever want you to say to anybody but me."

IT WORKED; she knew it would work, even without completely understanding why. In her faith in the tactic of total submission she felt herself delivering a kind of common-sense rebuke not just to her ex-husband and his lawyer but to legal minds everywhere. She stood shivering behind the councilman, out of camera range, on the front stoop of his Elmhurst row house for an hour and forty minutes, and he was so good she found it hard to doubt how sincere he was. Even with a unanimous motion to censure him in the city council, it was out of the news in four days.

Mona looked over Helen's shoulder as she typed up the invoice to send to Bratkowski's office. "Are you crazy?" she said. "This is government money we're talking about. Double it." Helen couldn't quite get herself to do that, but she did bump it up another few thousand, and they paid it without a word. A week later, Helen went through the day's office mail and found a Christmas card from Doug and Jane Bratkowski, with a photo of the whole family wearing matching sweaters. You couldn't really tell anything from a photo. Still, she stood it on her desk.

Can it really be this simple? she thought. As with the Peking Grill job, word of the agency's success seemed to filter out quickly and to generate an aura in which other jobs came their way, jobs that had nothing at all to do with the sort of apology wrangling she was starting to think of as her vocation, her accidental specialty. The aura seemed to magnetize even her life outside the office, and to bring other good news: Sara's dentist told them that she was the rare child who would not need orthodontia, for instance, and then at the end of the soccer season she was named all-county, the only Rensselaer Valley girl so honored. And then Helen got a call at home on a Saturday morning from Joe Bonifacio. While the various lawsuits were still far from settled, there had been one breakthrough, which was that Cornelia Hewitt's lawyers had agreed, for the sake of the child involved, to exempt the house itself from the list of court-frozen assets, on the condition that the deed be transferred to Helen's name alone.

"What does that mean?" Helen said softly; it was ten-thirty, but Sara wasn't up yet.

"It means that the house now belongs entirely to you, and that you are free to sell it and to profit by its sale."

"Isn't this something Ben would have to agree to?"

"He's agreed to it," Bonifacio said. "Done."

Helen's mouth still hung open after she got off the phone. Ben had to have worked all this out to his advantage, she told herself; he always had an angle, in any transaction involving money, at least—money and the law. In his fallen state he was paying no alimony anyway, though the court had vowed to revisit that, once the litigation against him was resolved and he was discharged from rehab. Belatedly she realized that she had neglected to ask Bonifacio if there was any new word on when Ben would be getting out—if indeed he wasn't out already; invoices from Stages went straight to the lawyer's office, so if no one thought to tell her, she supposed, she'd have no way of knowing. Broken or ashamed as he may have been, could he really be back in the world and not have made any attempt to contact, or even check on, his child? Not that she especially wanted him to, at least not yet. She almost called Bonifacio back to ask, but then Sara's bedroom door groaned open, and Helen dropped the phone on the couch.

The next night at dinner, which they ate in front of the TV, Helen hit Mute and said, "Sara, remember a few months ago, we talked about moving?"

"We did?" Sara said.

"We did. We talked about moving to the city. Not seriously, at that point, which I guess is why you don't remember, but anyway you allowed as how that was something you might actually like to do. Do you still feel that way?"

Sara's eyes were very wide. "I don't know," she said. "I guess."

"Okay, then," Helen said, "good to know," and she relaxed back into the couch and put the sound on again, trying not to smile.

All of a sudden it seemed that this Christmas might well be their last in that house, the only home Sara had ever known. When Helen called Mark Byrne at Rensselaer Valley Realty, the same agent who had sold the house to them fourteen years earlier, to let him know that she wanted to see about putting it back on the market—tentatively, discreetly, exploratorily—it was like he was over there pounding a For Sale sign into their lawn before she'd hung up the phone. There were offers right away—not great ones, but Helen resolved, without a word to Mark Byrne or anyone else, that she would accept the best offer they had in hand before New Year's, no matter what it was. Time to move on.

So in addition to her modest Christmas preparations—gifts for Sara, and a decent meal, and a clean house, and a little something for Mona and for Michael—Helen would have to scramble to find a halfway affordable apartment in Manhattan (two bedrooms, please God let them be able to afford two bedrooms, or Sara's wrath would be ferocious) and a decent nearby public school. Exciting as it was to be able to think of a future that extended further than their next heating-oil bill, Helen felt oddly guilty as well—more nostalgic than guilty, actually, but in some ways it amounted to the same thing. For all that had gone sour within it over the last few months and years, this was their home, and the faith in the future required to walk away from it risked seeming arrogant, even reckless. What was behind you had, for better or worse, a substantiality that what was still in front of you could not exhibit. It was a big moment, and Helen found herself wanting to mark it somehow rather than just slip from one season into another like an animal; and then she recalled that there was something she'd long wanted to do at Christmas to which Ben had always firmly said no.

"Church?" Sara said. "Are you nuts?"

"Just the Christmas Eve service," Helen said soothingly. "For a lot of people that's the only one they go to all year. Not the midnight mass. It starts at five, and we'll be home for dinner. Very mellow, lots of singing. Nothing too churchy."

"Why?"

"It's something I used to do as a kid. I'd like to do it again, maybe just to remind me of that. That's all. I'm not born again or anything. Please? For me?"

"Okay, I'll do it," Sara said. "On one condition."

Helen was shocked. "Thank you, honey," she said. "What condition?"

"I want to go to the movies before. Like that afternoon. A little of your idea of Christmas Eve, a little of mine. Okay?"

Helen beamed. "Sure. That sounds like fun. We could go see that movie *A Time of Mourning* that's just opened, I know it's at the Triplex, that's the new Hamilton Barth movie—"

"Uh, Mom? Did I say 'we'?"

"Oh. Well, okay. I just thought maybe you'd want to see *A Time of Mourning* and I know I would too—"

"Like I would pay eleven dollars to see some skeezy old guy you once made out with fifty years ago. Though I would gladly pay eleven dollars if someone could just scrub that image out of my head forever."

"So you'd rather go see something on your own?"

"Yes," said Sara, and something in her face, some studious attempt at expressionlessness, made Helen realize what was really going on here—oh my God, she thought, there's a boy. Someone she was going to have to say goodbye to.

"Fine," said Helen, coloring. "Just be back home no later than four, to change. No sweats in church."

After lunch on Christmas Eve, Sara rode her bike up the hill to the top of Meadow Close, and by the time she got out to the main road she didn't feel the cold anymore. She rode along the thin shoulder to the traffic light, across the five-way intersection where she always got honked at, over the highway bridge, and into town. There was very little parking for cars along the narrow main street, especially at this time of year, so behind the row of storefronts on the north side of the street it was all municipal parking lots, as if the town itself was just a façade built like a movie set. Sara cut behind the hardware store and rode through the silent lots all the way across town, even though she sometimes had to get off the bike to cross a guardrail or to thread her way between empty cars, because doing so reduced the chances of seeing anyone she knew. She passed the emergency exit behind the movie theater and kept going, past the blank rear walls of the jeweler and the Starbucks and the pharmacy, until she got to the lot at the back of a little family-owned Polish grocery all the way at the far end of Main Street, a mysteriously durable place where no one ever seemed to shop, with two small tables in the back in case someone wanted to sit and have a cup of Polish coffee. Sara leaned her bike against the concrete wall behind the recycling bins and walked through the back door, blowing on her hands, and there, standing up from one of the two little tables, was her father.

"Hi, sweetheart," he said. He must have just gotten there himself, because his overcoat, though open, was still on; he held out his arms and took her inside it, and the sensation of being warmed in that way struck something too deep in her, so that she stepped back out of his embrace almost right away.

He stood there grinning stiffly. "You look great," he said.

"Thanks," said Sara, and remained standing.

After a few silent seconds he laughed and asked, "And? How do I look?"

She considered it. "Less tired," she said.

"Thank you for coming," he said, which was such a weird thing for your father to say to you. They took off their coats and sat; the owner brought him a coffee and her a hot chocolate, which irritated her because coffee was what she wanted, but then he brought over these two amazing hot rolls with some kind of cream inside. She ate hers and started in on his. He brought out a tiny giftwrapped present and said, "Merry Christmas." She licked her fingers before taking it from him and put it straight into her pocket.

"Fine," he said, "but just be careful where you open it. I don't think you want your mom to find out it's from me. It's why I didn't get you something bigger."

"Are you coming home?" Sara said abruptly. "I mean just for Christmas Day or whatever?"

Ben flushed. "I don't think so. I don't see that happening. Not this year, anyway."

"Did you even ask her?" He shook his head no. "Why not? Afraid she'd say no?"

"Too soon," he said simply. "Too soon to ask her for anything, after what I did." He watched her eat. "Why," he said, "do you think she would have said no?"

"Probably, yeah," Sara said. "But anyway, not this year pretty much equals never, because Mom's selling the house. She says we're moving to the city." He didn't look as surprised by that as she expected him to.

"The thing I was really afraid she'd say no to," he said, "was this. Seeing you. Which is why I texted you directly, which I probably should not have done. But I don't want to talk about me anymore. We don't have a ton of time. I want to hear you talk. Tell me everything I've missed."

She told him about school, and about soccer, and about her new routine as a latchkey kid while Mom was at work, which Sara had to admit she sort of liked—a couple of hours with the house all to herself. She asked him where he was living now, and he just looked embarrassed and said, "Nearby." She didn't know if he expected to be asked anything about how he'd spent the last few months in rehab, but she figured he'd talk about that if he wanted to. Maybe he wasn't allowed. One thing he never said to her was "I'm sorry," but in a way she was glad he didn't, because it would have been too unlike him, and right now she just needed him to be as much like himself as possible.

Outside the front windows the streetlights started to come on. No one had come into the grocery the whole time they were there, but the owner was making no move toward closing the place. Ben paid the check and then pulled something out of his pocket and slid it across the table toward her: it was a movie ticket. "I stopped and bought it on my way here," he said. "It's for the one-forty show."

She looked blankly at him.

"So you have the stub," he said, almost proudly. "That's where she thinks you are right now, right? So now you have your alibi. In case she gets suspicious."

"Please," Sara said, standing up to put her coat on, leaving the ticket where it lay. "It's Mom."

3

NO ONE COULD TELL YOU MORE about narcissism than an addict, recovering or otherwise; and during Ben's first two weeks inside Stages, even though he wasn't technically addicted to anything, in all the talk about narcissism he'd recognized enough of himself not to feel like too much of an impostor there. True, when his turn came around to talk (that's all they did there was talk, in various configurations, over and over again until dinner), he had initially felt the need to amp it up a bit, in terms of the details of his drinking, his sexual compulsions, the destructive misbehavior that had left his life, and others, a ruin. And they could tell he was lying—they were expert at spotting it—but the funny thing was they read it as denial, they thought he was lying out of cowardice rather than fear of mockery or scorn for the relative luxuriousness of his problems. So he amped it up even further, until after a few weeks of group he had gotten quite good at it, so good even he couldn't always distinguish the manufactured shame from the real. By the end of a month he felt like a lifer there, with an inmate's sense of propriety and a protective attitude toward all the place's earnest rituals and customs. He was as shocked as could be on the Monday after Thanksgiving when at the end of a one-on-one his counselor, Paul, tapped him on the knee and said, "Benjamin, I believe your work here is done."

And the odd thing was that he had never felt more like an addict than he did on the day of his discharge: the world beyond that leafy, unmanned gate was suddenly a pretty scary prospect. His car was still in the lot. He let the engine run for a few minutes and tried to think what, of a practical nature, he should do. The first thing was to call the lawyer, Bonifacio, and tell him to close the escrow account they'd set aside for his treatment. He left a voice mail. The second thing was maybe to alert Helen that he was out? But then he recalled that that tie was no longer there, that they had severed it, legally and otherwise. He didn't know what he would say to her anyway—or to Sara, at least not yet. He hadn't spoken to his daughter in almost three months; the counselors had forbidden it for the first two, and even after that any phone call would have had to have been monitored, a condition Ben could not accept. In any case Sara would be in school with her phone turned off for another six or seven hours. Still, he had nowhere else even to point himself toward, no place of employment, no other home, and all his possessions outside of one suitcase were still in the house on Meadow Close, unless she'd stored them, or sold them, or burned them. He imagined he could feel the eyes of Paul on his idling car. Without coming to any conclusion about anything, he backed out of the lot and began the drive of forty minutes or so back to Rensselaer Valley.

As before, he made it most but not all of the way. A few exits east of his turnoff on 684, he had to pull over into the half-empty lot beside an office park because he thought he might be hyperventilating. Ten minutes later he got back on the highway; this time he made it all the way to the hill at the top of Meadow Close before stopping again. The house seemed almost to change its contours, to shrink or tighten against the bare trees and the cold, gray overcast. The yard looked like hell. A light was on in the bedroom window. He recalled that, in a fit of righteous remorse brought on by therapy, he had signed the house over to Helen while sitting on his bed one night in rehab; it was highly unlikely that she could have sold the place as quickly as that, but still, for all he knew some stranger might be lying under that light. He had no real right to go in there anyway, no reason sounder than whimsy to go anywhere. The fear whose physical symptoms he marveled at was not unmixed with other sorts of feelings, for in a way, he had to admit as he sat staring through the windshield with his hands in his lap, he now had exactly what he had wanted. He was a new man. Whatever step he took next would not be one he had taken many times, or even once, before. All that survived of his old life was the disgrace of its end, and there was something almost comfortable about that disgrace, about the burden of it; it seemed to be what he'd been courting all along, and now it was his. That was what had first begun to exasperate him about Helen, way back when: she believed in him too blindly, she refused to see how he bore the weight of what he was capable of. Out of nowhere, an amplified horn blasted right behind him and nearly put his head through the roof; a huge yellow Hummer drifted to a stop on his left, smack in the middle of the road, and the tinted passenger-side window, two feet above his head, rolled down.

"Is that Ben Armstead?" Dr. Parnell said.

The two of them turned off their engines and spoke through their windows. That Parnell was a boor and a prick and a windbag was something Ben had known for years, but never had he felt as repulsed by his old neighbor as he did now, when with a raised eyebrow and a puerile smirk he kept trying to convey to Ben that they were hypermasculine birds of a feather, that boys, whether driving obnoxious monster cars or nailing hot underlings in hotel rooms, would be boys. But he did at least invite Ben inside his home, and serve him a cup of coffee. And he did seem to understand something about the limbo in which Ben found himself, because out of nowhere he offered the use of a cottage he kept on Candlewood Lake, for fishing, he said. No one used it this time of year. Ben thanked him and took down the directions, and when he had finished his coffee he drove straight there.

The presence of candles and old wine bottles and a king-size bed cast suspicion on Parnell's claim that he used the cottage only for fishing. It was winterized, thank God. None of the few other cabins visible from its tiny back porch were occupied, even on weekends. Maybe in another month or so, Ben thought, when the lake iced over. In the meantime, the days crept safely by. He spent Christmas there, with the relief of a secret, cordial, but uneventful hour with Sara the day before to sustain him. He made no contact with his ex-wife but assumed that she knew he was out of Stages, that either Sara or Bonifacio would have found occasion to mention it to her. He'd had Bonifacio send her the rest of the escrow money, labeled as back child support. No response. Then, a few days after New Year's, when he broached with Sara the idea of arranging another meeting, she texted him peremptorily that they were moving—in fact had already moved, the previous weekend—to Manhattan. He was left to contemplate that during a raw, muddy January in which the lake ice never thickened to more than an inch or two. Even if it weren't his inclination, he wouldn't have had much choice but to wait: his future, in a legal sense at least, was still being negotiated elsewhere, without his direct involvement, and until that process was over, there wasn't much to plan for.

What had he done? It was a question he asked himself more in wonder than in regret. He couldn't even bring himself to regret the manner in which it had happened, the damage done to others, because the damage itself defined him now, defined even his flickering relationship to Sara, in that he had something to prove to her, though he wasn't yet sure what, or how. He had renounced himself: that was as far as it went. But that was pretty far.

It was a ten-mile drive to town, and there was nothing in town anyway, so Ben had little to do all day but think—not that different from rehab, really, save for the atmosphere of relentless silence. The cabin resembled Stages too in its technological isolation from the wider world, for it was socked in by hills and Ben's phone got no reception whatsoever. It wasn't wired for cable either. Once a day, sometimes twice, Ben would drive into town, park around the side of the Mobil station where he couldn't be seen from its front windows, and check for messages from his few remaining contacts in the world. In truth, if you left out all those emails that still came to him robotically for one reason or another, like bank statements and unchanging frequent-flier account updates, he was down to two correspondents. In the gray late afternoon when he was likeliest to catch her on her way home from school, he sat in the driver's seat with the heater on high and texted his daughter. This was both satisfying and frustrating, for Sara was a stingy texter, and he was left unsure whether this was a generational thing, or a measure of her own impatience and lack of thumb-typing skills, or whether she was trying to forget about him but lacked the fortitude to come right out and tell him so.

Hows ur new school?

Ok.

Hows ur new apt?

Sux.

She had an entirely new life, but you wouldn't know it from her lack of affect, if it even made any sense to criticize text messages for a lack of affect. At least she hadn't blocked him. After ten or fifteen minutes of this sort of exchange—she didn't know where on earth he was; she didn't seem to need to know—he'd walk into the Mobil station for a poisonous cup of six-hour-old coffee and a *New York Times*, and then he'd go back out to the car and call his lawyer.

That guy had turned out to be a find. If Ben still had a job himself, he would have hired Bonifacio in a heartbeat. Like most good litigators Ben had known, Bonifacio was a killer, a misanthrope, with the vengeful air of a man whose embarrassing delusions about the goodness of people had long ago been destroyed. Or maybe it was just that he knew how to hire a good PI, but in any event he had managed to turn up so much dirt about Cornelia Hewitt—including, delightfully, an affidavit that down at Duke she had slept with one of her professors—that they were able to settle the suit for what amounted, when compared to the nightmare scenarios of just a few months earlier, to pennies on the dollar. So Ben would still have some money left after all. The real financial winner in the end, though, was Bonifacio himself, who had even let slip to Ben, with a provocatory slyness, that he and his wife had briefly looked into buying Ben's old house when Helen first put it on the market.

But the criminal case, though manipulable, wasn't so easily closed. The sexual assault charge was, as Bonifacio had predicted, dropped before it could be dismissed, which indicated mercifully that there would be no trial, but also that there was some bargaining going on. Ben had little idea from day to day where things stood, or when the resolution might come. When the first of February passed—when he had been at Parnell's cabin on the lake, with nothing to do, for two full months, and the lake was finally frozen over, and he had read every ridiculous Tom Clancy and James Patterson book in the place, and it was dark and bone-cold even inside his car during the half hours he spent texting back and forth with Sara while she sat watching TV in her new apartment, before abruptly signing off *mom here gotta go* — he returned a call from Bonifacio and learned that even the best plea deal his lawyer could negotiate was going to have to include some token jail time.

"Twenty-eight days," Bonifacio said. "The DA says he can't go any lower. It's a high-profile case, and DWI is just such a political thing these days. Frankly, if you think about the position we were in three or four months ago, it isn't half bad."

Ben, though he felt oddly calm, was shaking. He turned the heat up another notch with his free hand. "It's a good deal, I know," he said. "Nice work on your part."

"Well, I went to high school with the guy," Bonifacio said.

"I assume you'll let Helen know?"

"Don't assume it," Bonifacio said coolly. "I represent you separately now, at least until you revisit the custody issue, which nobody seems quite ready to do yet. Apart from that, the only mandatory disclosures are financial. The money left over from escrow covers child support until, I don't know, the summer I think. I'll tell her where you are if she asks me where you are. Otherwise, it's not my place."

"Has she ever asked you where I am?"

"Not to date. She knows you're out there somewhere."

Wow, Ben thought. Good for her. "Does she know I've been in touch with Sara?"

"Ooh," said Bonifacio. "Not smart. In fact I think I'm going to have to pretend you didn't tell me that. Anyway, I haven't actually seen Helen in months. Of course, I haven't seen you in even longer. My biggest clients! We're all just voices in each other's ears now."

Ben would do his time at a minimum-security facility in a town called Mineville, north of Albany; Bonifacio had never been there himself, but he'd been assured it was the cushiest prison in the eastern part of the state. In ten days Ben would drive himself to the courthouse in Poughkeepsie, where he would surrender, make a brief court appearance to accept the plea formally and to allocute to his crimes, and then a couple of sheriff's deputies would drive him about four hours north to jail. Ben knew full well how all of this worked, but he let his lawyer go on explaining it anyway. Then he went inside, bought a shrink-wrapped roast beef sandwich and a can of beer, and drove back out to the cabin.

He was a pariah, a dead soul, and he was unsure how any of the various purgatories he was living through was ultimately going to return him to the world. He had gone from a life dominated by routine and obligation to a life wherein each day was almost perfectly vacant, and yet, when those pointless days began to count down from five, he felt the onset of panic at their ending. It kept him from sleeping more than about an hour at a time. He wasn't scared of prison, exactly. From what he knew of these places, this one wouldn't be that much different from Stages, only with plainer food and fewer meetings. The last days in the cabin came and went, seeming unfairly short, even though he had no way to pass them but to sit inside with his feet near the baseboard heater and stare out at the empty lake. He thought about making a run for it. He thought about trying to get some Ambien prescribed to him, but he did not know a doctor or even a single soul in this area beyond the fat kid behind the Mobil counter. Something kept him from calling Parnell and asking for this second, negligible favor. He did call Bonifacio to ask if the prison in Mineville allowed inmates the use of their phones: the answer was no, but they were allowed limited access to the Internet each day via the prison's own server. So he could still email Sara. The emails would be coming from a different IP address now; maybe she'd wonder about that, or maybe she wouldn't even notice it.

He decided that his fear was a function of simple instinct and that there was nothing to be done about it. On his last morning in the cabin he was awake at dawn, stripping the bed and sweeping up with a broom he'd found. Through the window, as the light slid over the frozen lake, he could see that there was someone out there, maybe a hundred yards offshore, sitting in front of a hole in the ice. The thermometer on the porch read nine degrees. Man, Ben thought. For what? He drank a cup of instant coffee while staring at the guy, who did not move; then he rinsed out the cup, put the key to the cabin on the lintel over the front door, and drove off to meet the authorities.

———

CRISIS MANAGEMENT was what she had learned to call it, but Helen's sense of her own particular niche in the world of public relations—in the realm, as Harvey had taught her to think of it, of public storytelling— didn't get much more sophisticated than that. She had no idea how to draw attention to her own achievements, or how to leverage the exposure (such as when the *Times* mentioned her in a sidebar after Brat- kowski was censured by the city council) that sometimes came her way as an accidental but still natural consequence of her success. She didn't know how to find new clients—she just said yes or no to those who ap- proached her, and in fact she didn't yet feel she had the luxury of say- ing no to anyone. She didn't know how, or else just lacked the aggression, to be the first one to cold-call whenever something went publicly wrong: a schoolteacher who was dating a student, a hair salon that burned a client's skin, a charity whose books were cooked. Her business model, and Mona's, was basically to pick up the phone when it rang. It was no way to get rich, that was for sure. It was a formula for getting by, and that's what they were all doing, with no sort of plan or even provision for the future, and with no one in her life who might offer her advice.

She did have some sense of what her skills were, even if they seemed less like skills than like instincts. She got powerful men to apol- ogize. Maybe women too, though she was a bit curious about that one herself since she'd never yet taken on a female client. The thing was, she seemed able to do it without even trying that hard. She got them to confess because they didn't seem to want to lie to her. Once this thresh- old had been crossed, it was a relatively simple matter to stand nearby while they confessed to the world at large via a TV camera or a micro- phone, though Helen frequently had the sensation that even in that broadcast moment the camera and the mike were still somehow basi- cally surrogates or fetishes, material symbols of herself.

Of course she worried too that this talent for inducing apology was maybe more of a lucrative quality than a personally attractive one. In the interest of avoiding hypocrisy, she took time to reflect that she was far from guilt-free herself. Her ex-husband may have had a lot to answer for over the last year or two, but the larger fact was he had turned from one sort of man in his twenties to a very different sort in his forties, and the only X factor to point to there, the only new element, was her. She had implicitly promised her daughter a warm, stable home—had taken her from the land of her birth and spirited her around the world on the basis of that promise—and now, when Sara wasn't in a gigantic and socially imposing public middle school where she knew no one, she was in a cramped one-bedroom apartment with her exhausted mother, ordering out for dinner, trying to remember to fold out the couch before falling asleep. (Helen had offered her the bedroom, but it was much smaller than the living room and had no TV in it.) And then there was Harvey's death, which groundless pride had kept her from preventing and which had changed numerous lives for the worse. Who was she to tell other people to confront their sins and move on?

Still, they kept coming, if not exactly in droves. In March she got her first corporate call, even if only a local one: Amalgamated Supermarkets, a low-end grocery chain that hung on as a stubbornly sane alternative to the efflorescence of Whole Foods and Gourmet Garages, had a PR nightmare when some young mother bought a bunch of bananas with razors stuck in them. She found this out by feeding them to her children, one of whom almost died. Helen read the story over someone's shoulder on the bus to the office, and for once her first thought was, I wonder if they'll call us. In fact they had left a voice mail already. She headed right back uptown to Amalgamated's corporate office, and, after a few minutes with the alarmingly young borough manager who had phoned her, she was fully if not pleasantly engaged.

"I hate it that you're here," he said. "It's like a visit from the Grim Reaper. And the thing is, we didn't do anything wrong. This is all so fucking unfair."

"What's unfair?" Helen asked him. He seemed young enough to be her son; he was somebody's son, more than likely, or he wouldn't have had an executive's job at his age.

"Ever tried to get a razor into a banana?" he said, a little louder than necessary. "You can't do it! It can't be done! I sat here at my desk last night and tried!" He held up his hands; three of his fingertips had bandages on them. "It is obvious that this broad did it herself, to try to work up a bogus lawsuit, because that's easier than getting a job and working, a lawsuit that we'll settle to make it go away, regardless of its transparent fucking bogusness, pardon my French, which is why I hate meetings with PR people, because PR people are always telling you to roll over and stick your ass in the air and settle, when every bone in my body is telling me we should fight this."

Helen felt the sort of counterintuitive calm blooming in her that she had learned to expect in these situations. "You think this woman fed her son a razor blade," she said, "to try to get grounds for a lawsuit?"

In reply the young executive—who was wearing one of those striped dress shirts with a white collar; Lord, Helen hated those shirts, they were like sandwich boards for assholes—reached into his top drawer, pulled out a file folder, and dropped it theatrically on the desk between them. "Her psychiatric file," he said. "I had a PI pull it yesterday, and he's got this much already. Would you like to have a look?"

"No," Helen said. "Here's what you do with that. You give it to your lawyer, and if you have already made another copy of it, you run that copy through the shredder. I don't want anyone here to refer to it in public, not even by accident, and the easiest way to ensure that is for no one to have seen it in the first place."

The man in the asshole shirt leaned forward, red-faced. Clearly it was going to take a little extra work to convert this guy. "I don't understand you people," he said. "You are giving this crazy bitch a license to steal from us. Where is this Harvey guy, anyway? I think a man might understand my point of view a little better."

You people? Whom did he think she was there representing? "No one is going to steal from you," she said. "That's what you pay lawyers to make sure of. They will go behind closed doors and they will probably take this poor, sick woman apart, but it is important that that happens where no one else can see it. I work in the realm of the seen."

"Okay," he said.

"What I'm doing for you has nothing to do with money."

"It doesn't?"

"Well, okay, it does," Helen said. "But only indirectly. That is, if you act correctly now, even against what you may think of as your interest, the reward will come to you and to Amalgamated later, down the road, as a result."

He had begun to smile obnoxiously. "I have a cousin," he said, "who's in a church like this."

Helen had no idea what he was talking about; she closed her eyes and shook her head once, to get herself back on track. "We have to think of it in terms of storytelling," she said. "Imagine how you want the customers to think of Amalgamated, say, two months from now. Then we begin to tell the story that leads them to that place. If it's a story of our guilt, of our desire to make amends, if that's how it begins, then so be it. You have to take the long view, even if it means making some sacrifices now in the service of that greater truth."

He tipped back in his chair. She could see he was coming around, just like they always did. "See, though, I keep coming back," he said, "to the fact that we very probably, very likely, didn't do anything wrong here."

"But you don't know. You don't know, I don't know, nobody knows. People want to believe you did something wrong, though. And if you keep denying what they believe, that just strengthens their suspicion. You're already guilty in their minds. But if you take it upon yourself, if you just agree to own it, then they're yours, then you're the one making the choices that drive the story from that point forward. If it helps you, you can think of it as a way of making up for other things you really did do, other more legitimate grievances people might have against you—a way to atone for sins you aren't even necessarily aware of."

He grinned, and shook his head. "Okay, Sister," he said. "You're hired. Now what do we do next?"

She raised her fee again, and they paid it without a peep; but she and Sara were still just scraping by, not in debt or wanting for anything but not setting any money aside either. Everything was so overpriced here. She'd been stupid to sign the lease on this Upper East Side one-bedroom, but it was in the district zoned for a public middle school everyone said was excellent, and so she'd grabbed it, even though Sara had only about four months of eighth grade left anyway and then the whole good-school panic would begin all over again. She'd told herself that if there ever came a day when the agency had paid all its debts and made its payroll and still had twenty thousand dollars in the bank, she would shut the place down and give the money to the seemingly re-sourceless Michael: she'd since lowered that hypothetical figure to fif-teen thousand, but in any case it was nowhere in sight. Expenses were few yet still managed, every month, to take her by embarrassing sur-prise. As for the sale of the Rensselaer Valley house, she'd accepted an offer back in December, but since then the process had slowed to a crawl, and though she checked in with Bonifacio once a week or so, they didn't even have a closing date yet.

Her great fear was always how her ongoing failure to restabilize their lives might be delaying Sara's recovery from all the trauma of the fall; but Sara, even if she didn't care to give her mother the satisfaction of admitting it, felt she was coping with uncertainty just fine. School, which under normal circumstances was pretty much your whole life at that age, now felt strangely and sort of exhilaratingly meaningless to her. She would be there for only one semester anyway, before everyone dispersed for the summer and then to high school. And it wasn't like Rensselaer Valley, where there was pretty much only one high school to go to, so that all the cliques basically just relocated to a new building. You overheard some kids talking about the SHS test, or about private school, and a few delusional girls who thought they were talented enough to get into LaGuardia or Sinatra. But the vast majority would scatter in June and head off in September to one of three sort-of-nearby high schools, each of them, from what Sara overheard, even more vast and unsightly and perfunctory and treacherous than whatever middle school you had just graduated from. Wherever Sara wound up next year, she'd be starting over, socially and academically, yet again. She'd moved to New York too late to take the SHS exam anyway, not that she would have passed it, even though everyone seemed to think Asians passed it automatically. She hadn't met anyone who'd passed it.

Unexpectedly, all of these aspects of her new life that should have depressed her — no friends, no sense of her own near-term future, ev-

erything and everyone brand new and a total cipher—made her feel
pretty bullish instead. It was like getting a cosmic do-over in terms of
who you even were. It wasn't just that no one seemed to know or care
who her father was. That was the kind of story that would have bored
an eighth grader to death anyway: it was more of an old-people scandal,
the type of scandal that would have been on somebody's parents' radar,
maybe, if she'd ever been invited to meet anybody else's parents, which
she had not. But it was fantastic, in a way, not knowing anyone or,
rather, being unknown to everyone. She wasn't really engaged in re-
inventing herself, not yet, but she had a strong and pleasing sense
of being dormant, like a one-girl sleeper cell, until she got the lay of
the land and figured out where and how she wanted the next few years
to go.

She was unused to so much time alone, not least at home, where
her mom, even without her former commute, was so tired at night that
there was zero supervision in terms of homework. But the homework
was easily handled anyway. It was such a relief after eighth grade in
Rensselaer Valley, where everyone stressed out constantly and bragged
about how little sleep they got. She couldn't believe how little everyone
here seemed to care about standing out in that way. It was really liberat-
ing. The school didn't have any sort of team sports program—even the
nominal playground was now filled with trailers brought in to provide
extra classroom space. Her mom did get it sufficiently together to sign
her up for an after-school basketball league on the West Side. Tuesday
and Friday she rode the bus back and forth to Broadway with her uniform on under her clothes. And that too was just unbelievably low-key
compared to what she was used to: no tryouts, no screaming coaches,
no practices even, just games. Just playing.

They ordered out for dinner almost every night—it was so easy in
the city, and so much better than home cooking, that not ordering out
seemed borderline perverse—and after the first several weeks that duty
too became Sara's. They'd eat in front of the TV, and sometime between eight and nine she would peripherally watch her mother's chin
sink down toward her chest, snap up suddenly, and then sink again for
good. It was awkward and sad, but, at the same time, Sara had little

desire for things to revert too far in the direction of how they used to be, because she liked being in charge of herself, of what she ate, when she went to bed, where she spent her time. One day she went to the movies right after school let out, by herself, and still got back home before her mom did; when asked how she'd spent the afternoon, Sara replied that she'd gone to a friend's apartment to study for a test. It was a totally pointless lie—her mother probably would have been pleased, if anything, to know she'd been to see a movie—but in another way it demonstrated perfectly the point that her time was now her own. So many things that used to define her just didn't signify that much anymore: New York City was full of only children, New York City was full of Asians, New York City was full of adoptees who wore their status on their faces, in their features' unlikeness to those of their mothers and fathers. There was a Facebook group for her school, and one for her grade as well, but she stayed off of them. She was pretty sure no one was talking about her on there anyway. She was neither hot enough nor weird enough, basically, to spark much social interest from either boys or girls, and on that score too she felt oddly but definitely relieved.

Even to her dad she seemed both there and not there at the same time. He emailed a lot but, for some reason, hadn't called or even texted for weeks. Maybe he still felt guilty about what he'd done, which, as she understood it, involved him trying to get over on some much younger woman who worked for him, getting his ass kicked by that woman's boyfriend, and then driving around drunk and bleeding afterward like some kind of maniac. It was pretty embarrassing and disgusting, to be sure, whatever this chick's age, which Sara didn't quite see the point of being shocked by—they were both adults. But to her the disappointing thing was that her father seemed to have done this not because he'd fallen in love or for any other logical reason but simply because he had freaked out—his life had seemed intolerable to him— and parents just were not supposed to do that. Apart from the sexual element of it, she felt she understood his state of mind easily enough— this cannot be my life; this cannot be my family; my real life and family must have been left behind somewhere else—because everybody felt that way sometimes, but you were not supposed to give in to that feeling at his age, at least not if you had agreed earlier on to become some girl's father.

For a while she got an email from her dad at the same time every day. All he did was ask her questions, as if to make up for the period in which he'd had to feign interest in her, and no detail was too small to escape his anxious attention: if she mentioned playing a basketball game, he wanted to know what the score was, and if she told him it was 24–22, he wanted to know who'd scored the winning basket. Even when the names meant nothing to him. Sometimes she'd text him, but he would never reply. She still hadn't mentioned any of it to her mom; she had a sense of the panic and fury that would lead to, and as weak as her connection to her father was now, she didn't want to lose it again. Besides, if her parents could just decide on their own one day that their lives were now separate, who was anyone to tell her that her relationships with them couldn't be kept separate as well? One night when her mom was out unusually late, Sara called him but just got his voice mail: she left a message, but his email the next day read very much as if he hadn't heard it. "Did u lose yr phone?" she emailed him. No reply. Finally she sent him an email saying that she understood if he didn't want to talk about himself because he felt guilty or whatever, but that it was starting to seem weird to her that he wouldn't even tell her where he was, where he was living, where he was working, etc. Was she ever going to see him again? The next day, same hour as every day, she opened an email from him, this time with the subject line "confession time":

"The reason I haven't told you where I am is that I'm ashamed of it. I thought that losing my home and my family would be the price I paid for my behavior over the summer, but it turns out there was more of a price than I thought. I am an inmate in the Mineville minimum security prison, which is about two hours north of Albany. It's not a rough or dangerous place at all, but we aren't allowed phones, and I get access to the internet only at a certain time of day, i.e., now. It's a 28 day sentence and I've already served 22 of them. I thought I could keep it from you for 6 more days; I should not have tried to keep it from you at all, but I hope you at least understand why I did. Please forgive me, for this and for everything else. You deserve much better from your father."

That night there was no food in the apartment, so she met her mother for dinner at Hunan Garden, where the service was fast and they offered bad but complimentary white wine. When their plates were cleared away, and Helen tried unsuccessfully to stifle an expansive yawn, Sara said, "Mom, do you know where Dad is living right now?"

Helen was taken aback. "No," she said. "Actually, I don't. I know he's out of that Stages place. The child support checks come via the lawyer's office, which makes me think he doesn't really want any contact with me at this point, which is fine. I don't really want any with him either. We're officially divorced, so as long as he fulfills his obligations to you, I've pretty much given up my right to keep tabs on where he is and what he does."

Sara searched her face. There was no way she was lying. She really didn't know. Her mother had always been a poor liar.

"Do you think there's any way," Sara said, "that the two of you would ever get back together?"

Helen's mouth fell open. It wasn't an unusual question for a child to ask, of course, but through all the drama and upheaval of the last seven or eight months, Sara had never once asked it. Still, it was a rebuke to Helen that this moment should have caught her with her guard down so completely. Of course, of course she wanted Ben's and Sara's relationship to be repaired, but only when the time was right, only when she could feel confident that he was sane enough not to hurt her again: as it stood, she had no idea how much of an unfiltered, impulsive wreck he might still be. She'd resolved never to badmouth him in front of Sara, but that had wound up meaning that she never mentioned him at all. Just be honest, she told herself now: she knows when you're lying anyway. "No," Helen said, not harshly. "The way he treated us is something I can't really forgive. But there's no law that says it has to be the same for you as for me. Do you want to see him? It's totally natural that you should. I've sort of been waiting for him to make the first move there, but you're right, I've let it go way too long, I can call the lawyer tomorrow and—"

"No," Sara said quickly. "I mean no thank you. Maybe soon. I was just wondering."

That Friday she took the crosstown bus to get to basketball, but they were detoured all the way to Ninety-sixth Street just because one block of Amsterdam was cordoned off for what looked like some sort of religious festival. Passengers were swearing and rolling their eyes. The air smelled great, though—like meat, basically—and Sara, on a whim, got off the bus and watched it roll away. She spent the next hour or so wandering by herself on the fringes of the festival, watching a short and inscrutable parade, checking out what was for sale. For a dollar she bought a huge empanada out of a cart; it was so good she went back for another one, but by then the cart was gone and traffic was starting to flow again. She made her way back down to Eighty-sixth and got on the eastbound bus for home, where she changed out of her uniform and then checked her mother's email every few minutes until a message came in from her coach, not mad at her for ditching, just making sure she was okay. She deleted it. An hour or so later, Helen came home from the office. "How was your game?" she said. Sara told her that her team had won a thriller, 30–29, and that she'd hit the winning shot.

CLIENTS NEVER CAME TO THEIR PLACE, which was just as well, since it was a gloomy, underpopulated setting: just the two women, working side by side in the outer room, while Harvey's office sat there empty like a particularly dusty shrine, except on the days when his son came in. Those days had grown more frequent as the winter went on, even though the website on which he was nominally working was nowhere in evidence, or even mentioned much anymore. He was clearly a creature of habit, and he seemed to have nowhere else in particular to go. In the afternoons he would walk through the unlocked door, nod uncomfortably to Helen and Mona, go into his father's office, and close that door behind him. One Monday before he arrived (he never made it there more than an hour or two before the end of business), Mona stood up from her desk and marched purposefully into Harvey's office to boot up the computer and check its Internet history: a while later she came out looking more confounded than sheepish and reported that he seemed to spend most of his time posting comments on a variety of music blogs, something he could just as easily have done from his home in Brooklyn. "No porn, at least," she said with equal parts relief and bemusement.

So other than Michael at three o'clock or so, and the mail delivery about an hour before that, the door to Harvey Aaron Public Relations seldom swung open during business hours, which did at least lower their level of self-consciousness during stretches of the workday in which there was no real work to do. Helen could, for instance, at her desk on a Friday morning at 9:30, allow herself to finish the *Vanity Fair* profile of Hamilton Barth she had started reading on the train. She always read anything about Hamilton that she came across, hoping mostly for some reference to their old school or their old hometown. But he never seemed to want to talk about it, or maybe they just never asked him. He usually had loftier things on his mind.

"Barth, in town for the film festival, had asked to be moved from his hotel because the windows didn't open," Helen read. "He wound up instead at an efficiency motel a few miles away, where the windows were indeed open, though the curtains had to be kept closed because of all the photographers in the parking lot. Clearly restless, he suggested we decamp to the Art Gallery of Ontario, where there was an exhibition of Motherwell drawings. I asked him what time he needed to be back for that night's premiere; 'I was hoping you knew that,' he grinned."

Mona picked up the office phone, as she sometimes did when she was bored, just to see if it was working.

"'I'm not afraid of death,' he said—apropos of the Motherwell we were looking at, or perhaps apropos of nothing—'but I resent it. I think it's unfair and irritating. I know I'm not going to get to all the beautiful places I want to go, I'm not going to read all the books I want to read, or revisit all the beautiful paintings I want to see. There's a limit.' He paused. 'I mean, I understand limits are good for character and all that, but I would rather live forever.'"

A soft knock on the office door caused both women to jump in their seats. Helen dropped the *Vanity Fair* facedown on her desk and reflexively pretended to be typing something.

"Come in?" she called out, shrugging at Mona.

In walked a white-haired man in an excellent suit, with fashionably tiny glasses held up by large cheeks. Actually, what enlarged the cheeks was his smile, which was constant, even as he took in, without having to so much as crane his neck, the entirety of the operation—the two women at mismatched, perpendicular desks in the outer office, the inner room, at this hour, open but unoccupied.

"This is Harvey Aaron Public Relations?" he said. Helen nodded. He looked a bit like Harvey, actually, or maybe just of Harvey's vintage, like someone Harvey would have avoided at his own high school re-union because of the man's conspicuous aura of success.

"I won't ask for Harvey himself, because I know he's sadly no lon-ger with us," the man said. "I take the liberty of calling him Harvey because we actually met once, probably twenty years ago. More than twenty." His smile seemed to refresh itself. Helen and Mona were still seated with their fingers over their keyboards. "But may I ask, which of you ladies is Ms. Armstead?"

Helen, absurdly, raised her hand. The white-haired man looked again at Harvey's empty office, as if he had not noticed it before, and said, "I wonder, if you're not too busy, if I might have a few moments of your time. That is," he said, turning his gaze graciously upon Mona, "if you don't mind."

Skepticism had flared Mona's nostrils. "You from the government?" she said. "Because you seem a little bit like somebody from the govern-ment."

Helen shot her a stricken look, even though she too had an instinct that this man was not some prospective client. Too untroubled, maybe. He seemed like he was pretty happy with the public image he was pro-jecting already.

"Not at all," he said. "My name is Teddy Malloy." The way he said it, he clearly expected it to make some impression; Helen felt at fault for having no idea who he was. He extended his hand toward Harvey's office door, graciously and presumptuously at the same time. "Shall we?" he said to Helen.

At least he let her take the seat behind Harvey's desk, she thought as he closed the door after them, though he couldn't have been smart enough to know how wrong and off-balance it made her feel to sit in Harvey's old swivel chair. "Well!" he said pleasantly as he sat, folding his hands over his stomach. "So you are Helen Armstead."

Helen smiled weakly. "What can I do for you?" she said.

"You're the woman who handled Peking Grill, yes? And Amalgamated Supermarkets? We've been watching your work for some time now, with greater and greater admiration."

"Who's 'we'?" Helen said politely.

His smile widened a bit whenever she spoke, but then he just resumed what he was saying as if she hadn't spoken. "Crisis management is, as I'm sure I don't need to tell you, the fastest-growing sector of our business by far. I'm old enough to remember the days when influencing the public discourse was just a matter of taking gossip columnists out for lunch and getting them drunk. But now of course with the Internet—"

"You're in the public relations business too?" Helen said.

This time his eyes met hers. The smile, she was beginning to understand, was a sort of catch basin, or surge protector, for emotions of any kind; wide as it was already, it seemed almost to flash a bit when he realized his name had meant nothing to her. "Yes," he said. "Forgive me. I am the chairman of Malloy Worldwide, which is, for lack of a better term, a PR agency, the sixth largest PR agency in the world. We have offices in Los Angeles and London and Tokyo and Rome, as well as here in New York. We have about twelve hundred employees, including eight full-time members of a crisis management team at our main office, which is about twenty blocks north of here. It's a company that was started by my uncle, actually, but I've been chairman since 1979, which is when he passed away."

A silence ensued. "It's funny," Helen said, "just because Malloy is actually the name of the town where I grew up."

"How about that," Malloy said.

"Listen," Helen said abruptly, "can I get you anything? I really should have asked that before we sat down. I guess we're a little rusty. We don't get that many visitors here."

"You're very kind," Malloy said, "but no thank you. You've proba-

bly already figured out why I'm here. We follow the trades, of course —
we're not so arrogant as to think we can't learn from our competitors,
however small — and it's clear that when it comes to the art, if I can call
it that, of public-image repair, you have an extraordinary gift. I have
come here to try to hire you."

Now was the time for her to say something. He waited patiently.
"Well," she finally managed to produce, "it's a complicated situation
here."

"So I see. In fact, now that I'm here, it's unclear to me whom I'd be
competing with for your services. Who owns this place, now that Harvey is no longer with us? Who pays the rent?"

"No one, really," Helen said, cursing the blush she could feel coming on. "I mean, technically it's Harvey's son. But when Harvey died,
there was actually some outstanding debt that we hadn't known about,
and my colleague, Mona, and I decided to work off, and collect on, the
existing contracts, so there'd be something more than just legal head-
aches for Michael to inherit. He doesn't work here himself, though he
does come in from time to time. Fairly often, actually. He's a little bit
of a lost soul."

Malloy pursed his lips. "Remarkable of you," he said. "So then the
plan was really to wind the business down all along."

"Well, yes, that's the plan. It's just — it's taken a bit longer to climb
out of the hole, to be honest, than I'd first calculated. The pure business end of things — it's not my strong suit."

"No, it wouldn't be," Malloy said.

"Excuse me?"

He lifted his eyes to hers. "I only meant that you have a gift," he
said gently, "and that gift has nothing at all to do, strictly speaking, with
business. This is why I wanted to come to talk with you in person." He
tapped his fingertips together, thinking. "Would you know how much
the debt consists of, right at this moment?"

She would have been embarrassed to tell him how small an amount
it was, how shallow the hole they were laboring to get out of. "It isn't
just a matter of getting back to zero, at this point," she said. "I have re-
sponsibilities, to the others here, to existing clients —"

"I see that," he said indulgently. "What if, then, rather than hire you, we simply bought out the agency, from Harvey's son? And then, what's the right word, absorbed it? That would take care of the debt and then some, I should think."

Helen's heart started to pound. She was afraid to ask him what he thought the whole operation might be worth. It was part of her lack of business acumen that she wouldn't have considered it worth a cent to anybody but her.

"And what about Mona?" she said, surprising herself. "I couldn't just put her out of work. She has a family."

"We would offer her a job," Malloy said calmly, "though at this point of course I'm unacquainted with her particular skills. As an alternative, we could offer her a very fair severance package."

Helen sat back in Harvey's chair. An old line of the nuns' kept sounding in her head: *Close your mouth,* they'd say, *you look like a trout.* Nothing like this scenario had ever even occurred to her, which made her reflexively search for reasons why it wouldn't work. She couldn't come up with any right away. Still, what she felt most was not excitement or relief, but fear.

"Why are you doing this?" she asked him.

He leaned forward, his elbows on his knees. "I'll be honest," he said. "I don't care about these other people—though I understand why you do. But not many people, Helen, can do what you do. Nor can they be taught to do it, even though business schools make a fortune pretending otherwise. It's a calling. This is why I came here myself today to try to persuade you, instead of just sending one of my managers to do it. Think of it this way. This place, it's like your training ground. But there's a whole world out there, where a lot of people need your help. It's time to expand your mission."

Fifteen minutes later, when Helen had seen him to the door, she turned to acknowledge Mona's direct, skeptical stare with as much of a poker face as she could muster. She knew it wasn't worth much, her poker face; people had told her so all her life. "What the hell was all that about?" Mona said.

Helen smiled nervously. "Turns out that man works at—"

"I know where he works. I Googled him while I was sitting out here by myself staring at that closed door. So what did he want?"

Helen walked to her desk but did not sit down; she put her hands on the back of her chair. "Do you want to go out and have lunch today?" she said.

Mona pulled her head back. "What," she said softly, "you mean together?"

Helen nodded soberly.

Mona looked around the surface of her desk, picking things up and putting them down again. She looked at her watch: it was only about quarter past ten. "Listen," she said, "if it's bad news, just please give it to me now, I'm not good at waiting. I don't know why people always think you need to be eating something when you get bad news."

"It's not bad news," Helen said. "It's . . . well, it's either good news or no news." By which she meant, though of course Mona could not have known it, that if Mona was not amenable to the offer, in any of its forms, they would turn it down, and things would go on as they had been.

"Okay, then," Mona said, without much confidence. "I'm going to make you take me someplace nice, though, if you're gonna torture me like this."

"No problem," Helen said, smiling.

Five minutes later, Mona grabbed her bag and said, "The hell with this. There's a Hot and Crusty on the corner. Let's go."

When they were seated at a tiny Formica table for two with their coffees and a gigantic cranberry muffin cut in half, Helen told her that Teddy Malloy had come to buy out the business and to offer them both jobs at Malloy Worldwide, jobs whose salaries, she now realized, she had neglected to inquire about, though they seemed bound to be better than what the two of them were currently taking home.

"You mean you," Mona said. "It's you he wants, not both of us. He didn't even talk to me. Why would they need me anyway? I'm good, but I'm sure they got people who can do what I do."

"Well, he does," Helen said. "He wants to hire us together." She took a long sip of her coffee and watched Mona pick a hunk out of her half of the muffin. "Although he did present an alternative offer, for you. If you didn't want to go work there, he would offer you a severance package."

"A severance package?" Mona said combatively. "So I'd be fired, is what he means."

"Well, sort of. It's not your usual deal. He'd offer you a year's salary."

Mona stopped chewing for a long moment, then hurriedly resumed until she could repeat, "A year's salary?"

Helen nodded. "Also COBRA benefits for up to a year if you needed them. So that's pretty generous. But, Mona, I don't want you to feel like you're being—"

"Done," Mona said, and she laughed. "Sold. Accepted. Let's call this old dude right now before he regains his senses or dies or something."

Helen felt stricken. "Just like that?" she said. "You don't need to think about it? You're not curious what this Malloy place would be like, or what it might be like to do what we do at a place with some resources?"

"Someone offers you a year's salary," Mona said, "you take it. That's just basic sense."

"But don't you—don't you want to keep working?"

"Who says I won't keep working? I'll get another job of some kind. There's lots of them out there. I'm not the type to sit around and do nothing. But if I play it this way, then it's like I have two salaries for one job. Why would I . . . What?"

"Nothing."

"Are you *crying*?"

"No," Helen said, though she was a little.

"Good Lord," Mona said. She sat back in her undersize chair and stared at Helen less in sympathy than in puzzlement. "It's just a job. For you, too, I mean. There's lots of jobs out there a smart, hardworking person can do. Jobs are for making money, so you can take care of your own, and maybe give them something nice once in a while that you didn't have. Isn't that what it's about? You're a single mom, you must know what I'm talking about."

Helen nodded, and wiped her eyes with a scratchy paper napkin. "Sure," she said, "but we built something together. We kept something alive. You and me, just the two of us. Doesn't that mean something to you, at least a little bit, besides just a paycheck and health insurance? I mean, I know we aren't really friends, but I'm never going to see you again, am I?"

Mona reached across the tiny table and squeezed Helen's fingers. "It don't mean I don't like you," she said. "I do. But in my opinion? You have always gotten worked up about the wrong things."

Helen nodded and squeezed Mona's hand, eager for it to be over now. When they got back upstairs, she went straight into Harvey's office and shut the door; she phoned Teddy Malloy to accept his offer, left a message for Scapelli the lawyer, and then she took a deep breath and called Harvey's son. "Cool" was all Michael said, though in a cracked tone suggestive of shock; then he asked her how soon he could expect the check, not out of avarice or impatience, she could tell, but out of need. It wasn't important that he be grateful. It was more that she was hoping that what she had just done for him had cemented a bond between them. But she was never going to see him again either. She could tell just from the quaver in his voice that it was too much money for him, that he knew he was going to blow it. He had no one to help guard him against himself. But she had to be able to let these relationships go. They were never all that real to begin with, she told herself, notwithstanding her sadness over their end. You couldn't feel responsible for everybody.

4

"THERE'S A HEALTH CLUB on the third floor," Yvette said; "your key card opens it. If you need a locker, send me an email and I'll get you set up. It's twenty-four hours, with the exception of the pool and the Jacuzzi, for obvious reasons." Nothing was obvious to Helen about any of this. She just kept trailing behind Yvette, who was the office manager and who looked like a catalogue model, nodding and making noises of assent and wishing that the needlessly comprehensive tour of Malloy Worldwide's facilities would terminate at Helen's own desk, which she was eager to get behind and gather herself a little. She carried over her shoulder a new soft briefcase that had in it only a *New York Times*, a pen, a yogurt, and a plastic spoon.

"On the fourth floor is the staff cafeteria," Yvette continued. She walked like most people ran. "You'll get another card—a lot of cards, right?—that's good for the employee discount there. You can pay cash if you want, though most people just have it deducted from their paycheck. The food"—she turned around to confide in Helen—"is really good, I have to say. I mean you know it's just to encourage you to stay in the building and take shorter lunches, but still. The whole place is nut-free, though, for obvious reasons, so you'd have to go outside the building if you're, you know, desperate for nuts."

A glance into the cafeteria, occupied at this hour mostly by people waiting in line at the cappuccino bar, was enough to tell Helen that she probably wouldn't be eating there all that often. She was now immersed in the world she had taken notice of when she first started job hunting in Manhattan, the world where people her age were nowhere in evidence, where she was, or felt, old enough to be everybody's mother; she did not see herself sitting at one of those long tables in one of those clusters of skinny women in their twenties, complaining about whatever it was such creatures thought they had to complain about. Only some of them were from Malloy—they shared the building with, among other enterprises, a casting agency and a website devoted to shopping. The notion of cheap food did still have a strong pull; Helen had to keep reminding herself that she had not just a new job but a new salary, and so saving a few bucks on lunch was no longer the imperative it had been just a few weeks ago. Still, she thought she would bring her lunch most days.

"And here we are at your office," Yvette said suddenly. It was indeed an office—not a cubicle, as she'd feared—and she felt a surge of pride at the sight of her nameplate on the wall outside the door, even though the plate was attached with what looked like Velcro. She just wished she'd been paying better attention to how they'd gotten there. She laid her briefcase carefully atop the empty desk. Pictures, she thought—that's what people put on their desks. Tomorrow she would bring in a few framed pictures of Sara, if she could figure out which still-sealed box she'd packed them in when they left Rensselaer Valley. "I'll leave you to it," Yvette said, still on the threshold. "You have my email if you need anything. Good to have you with us." Helen smiled her thanks. The tour had lasted nearly an hour, and most of it had been about the aspects of office life that did not involve actual work; not once had Yvette referred to how Helen was expected to use her time when she was not exercising or smoking or eating or taking a Jacuzzi.

Though Mr. Malloy had been clear that this was a full-time position, still Helen had imagined herself, in the weeks before she started there, as something like a consultant, on call for new or longstanding clients in case of some extraordinary public-image emergency; she couldn't imagine that there would be some crisis to deal with, some nominal fire to put out, forty hours a week. About that she turned out to be mistaken. Back at Harvey Aaron they had sometimes waited around for days with only scutwork to do, until some sort of scandalous event would trigger the process by which she worked and got paid;

here, though, as it turned out, the demand for their time was almost more than they could keep up with. Part of it was that the term "crisis" was defined at Malloy in a way that was sometimes so petty it would have seemed comic under less exigent circumstances: her first week on the job, Helen was called in on a Saturday because a Broadway play in which one of their clients had invested had gotten panned in *The New York Times* the day before. But part of it too was that Malloy was an operation whose true range Helen simply hadn't understood when she signed on with them. They had thousands of powerful clients all over the world, and at every moment of the day there was at least one of them, paranoid and imperious, who was being perceived, fairly or otherwise, as having done something wrong, someone who saw where the story of his life was headed and wanted to redirect it.

She had a boss, or more strictly speaking a supervisor, a very good-looking young man named Arturo—gay, she was quickly and preemptively informed, as if the notion of a straight Arturo would keep her from being able to concentrate—who cultivated an air of knowing what you were going to say before you had quite finished saying it. Every morning at ten-thirty the Crisis Management group met in the conference room on the fifth floor, a room known among the staff as the Fishtank because of its glass interior walls. There was one of those single-cup coffee machines, and an array of pastries and fruit, though that had usually been thoroughly picked over by the nine-thirty meeting of the Promotions group.

Arturo's oversight of the individual members of the group was intimidating but loose. The ten-thirty meeting was often the only time all day he spoke to them. Most crucially, though, he was in charge of assigning them to new clients, or to old clients with new crises, and in this area his disregard of Helen's particular skill set, not to mention the limits of her previous experience, was so perverse she wondered if it was intentional. She had a hard time imagining that he wouldn't have known she was his own boss's personal hire. But Mr. Malloy was more of a specter than a presence there—his office, though only three floors above theirs, had its own elevator, so sightings of him were rare—and with a rigorous impartiality Arturo felt free to assign her to the aggrieved

Broadway investor, and to an online-gaming company whose IPO valuation was threatened because its CEO had just died, and to other clients who often seemed as puzzled by her anxiety as she was by theirs.

One Friday morning in the Fishtank, Arturo laid out for them the news that feuding board members at a cellphone-chip manufacturer they represented—one of those companies you've never heard of that turns out to dominate a whole vital corner of your world—had been secretly taping one another's conversations, both on the phone and in person, and that the transcripts had been leaked to *The Wall Street Journal*, which was going through some high-level legal review, even as they spoke, to see what they could safely publish and what they could not. "Ashok will take you through our response," he said, nodding curtly to another member of the group, a diffident young man (they were all young to her) whom Helen had pegged as decent, despite his nervous adherence to a handful of business school aphorisms.

"It goes without saying that we have to get out in front of this," Ashok said, and everyone, including Helen, nodded; but it turned out that what he meant by getting out in front of it was that they should mount an all-out attack against *The Wall Street Journal*, focusing on the morality of profiting by someone else's criminal act.

"Does that mean we can question whether the tapes themselves are even genuine?" said Shelley, who sat next to Helen at the conference table. Not by accident: Helen always tried, at these meetings, to sit beside either Ashok or Shelley, a rock-bodied young woman who also managed to exude a kind of good-heartedness despite the rapidity of her speech and the fact that she had a rather uncorporate and scary tattoo of someone's initials on the back of her neck. You couldn't always see it; it depended on what Shelley was wearing that day.

"Probably not," Ashok said. "There are dozens of hours of these tapes, from what I'm told. I don't think we want to engage them on the level of authenticity. Anyway, the first course of action, in this type of situation, is to dirty up the messenger, if that's possible. And here it seems most definitely possible. Everybody hates Murdoch. Everybody values privacy, and this whole dispute has its root in illegally bugged convos, which are basically stolen goods."

"What's on the tapes?" Shelley asked.

Ashok frowned. "See, even just asking that moves the conversation—"

"I know," Arturo said. "Still, it's information they should probably have."

Ashok sighed. "Price-fixing," he said impatiently. "Buried in these hundreds of pages are some arcane discussions about price-fixing. But that is information that stays within these walls, because it is not relevant to the problem at hand."

The hell it isn't, Helen thought, but she stayed quiet as the requisite tasks were assigned, none of them to her. This was her first real experience with a corporate job and its attendant hierarchies, and her chief aspiration for now was to avoid giving offense. Older or not, she wasn't so proud as to assume that her instincts were better than other people's. Ashok enlisted Shelley's help in writing an anonymous blog that would attack the *Journal* and Murdoch for their greed in rushing to cash in on someone else's crime and thus interfering with the workings of the justice system. The fictional blogger, claiming to have a mole inside the *Journal*, would release piecemeal everything the Crisis Management group knew about conflicts inside the paper, as well as some other allusive nuggets Ashok would simply make up, for instance the suggestion that the *Journal* might have paid for the tapes not after the fact but before. Two other members of the team were directed to set up a nonprofit entity called Americans for a Responsible Press, which would begin placing print ads exploiting the average citizen's push-polled contempt for the immoral tactics of the media. They talked about staging an actual rally outside the *Journal* editorial offices; but that would mean hiring actors, with obvious attendant risks, and so Arturo wistfully declared that proposal tabled for now.

They carried these plans out over the course of ten days, never knowing how close the *Journal* was to publishing its story. Helen spent the better part of those days on a different case, arranging photo ops for a hedge fund manager who had started a charitable foundation to overhaul public schools, first in the city and then, after what he viewed as his inevitable success at home, across the country. The photo ops had to be the sort at which no reporter could ask this client a question, for his chronic problem was that he couldn't keep himself from publicly insulting the teachers, administrators, families, and even children he had supposedly devoted his time and expertise to helping. "Charity" seemed to Helen an odd word to use in connection with what seemed more like a campaign of aggression, but she tried to see the best in people, and surely the goal was a worthy one. She went to every ten-thirty meeting and offered her update when asked, even though what she was doing didn't seem to her strictly like crisis management work.

She ate in the cafeteria with Shelley and Ashok once or twice a week. The food was remarkably good, and their youth gave her cover. Shelley was maybe twenty-eight, but what made her really imposing was her level of physical fitness. Her arms alone, at which Helen had to remind herself to stop staring, must have amounted to a part-time job. Ashok, whenever the subject came up, looked embarrassed and mumbled something about a gym membership that he never had time to use. Though Shelley in particular loved to pump Helen for her backstory, neither she nor Ashok ever made much reference to their own lives outside the office. Once, when Shelley got up for another Vitaminwater, Helen—curious how well these two work friends even knew each other—asked Ashok with a conspiratorial smile what was up with that tattoo on the back of Shelley's neck. Not to sound like an old lady, but weren't they generally supposed to be somewhere less visible? Did everything these days have to be so out there? He did his best to smile back at her before answering.

"She lost a child," he said. "Those are his initials."

And as chastened as she was by that, Helen never forgot Ashok's weak but carefully complicit smile, which was obviously meant to help her feel less guilty in retrospect for having accidentally made light of something tragic. She was right about him, she decided.

Her salary was now almost ninety thousand a year, plus insurance and access to a car service and other assorted little freebies such as coffee that her colleagues didn't even take into consideration but that Helen, not long ago, was penciling into her budget every week. Suddenly there was money in her and Sara's lives that was not only sufficient but dependable. Certainly they could now afford to live somewhere nicer than the cramped two-room rental they'd been in since January. Looking for a place to live in Manhattan, though, was absurdly complicated and labor-intensive. Helen wasn't really working longer hours now than she had been at Harvey's office, but she did have much less freedom to take off for an hour or two in the middle of the day in response to yet another excited phone call from some broker.

"There's Brooklyn," Sara said when they were discussing it at breakfast one Sunday.

"Sweetheart," Helen said, cutting in half a warm everything bagel, "I am going to let you in on a little secret. I am too old to figure out where everything is in Brooklyn."

In the end, she decided that another rental, even if it were bigger than this one, would only put them through the trauma of packing and moving again; they would wait until it seemed reasonable to start looking for a place to buy. That day might already have been upon them had the sale of their old house in Rensselaer Valley, upon which their original plans had naïvely depended, not fallen through. The buyers had started postponing the closing with demands that escalated in ridiculousness—a second well test, a certificate from a tree surgeon, replacement of the foam insulation in the garage—and when Bonifacio began skeptically looking into them, he discovered that the husband had recently lost his job, and their financing had been pulled. He wanted to tell them to take a hike, but Helen had suggested waiting to see if they could bounce back and get approved for another mortgage. They couldn't, though, and eventually they withdrew entirely, and Helen had earned her lawyer's scorn by returning this time-wasting couple's deposit even though they weren't entitled to it. They had a one-year-old son.

In the end, the *Journal* mined the bugged phone conversations not for one story but for almost a dozen—one every day for a brutal two weeks, as if to manufacture the fiction that the tapes themselves were still being feverishly transcribed, with the most damning moments reprinted as eye-catching sidebars. It was a war of attrition, which Ashok and his team were ill-equipped to win. His grassroots offensive, however loving the craftsmanship with which it was faked, was roundly ignored. Finally the day came when the CEO of the chip company tendered his resignation, along with most of the board of directors. Apart from a hopeful uptick on the day the resignations themselves were announced, the company's stock fell steadily through the floor.

Helen took no pleasure in the air of panic and failure that seemed to suffuse the Fishtank during these weeks. She lay low and took meaningless notes. Then one Monday morning Arturo began the ten-thirty meeting by announcing that the chip manufacturer's reconstituted board of directors had just fired them, and the recriminations began.

"Did anybody besides me even look at that blog?" one group member said disdainfully. "It read like a child wrote it. Even the comments sections were full of people calling bullshit on it."

"It didn't matter who wrote it," said another voice, "or how well. It's an old-school tactic. It's a Neanderthal, first-year-business-school-textbook idea. Ivy Lee would have thought it was stale."

Ashok, clearly panicked, hit the table with the heel of his hand. "How nice to hear from you," he said, "finally, after all these weeks. I certainly didn't hear a word from you back when we were looking for ideas. Of course it's much easier to wait like a vulture and then say how you would have done things differently. And Ivy Lee was Ivy Lee for a reason, by the way—"

"Enough," said Arturo. He stood up from his chair, buttoned his jacket, and turned upon them a stare so ostentatiously cold that a less handsome man could never have pulled it off. "Nobody is getting fired over this," he said, "so there's no need to start eating each other. Look. We can argue about strategy in here all we want, but what we do outside this room—what we do in the world—is predicated on belief. Everybody has to pull together, everybody has to believe in the idea at hand just as you would if you thought of it yourself. Everybody has to not just understand but completely internalize what we are fighting for. You can't be an impartial advocate. You are either all in or you are part of what we're fighting against. Do you understand what I mean when I use the word 'belief'? Not a performance, but the real thing. Not 'I will act *as if* my client is in the right.' The public sees through that in a second. And I see through it. Doubt is a cancer, whether it's doubt in our strategy or doubt in the people we represent. The distinction doesn't matter. Cancer is cancer. When you walk out of this room in a minute, do it with a sense of your mission on the other side. And if you can't do that, don't come back at all."

He closed his briefcase and left the room. They watched him through the glass walls all the way to the elevator bank. "Wow," Shelley said. "Extra hot when he's angry."

Helen, despite herself, was stirred. There goes a leader of men, she thought. I could never do that job. The more she thought about Arturo's words, the less sure she felt what he was actually talking about—it was really just sort of a variation on my way or the highway, with a little Messiah complex thrown in—but still, he was right, it wasn't just about what you said to the world, it was about what was in your heart when you were saying it.

FREEDOM FROM HER FAMILY, freedom from a sense of place, freedom from peers who knew all about her, freedom from familiar objects: all of this had happened to her once before, Sara reflected, but not when she was old enough to remember any of it. "Rebirth" was too strong a word, maybe, but it was both truer and more mischievous to say that she felt like she was up for adoption again.

Here was one of the differences between her parents: she knew she could never figure out her father's email password in a hundred years, but it had taken her all of five seconds to correctly guess her mother's, which was "Sara." Sara sent an email, from her mother's account, dropping out of the basketball program entirely; she carefully deleted both the sent email and the coach's understanding reply. She still rode the bus across town every Tuesday and Friday after school, though, usually just to wander in and out of stores or, when the weather got a little warmer, to lie on the grass embankment between the West Side Highway and the Hudson River, a spot she found soothing and also far enough from most human traffic that detection wasn't a worry. Once in a while she'd take a picture of the river and upload it straight to

Facebook, less for the benefit of her few friends from school who might see it than just to create some record of where she was. Sometimes these friends would respond, sometimes they wouldn't, and then one day a few of them came and surprised her en masse, two she knew and three others. They sprinted across the highway like idiots to reach the embankment, rather than go two blocks out of their way to take the underpass.

They sat and watched the boats, Sara's cheeks growing hot in the midst of them, talking about nothing—mostly waiting for some jogger to go by, or for some middle-aged guy to emerge from below the deck of his weathered boat, so they could fall silent and then mock him after he'd disappeared again. One of them, a boy in a green army jacket and a sad Jewfro that the wind off the Hudson kept shaking like some kind of jello mold, had a pocket-size bottle of Jägermeister with him; but after one swig everybody pretended they were buzzed just so they wouldn't have to taste it again. Sara's sort-of-friend and chem lab partner, Tracy, seemed to want to cultivate the impression that she was with one of the other guys, a fellow eighth grader named Cutter (at least that's what he had named himself), whose family, she'd heard, was more well off than anyone else's in the school, which, because he was black, probably shouldn't have seemed ironic but did. Cutter kept catching Sara staring at them, which was not cool; she made herself look instead at the tide racing upriver toward the George Washington Bridge.

She heard his voice on the hill behind her, diluted by the pulse of traffic sounds from the highway, and then she realized he was saying, "What's her name?"

"Sara," someone answered him.

"Hey, Sara," Cutter said, "you live near here?"

She swallowed. "No," she said, "I'm all the way across town. Not too far from school."

"So you just like boats?"

She laughed, still without looking at him. "My mom thinks I'm playing in a basketball league," she said. "But I just come here."

"Why?"

"I don't know. 'Cause I like boats?"

"What about your dad?" Cutter said. "Where's he think you are?"

"Don't know," Sara said, but none of them heard her because they were all yelling at Cutter to try minding his own fucking business and stop asking people personal questions. "This is why no one will hang out with you except us," the Jewfro guy said.

Next Wednesday in school, Sara was standing in the cafeteria line, which stretched out the door, when she felt a hand on her shoulder. "Hey, boat girl," Cutter said. "What's your first class after lunch?"

"English," Sara said.

He snorted. "Come on," he said. "It's a beautiful day." He took her hand, which kept her from dwelling too much on anything else that was happening as they walked straight through the kitchen and out the fire door onto Seventy-seventh Street. He hailed a cab going west, and at first she thought he wanted, for some bizarre romantic reason, to go back to the embankment by the boat basin where they'd met, but no, the cab kept going south all the way to the Hudson ferry slips, where he bought them two tickets for the Circle Line. They sat on the deck—it was two-thirds empty, no one but out-of-season tourists and a couple of lame class trips—and circled the island of Manhattan, watching the sun split by the peaked tops of the buildings, the silent cars, the way the crosstown streets would open up to their full depth just at the moment you passed them and then flatten out again. Cutter pushed her hair out of her eyes with one finger. Sara felt a bit like she'd heard drugs were supposed to make you feel—dangerously receptive, like in the future it was going to be too hard to resist knowing that you had the power to feel this way again.

"Better, right?" Cutter said. She looked at him quizzically. "To be the one on the boat," he explained, "getting looked at by the people on the shore."

He had a thing for boats, it turned out, even though they were no great novelty for him since his family owned one, which they kept at their place out in Sag Harbor. It was a little disappointing to Sara to realize that that was the initial basis of his interest in her—that she re-flected an interest of his own. On the last Friday of the nominal basketball season, he took her to ride the Staten Island Ferry. The ferry itself was about the least quaint thing imaginable, and the harbor was surprisingly crowded, and if you looked too closely at the water it was pretty full of garbage, but Sara loved it anyway, in large part because of the uncharacteristic smile it put on Cutter's face. When you got to Staten Island there was really nothing to do—some storefronts, an empty baseball stadium, MTA buses that went God only knew where—but there was the ride back to look forward to, with Manhattan expanding in front of you, as you tried to pick out from the forest of mismatched structures along the water the one small maw toward which the ferry was pointed.

She'd never been anybody's girlfriend before, and she wasn't sure she was now; the most official-seeming aspect of it was that Tracy wasn't speaking to her anymore. She and Cutter never went to each other's homes, though if the weather turned wintry again and they kept hanging out like this, she could see how that was going to emerge as an issue. For now they dated the way she imagined two homeless people might date. The first time he tried seriously to make out with her, they were on a bench on the East River promenade, and she was freezing. She pulled her head back and looked into his desire-clouded eyes.

"What is your real name?" she said, stalling. "I don't see how I can kiss a guy when I don't even know what name your mother gave you."

He shrugged. "What name did your mother give you?" he said.

Which undermined her just enough to make her want to end the conversation; she unzipped his jacket so she could get her arms inside it for warmth, and kissed him until she could feel that her whole throat was bright red.

He talked a lot about adoption, actually, and about race, with passion but with no sense that these were subjects about which she might know something he didn't. He claimed that a lot of people assumed he was adopted, since he was black and had money. Sara had never seen any instance of this assumption, though, and she decided that it was probably something that had happened to him one time but had become such a big deal in his mind that his recollection of it had swelled. It was true that no one knew why his family had him in public school when they had the resources to send him anywhere they wanted. Liberal guilt, Cutter said: it isn't just for white folks. Though in the next breath he'd insist that he wouldn't go to one of those elitist private banker-factories if you paid him to. Not many of his friends had actually seen where Cutter lived, but those who had, or said they had, all agreed solemnly that it was enormous.

"I have everything," Cutter said to her, "but people are afraid of me because they think I feel entitled to what they have. Because I'm black." They were sitting on a stoop just off Park Avenue, near Ninetieth Street, having cut last period; now other schools were letting out left and right, and sometimes they'd watch a pack of younger kids go by wearing uniforms and texting on their phones. Cutter and Sara were passing a pint bottle of warm cranberry vodka in a paper bag, though Sara had stopped after two revolting sips; now she just took it from him and then passed it back a minute later, while he was talking.

"White people are afraid of us, because they project their guilt onto us. They assume that we spend our lives thinking about them, measuring ourselves in terms of them. That's what gives life to their guilt. It's guilt over racism, but the guilt itself is racist, right?"

This wasn't a side of him Sara particularly enjoyed, though she was impressed that he thought about this conceptual stuff at all. She wished there was a way to get rid of the vodka, because that seemed to draw it out of him. The only way to get him to drink less of it was to drink more of it herself. She had another small swig and passed the bag back to him.

"I don't really see people reacting to us like that, though," she said, in a near whisper she hoped would induce him to lower his own voice.

"Well, not so much to you, because you're Asian," he said. "That's a whole other set of prejudices."

"Okay," she said, a little irritated, "thank you for the deep insight into my Asianness, but I meant I don't see people reacting like that to you, either."

Another group of middle school boys in blazers made their way down Ninetieth Street; one, who looked about ten, stopped right in front of them to tie his shoe. He had an iPod in his ears and showed no awareness that Sara and Cutter were looking down on him from just a few feet away.

"You don't," Cutter said, with a muttered, throaty laugh. The boy in the blazer straightened up and moved on. Cutter stood and hopped down the steps.

"Hey," Sara said weakly. She thought he was angry and ditching her. Instead, when he caught up to the boy in the blazer, who'd fallen behind his friends, Cutter tapped him on the shoulder and started talking to him. They were only about thirty feet from the intersection, in front of a townhouse whose courtyard was filled with manicured bushes. Whatever they were doing or saying, Sara couldn't make it out—Cutter's back screened her from seeing much more than the loafers on the boy's feet. Then the feet turned and ran toward Park Avenue, and Cutter spun and walked leisurely back to the stoop, a grin on his face so wide it opened his whole mouth in wonder, and in his hands the boy's iPod, as well as what looked like forty or fifty dollars in cash.

"I didn't even ask him for the money," Cutter said, shaking his head delightedly. "How fucked up is *that?*"

JAIL, FOR ALL HIS FEAR OF IT, had proved mostly just another iteration of the limbo in which Ben had been living for six months now. It even, like Stages, housed one or two minor celebrities who might brush by you on their way to the cafeteria or the gym, acknowledging with a rueful smile that they were who you thought they were. And on the day it was over, Ben once again was released into the bright sunshine with his car keys, less than a hundred dollars cash—though to be fair he still had access to much more money, in accounts in various places—no home, and nowhere special to go. To those who knew him, he was defined by his transgressions now, by the things for which he would not be forgiven, and, as rough as that was, it seemed pathetic to think about going to some random town or city just to start all over again—to pretend, at his age, to be anyone else. Not to mention that, in order to get at his money, he would have to make at least one trip to Bonifacio's office and sign a few instruments he might well wind up drafting himself. Half out of spite for himself, therefore, and half out of the absence of other pressing business of any sort, he took the bus to Poughkeepsie, where his car was still parked, crossed the thruway, and ended up back in Rensselaer Valley. First he stopped and checked in to a motel just off the Saw Mill, a motel he had driven past ten times a week for the last fifteen years but had never been curious enough to see the inside of. Everything he owned fit in one bag now—well, maybe not everything, but having no idea where your belongings were was pretty damn close to not owning them anymore. Storage, if that's where they were, was where they would stay. Offhand, he couldn't remember what, other than a whole lot of suits and shirts and neckties, was even in there.

He was starving, but when the route to town took him past Meadow Close, he couldn't resist turning in for a quick look. A few months of neglect weren't really enough to change the appearance of a house; still, he inhaled sharply when he saw it, dark and clearly uninhabited, sitting in a chaotic brown yard that must have been giving Parnell and their other neighbors fits. The paint job was holding up, and the shutters were open and hung fine, and yet it still managed to look like a place where a disaster had happened. Kids would be daring each other to hit the windows with rocks before long. He had an urge to get out of the car and walk around the back to check on the screened porch. But it was the middle of the day. He pulled into Parnell's driveway, backed out again facing the other way, and continued into town.

He parked his car on Main Street and walked up and down, peering into familiar shop windows, absorbing the looks of surprise and even horror on the faces of those who still recognized him, which happened maybe half a dozen times. He stopped in to the Polish grocery where he and his daughter had met back in December, and he ordered another one of those cream-filled rolls; hungry as he was, after a month of prison food it was so rich he couldn't finish it. Then, on his trip down the opposite side of Main Street, in the shade of late afternoon and the corresponding chill, for which he was not appropriately dressed, he passed the hardware store, and the shingle that hung by the stairs running up the side of the two-story building, leading to the Offices (the "s" was a hilarious touch, Ben thought) of Joseph Bonifacio, Attorney at Law.

"Jacob Marley's ghost!" Bonifacio said when Ben walked in. It took him a surprisingly long time to stand—he'd had his feet on his desk and was watching something on his computer. "I should have marked my calendar. But honestly I was pretty sure I'd never see you again. Certainly not here in the Valley. Returning to the scene of the crime, eh what?"

"Something like that," Ben said.

"Well, listen, let's have a drink to celebrate the end of your sentence. That is, if there's a bottle of anything around—well, what do you know?" he said, producing a bottle of Jameson from the top drawer of his desk. "What are the chances of that?"

It was about four-thirty, and an hour later—during which time Ben didn't hear the office phone ring once—the lawyer invited his client over to his house for dinner. There was a real edge to Bonifacio's aggressive friendliness, an edge Ben thought Joe himself was mostly unaware of. He seemed proud of how small and cluttered and poorly insulated his house was, proud that someone like Ben—just the kind of privileged guy he'd always hated—was brought so low as to have to be grateful even for the tepid, perfunctory dinner put before him by Bonifacio's resigned and surly wife.

"So how long are you back in town for?" she asked him. "Just picking up some things?"

He struggled to finish chewing a rubbery piece of beef. "I don't know," he said. "I don't really have any plans, to tell the truth. I guess I just came back here to regroup."

"Regroup for what?" she said skeptically.

"Not sure. I'm thinking."

"Thinking about what?"

"Ginny, let's not be rude to company," Bonifacio said. "My client has paid his debt to society. Also his bill, which puts him in rare air around here. So as far as we are concerned, he is washed in the blood of the Lamb."

Ginny shrugged and began clearing the table. "You'll have to go back to work," she said to Ben without looking at him. "Everybody has to work."

"Demonstrably untrue," Bonifacio said.

"All I really know how to do is practice law," Ben said, "but with a prison record, that might be difficult for me."

"Anyway," Ginny said, pointedly on her way to the kitchen, "one lawyer is already plenty for a little town like this."

Ben and Joe looked at each other, eyebrows up, realizing together what Ginny had been talking about all along: she was worried that Ben was planning to open up his own law office in town and drive her husband out of business. In her mind this was how well-off people behaved, and Ben had to hand it to her—as stereotypes went, it wasn't a bad one.

"I wouldn't worry, honey," Joe said, struggling not to smile. He had been drinking Jameson, however leisurely, for at least three straight hours now. "Ben's a smart enough guy to know that he'd be better off hanging his shingle in some town where he has less of a preexisting reputation as a scumbag."

Ben smiled; then, to get off the subject, he said, "Joe, can I ask you something? I drove by my old house earlier today, before I saw you, and it looks very much like no one's living there. You handled the sale for Helen, right? Is it some kind of absentee owner or something?"

"No. Well, yes, in the sense that the absentee owner is your ex-wife. The sale fell through, although it took months to declare it dead because Helen kept giving these deadbeats extra time. It's still technically on the market. Not a great moment for real estate around here, in case you hadn't noticed."

"Are you kidding me?" Ben said loudly. "What the hell is she living on?"

Joe shrugged, as the ice from the bottom of his glass hit his teeth again.

Ben returned to the house on Meadow Close the next morning. First he looked through the intact porch screen while standing on the back lawn; then, on a whim, he tried his key in the front door lock. It still worked. All the furniture was gone, and the rooms smelled of moisture and what was probably mice. He stood in the center of each empty room. He opened all the windows and then, before leaving, shut and locked them again.

It felt strange, after that, to go sit on his bed in the motel room. He held his phone in his hand and reflected that it—a cellphone—was probably the closest thing in his life to a home right now, the object most linked to his sense of identity and with the longest association to his past. *Whats a good time to call u?* he texted Sara, and she did not reply. Then it occurred to him that she might have thought he was still in jail upstate, but when he texted to let her know he was out now, she wrote back *yes I know I can count.* She did not ask him where he was.

Two nights later Bonifacio called him when he was watching TV in the motel room and said, "Listen, I have a proposition for you. You're a trusts and estates guy, right? Or were. Anyway, I just caught a probate case that is a real bear."

"Who died?" Ben asked.

"You know the Feldmans, who live on Colonial Ave.? Husband was a commodities trader?" Ben did know them, a little; he saw Jay Feldman ten times a week back in the early years, when he used to take the train. "Well, he died of a heart attack while jogging, if you please, and the weird thing is the Feldmans were like two days from finalizing their divorce when it happened. Anyway, it's a mess, and I was wondering how you'd feel about coming in for a week or two to help me sort it out. If you're not doing anything."

Bonifacio was loving this a little too much, Ben thought; but he agreed to it anyway. For a week, he sat in a folding chair with his feet on Joe's windowsill and helped him craft a brief on the angry widow's behalf that was bound to blow the mind of whatever hack rural circuit-court judge caught the case. The bottle of Jameson usually came out of the drawer around four o'clock. Ben understood that it was tied in some way to the difficulty Bonifacio had not with his work but with going home. At the tail end of the Friday before his court appearance on behalf of Mrs. Feldman, Bonifacio brought up with Ben the question of money.

"It'll have to be under the table," Bonifacio said. "I hope that's not going to cause you any problems. I can offer you two grand. I know you're worth much more, but I mean, look around you." He waved with the glass in his hand to indicate the tiny lamplit office, the sun already descending behind the muddy train station across the road. "It's all I've got."

The proper thing for Bonifacio to do, Ben knew, was to offer him instead a cut of the eventual settlement; but he didn't care to pursue it. He had something else on his mind.

"Keep it," Ben said. "I was happy to help out. You did plenty for me, so it's good to give back."

"I did do good for you, didn't I?" Bonifacio said. "I mean, I couldn't keep you out of jail, I am sorry about that, but you were able to hold on to a fair amount of money in the end, considering you were getting prosecuted and sued and divorced at the same time."

Ben raised his glass in salute. "Very true," he said. "Which is why I don't need your lousy two grand."

Bonifacio laughed. "Have it your way," he said. "Regardless, you were the best little assistant I've ever had around here."

Really, it was like he kept digging around until he stumbled on the remark that would make you want to slap him in the face. That seemed to be what he wanted. No wonder he didn't appear to have other friends in town. Ben drained his glass and held it out cheerfully for a refill.

"You make a better lawyer than a boss," he said. "And you're still the only advocate I've got. Which brings us to new business. I have a job for you."

A NEW KOREAN-MADE ECONOMY CAR got a "Satisfactory" rating from Consumer Reports, whereupon the Crisis Management team assembled as immediately and instinctively as a team of superheroes; but then most of their subsequent time and ingenuity was spent moving ninja-like through the immense trivialities of the various social networks, countering complaints, planting favorable remarks. The question of whether the client might instead address the crisis by building safer cars was a nonstarter. Helen understood that once you got out of the realm in which your clients were individuals with whom you sat down face to face, your power diminished, and your thinking had to change; still, though, even their most detailed and intense strategies often seemed to her like confoundingly small potatoes.

A company that made artificial knees hired Malloy the week an FDA report was released suggesting that the knees were failing far more quickly than predicted and that the resulting complications had contributed to one death. The two orthopedic surgeons who had invented the device, which, having enriched them beyond the dreams of avarice, was now poised to ruin them, were turning on each other. One insisted almost dementedly that the device was working exactly as intended and that, since any response to the charges only gave them further credence, they should be ignored. The other, whose lawyer seemed to have all but moved in with him, said that silence equaled guilt, but that there was a way, in these matters, to apologize without actually admitting anything, a way that only lawyers understood.

"This is what happens when people's attorneys get involved," Arturo said at the Fishtank meeting where this new business was introduced. "They specialize in selfish thinking. So what does he suggest we ask people to believe about these failing knees?"

"Acts of God," Shelley said, "was I believe the phrase he wanted us to use."

Arturo snorted. "There are no acts of God anymore," he said. "Americans believe in negligence. Helen, what do you think?"

This was a question Helen had never yet heard in the weeks of her employ. "I'm sorry?" she said.

"About the notion of the non-apology apology. You're supposed to be the apology expert. This is the word from on high, anyway."

Everyone turned to look at her. "Well, it has to be sincere," she said, reddening. "It has to be sincere and thorough. If it gives off the whiff of having been vetted by a lawyer, to me that's worse than saying nothing at all."

"But it will kill them," one of the other group members said. "If they get up there and say hey, our bad, our knees don't work the way we thought they would, no way they stay in business, at least not with this product."

"So, Helen, you're suggesting we counsel our client to embrace their failure?" Arturo said.

Helen, unused to being asked to justify her instincts, faltered, and there was an awkward pause.

"I can sort of see it, actually," Arturo said at last. "If you want to be resurrected, you have to be dead."

The following Wednesday, Helen was gathering her things to leave for home and maybe make Sara a decent dinner for once when Arturo popped up unprecedentedly in her office doorway, his hand on the shoulder of a miserable-looking Ashok. "We're looking for the sorry maven?" Arturo said brightly. Poor Ashok, on a cold streak as it was, had been battling all week with a roomful of unsmiling dogmatists who handled in-house PR for Pepsi. New York's city council, they were reliably informed, was about to reintroduce a bill to establish a so-called sin tax on sodas, which, even if it didn't significantly harm their sales, would lump them in with cigarettes and gambling and open a sort of moral door that everyone agreed should stay shut if at all possible. Such was their panic that Ashok's mild proposal, at a meeting that morning up at PepsiCo headquarters in Purchase, of a "two-pronged approach" — one prong of which was admitting that it was theoretically possible for a person to drink too much Pepsi — had led to their demand that he be fired.

"I'd like you to go up there tomorrow," Arturo said. He was composed and smiling, but the expression on Ashok's face hinted at a recent closed-door reaming. "The two of you, though I think it's better if you do all the talking. Mr. Malloy tells me you're good at apologizing, so let's see those mad skills in action, okay?"

He didn't have that last bit quite right, of course, but Helen saw that Ashok's job might be in the balance, and so she said okay. The next day she sat at a conference table across from six people in suits; their designated spokesperson was, refreshingly, female, though whether that might make Helen's own task easier or harder, she had no clue.

"Obviously we have to get on an attack footing as quickly as possible," the woman said. She looked about twenty-two, except for her taut corporate hairstyle, which was forty or forty-five. "We should paint this as the work of an out-of-control government. In that folder I brought you"—she reached over and tapped it—"are some polling numbers on various key phrases. 'Nanny state' is second highest but also shows the highest increase since the last time we polled. We'll want to hit that one hard."

Helen flipped listlessly through the research. "Americans Against Higher Taxes?" she said. "What is that?"

The Pepsi woman looked confused. "That's the nonprofit we established to serve as sponsor for our TV and print ads against the bill," she said. "To make them look like PSAs."

Helen pinched the bridge of her nose. "I feel like you're reacting emotionally," she said. "In terms of long-range thinking, I know you know better than this. This kind of aggression ultimately gets you nowhere. Soda is not particularly good for you; in conjunction with other things that are not good for you, it can affect your health. You can keep contesting the facts, or commissioning new studies. But do you really want to keep bailing the boat, or do you want to get in a different boat?"

The Pepsi woman sat stone-faced.

"Well, whatever, the point is you have to adapt. Fifty years ago cigarettes were being marketed for their health benefits, for goodness sake, but if you tried that today you'd be laughed out of business, right? So here's what you do: you admit it. You take away their weapon. You admit your complicity in the sins of the past, because that way you take the past out of the conversation. You resolve to conduct yourself differently in the future, and then—you know what?—you conduct yourself differently in the future. This is how you stay in business. People relate to brands as if that relationship were emotional. So you have to play the role they want you to play, you have to personify it, and ask forgiveness the way you would if you were talking one on one. The first thing you do is kill off this ridiculous Americans Against Higher Taxes. People are too smart for that nowadays. You can't predicate your PR strategy on the idea that people are morons. Whose gem was this idea, anyway?"

"Yours," the Pepsi woman said irritably.

Helen did not look over at Ashok. Instead she got them to agree to at least try to draft a hypothetical release in which they applauded the motivations of health-minded politicians and looked forward to playing a leading role in helping Americans of all ages live longer. They'd call it The Next Century Initiative or something forward-looking like that. She wasn't positive they'd be able to go all the way through with it, but the look on Ashok's face as they rode back to Manhattan in the town car—the look of a man who'd been called down from the gallows— made the day feel like a success in any case.

The next day—again, just as she was packing up to leave for home—he walked into her office and gently shut the door behind him. "I just wanted to say thank you," he mumbled.

"No problem. They're living in a kind of bubble up there, that's all. Sometimes you have to explain your client to people, sometimes you have to explain people to your client."

"Right. So listen, I was thinking that, being at home with your daughter, you probably don't get out much—"

"I don't know that it's as bad as all that," she laughed, though in fact it was.

"—and I have these two premiere tickets for *Code of Conduct* next Tuesday night. Julie in Promotions gave them to me. I thought maybe you'd like to go."

"Tuesday," she said, thinking how nice it would be to do something with Sara, to let her share in a big-city perk. "It's a school night, of course."

"Sorry?"

"You remember the whole school-night phenomenon? But I don't think Sara would mind if I made an exception this time. Thank you. We'll take them."

"Ah," Ashok said. He turned to look behind him at the closed door. "Well, you're very welcome. I mean of course I couldn't use them, which is why . . . So Sara is your daughter's name. Very nice. Okay then." But he didn't move.

Did I say something wrong? Helen thought, and then it hit her: he was asking her out. He was asking her out on a date. Sweet Jesus. It was staggeringly inappropriate of him; and yet her first reaction was shame at having humiliated him by not even realizing what he was doing, by not taking him seriously enough to say a proper no.

But he had to be fifteen years younger than she was. Maybe more. She had no idea what to make of it. Maybe he had some kind of depraved mommy issue. Maybe he sensed that she was somehow ascendant around there and was just trying to advance his own career. In fact maybe he *knew* she would say no, but gambled that the flattery of his asking her at all would linger and maybe work to his advantage down the road. Because who would ever ask her out, right? An old lady like her? Why not give Grandma a little thrill?

"I never said we don't get out much," she said, a little more angrily than she meant to. "She just turned fourteen. It's not like I'm upset she's not out more. What is Code of Whatever, anyway?"

"It's a movie."

"What's it about?"

"What's it *about*? I don't really know."

"Who's in it?"

"Hamilton Barth, Minka Kelly, Bradley Cooper."

Helen's eyebrows shot up.

"Why do we get tickets?" she said.

"Because we get tickets to everything."

"But I mean do we represent all of these people? Is Hamilton Barth a client of ours?"

"Not really. I mean, in a sense," Ashok said, relaxing as he saw her expression change. "We represent the studios, the studios make movies with him in them, so you could say he's sometimes a client of ours. You're a fan?"

"So he'll be there?"

"I imagine they'll all be there. You know how it is with him. He's expected, but there's always some suspense."

Helen smiled.

"So you'll go?" Ashok said. "Great. I'll tell Julie to put you on the list. It's at the Ziegfeld."

Helen knew her daughter well enough not to overplay the element of glamor in attending a red-carpet premiere; at Sara's age, what you wanted most was not to be looked at too hard or by too many people. "It's supposed to be a good movie," Helen said, "and we'll get to see it before anybody else, and we'll get a good look at a bunch of celebrities probably." She did not mention Hamilton, in order to spare herself the torrent of eye-rolling abuse that name always provoked.

"I don't have to buy a new dress or anything?" Sara said warily.

She was a very different girl than her mother had been. But they were all like that now. "You can wear what you want," Helen said, "within reason."

"Cool," Sara said. "And I have to go with you?"

These moments had been coming more regularly of late: cold-eyed expressions of disregard from her own daughter, made more stunning by the offhandedness with which they were delivered. Helen had been spoken to disrespectfully for at least two years, but this was different. Remarks like this used to be intended to hurt her, which was hard but at least comprehensible. Now it was more like the effect of her words didn't matter to Sara at all. She even looked a little different lately, in the face mostly. She was spending more time out, at night and on weekends; Helen thought maybe there was a boyfriend in the picture, though she had made the mistake of asking about it only once. She'd signed Sara up for weekend soccer, but for some reason Sara had actually extracted from her a promise not to attend the games. She said her mother's presence, since unnecessary, would be embarrassing.

The insults, though, were not the issue; the issue was that they made Helen feel her child was slipping away from her. She kept trying to think of new approaches. They ought to take more advantage of the city, Helen knew, and go to museums together, or to shows or on walking tours. They ought—both of them—to be a little more cognizant of their own good fortune and find some volunteer or charity work that they could do together, preferably on weekends. Not that arresting Sara's drift was a simple matter of tacking on a few supplementary lessons in culture and humility. Helen's own positive influence was, she feared, being trumped by unseen bad ones, and in that light she started wondering about how to get Sara out of that awful school all the published rankings had told her was so good. Forms were already beginning to show up in the mail from the high school she was slated to attend next year, a place reportedly, as even Sara admitted, not much different from where she was now, just bigger, and therefore likely worse. Why not private school instead of public next year? Helen thought; but when she called Trinity to ask if maybe there were still spaces left for the fall, the woman on the other end actually laughed, before apologizing politely and profusely, saying she had assumed Helen was kidding. Maybe for tenth grade, Helen resolved. They'd come up with the money somehow.

"Stop trying to improve me," Sara would snap when topics such as this came up. "Like you're so perfect." Helen was terrified by the guilty thought that it was all some delayed reaction to the trauma of the move, or of the divorce itself—that she herself might be a source not just of love but of damage. But if her own actions had contributed to this damage, then her own actions could put it right. Not that she was willing to take all, or even half, of the blame for events that had knocked Sara off the loving equilibrium that, as a child, she'd always shown. But Helen was the parent who stayed, the one who was always right there, so naturally she was the one who got excoriated. One day soon she would get up her nerve to pursue the issue of contact with Ben, but, truth be told, she was scared he would use the opportunity to open up the custody issue too, and that she could not handle just yet. Anyway, she scolded herself, wanting to share some of the burden of getting insulted was not a very admirable reason to try to bring Sara's father back into their lives.

It was true that most of the celebrities at the premiere would be people whose names and faces meant nothing to Sara or anyone else her age. Still, they were going to spend a few hours inside the barricades of that world where movie stars came and went. They were going to walk a red carpet, even if they did so hours before the carpet was cleared for those whom the tourists and gawkers and photographers really wanted to see, even if the sight of a middle-aged mother and her daughter in fancy dress would cause people to turn away in disappointment or derision. It had to mean something to her daughter, whether she was capable of admitting it or not, that, having fallen so low together in the world, they had now risen to the level where they were, if nothing else, visible again.

Helen, at any rate, grew excited about it, and even permitted herself to fantasize that she might get to say hello to Hamilton Barth, or sit near him in the roped-off VIP seats, maybe talk about old times, introduce him to her child. She knew this was not how these tightly scripted public events generally worked, but she indulged the thought anyway. And then her sense that life in general was on the uptick was boosted further when she got a rare phone call from their lawyer from the dark days up in Rensselaer Valley, Joe Bonifacio. She felt fear in her throat just at the initial sound of his voice, but it turned out he was calling with excellent tidings. A new buyer had emerged for their empty house. She hadn't given up on that, of course, but the fact that the house was long since paid off in full kept its existence from weighing too heavily on her mind day to day.

"Not that I care," she said happily, "but how far did you have to come down in terms of price?"

"The buyer has offered the full listing price—"

"Are you *kidding*?"

"—in exchange for a few considerations regarding the closing. Chief among these is that he would like his identity to remain anonymous. He won't be present at the closing itself, and he has given me his proxy to sign all affidavits, et cetera, on his behalf."

"What about financing? Won't all this secrecy be a problem there?"

"He will pay cash."

"Oh my God," Helen said. Into their lives, already stabler than they were used to, was about to drop $315,000 in cash. "What is this guy, like some kind of celebrity or something?"

"Yes, actually," Bonifacio said coolly. "He is something of a celebrity, and for that reason would like everything done as quickly and as secretively and uncontentiously as possible. A fast closing. Is that acceptable to you?"

Helen allowed that it was. The day before the premiere, she took the afternoon off from work to ride the train back up to her old hometown and sit in Bonifacio's threadbare office and sign a stack of docu-

A THOUSAND PARDONS | 121

ments, and their last tie to their old life was cut. She was surprised not to feel any more ambivalence or nostalgia than she did. Mostly she just felt an unfamiliar pride. From the shipwreck of her marriage, with no resources at all, she had made a new existence for herself and her daughter, and that existence, at the present moment, would have to be counted a roaring success.

Movie theaters had basically followed the model of airplanes—what once had a now all but unimaginable aura of luxury had become as depressingly cost-efficient as possible—but the Ziegfeld had been left sufficiently alone that it could be pressed into service on nights when a little old-Hollywood glamor was on order. Helen had been instructed to arrive no later than five-thirty even though the movie didn't start until eight. She understood why. Sara did too, she was sure, though that didn't stop the poor girl—who looked amazing, Helen thought, amazing and pitiably self-conscious at the same time—from denouncing the whole operation as a perfectly refined symptom of everything fake for which she somehow held her mother responsible. They got out of a yellow cab at the end of the block (as far as the traffic cop posted there would let it go) and walked to the head of the pristine red carpet, where the spotlights were turned off and dozens of photographers, who had to get there early to secure their positions, fiddled irritably with their equipment. Helen wasn't sure whether to savor the moment and walk leisurely with her head up, smiling, or to speed into the theater as discreetly as possible. Sara walked almost directly behind her about halfway through the bored gauntlet, and then, incredibly, she stopped dead and answered her phone.

"Sweetheart," Helen said reproachfully, but Sara held up a hand to silence her. She was reading a text; whomever it was from, it put a welcome smile on her face, and she flipped the phone around in her hand and began snapping pictures of the paparazzi. "Smile!" she called out, and one or two of them did, though most simply looked annoyed with her for daring to clog up the charged public space with her ordinariness. Sara's phone beeped at her again as she was holding it aloft for another photo; she brought it down, read what was on the screen, laughed, and started texting back.

"Sara!" Helen said and put a hand on her shoulder. Sara shook it off. "Who are you texting?" she said, leaning next to her daughter's face to try to look at the screen; she got a whiff of something sweet and medicinal. "Fine," Sara said, closing her phone, and marched toward the theater doors, her mother trailing behind.

They were hustled into a very plain-looking reception room full of catering tables, where they spent an hour stuffing themselves with finger food while glancing at a closed-circuit video monitor fed by a stationary camera trained on the same carpet they had just crossed. First came a trickle of anonymous corporate invitees just like them, overdressed people who walked off the bottom of the screen and then appeared a few seconds later in the doorway of the reception room, trying to look nowhere and for a familiar face at the same time. Helen was sorry to see that no one else had brought a young son or daughter. Then came a second round of people, who apparently were well known if you were part of the movie industry, judging by the little, indiscreet grunts of recognition Helen heard moving through the crowd.

"Who's that guy?" Sara said.

"Not a clue," said Helen.

Sara shrugged. "They're going to wait until the last of the genetically inferior walks the red carpet," she said, "and then they're going to seal the doors and turn on the gas."

Her mother was turning to ask her to keep her voice down when a more serious ripple went through the room, and Helen felt her shoulders squeezed as others abruptly tried to work their way toward the door separating them from the lobby. She turned to the screen and saw a face she recognized, though she had no memory of the name, and then a beautiful young woman who was either Amy Ryan or Amy Adams. She didn't dare ask anyone—certainly not Sara; when she got into a certain mood, anything you said to her was a provocation—which Amy it was.

"Pretty sure," Sara said, "that I am the only Asian person here."

"Oh, I'm sure that's not true," Helen said, trying to conceal her surprise; that was exactly the sort of thing she'd always taken comfort in Sara not noticing. She kept her eyes on the screen. Though the camera angle excluded the arc lights themselves, you could tell they were on from the glow that now framed the faces on the video feed; and every time they heard the lobby doors open, the sound of a kind of dull human panic reached them from outside until the doors swung shut again. They weren't really on the inside, Helen thought, where they could see what was going on, but they weren't on the outside either; she didn't know where they were. And then there was a collective octave change as the crowd saw Hamilton Barth step out of the carousel of limousines.

The other guests had already begun to exit the reception room, to find good seats and to get a good, clear, casual look at the famous in the flesh before the lights went down; so Helen, with everyone suddenly drawing away from her, could hear for the first time that there was now an audio feed on the monitor as well. Two well-dressed men, just good-looking enough to be unobtrusive, stood on either side of Hamilton with their hands on his two elbows.

"He's bombed," murmured Sara, startling her mother, who hadn't realized she was right there. "Nice. He's so hammered he needs two guys to hold him up."

But Hamilton, handsome and curious and wincing a bit from the noise, clearly wasn't bombed, and they weren't holding him up—their touch was too light for that. While pretending to look elsewhere, the two men—who might have been co-workers of Helen's at Malloy for all she knew; where else would you drum up people to perform such a task?—were trying their best to shepherd Hamilton into the theater as quickly as possible, to keep his feet moving before some beautiful woman in a gown holding a microphone could step into his path and arrest his attention, which was of course exactly what happened next.

"Hamilton!" the woman shouted at him. He stopped dead and drew back a little at the sight of her. "Hamilton Barth! What a night! How excited are you to be here?"

"How excited am I?" Hamilton said, shouting over the screams of those behind the ropes—shouting, it seemed, over the strobe of flash-bulbs. He was grinning, a little gamely and a little condescendingly, and crow's feet ramified handsomely around his eyes like pond ice someone has stepped on a little too soon. "We're all overexcited, right! Did your mother used to tell you sometimes that you were getting over-excited? Mine did! What's your name?"

He brushed his hands through his hair, mostly as a way of getting his elbows out of the palms of his two escorts, who were already visibly worried.

"Everybody's here tonight! You must have lots of friends here for your big night!"

"I don't really have a lot of industry friends, actually," Hamilton said ruminatively, as if they were having a serious conversation at the tops of their voices, "because if you have a lot of friends in the industry, then you wind up spending a lot of evenings like this one."

"Tell me about this movie," the woman with the microphone said through her dozens of teeth. "Was it—"

"Maria," Hamilton said. "Is it Maria? Not that you look like you would be named Maria, just I suddenly feel like we've met before."

"Wow!" said the woman who might plausibly have been Maria. "So there's already Oscar buzz about this movie. What was it like mak-ing it?"

"What is your job?" Hamilton asked her, in the friendliest possible tone. "What do you do?"

The woman's openmouthed smile gave way to uncertain laughter. The microphone dropped an inch or two.

"No, I'm sorry, right, the movie, the movie," Hamilton said. "Well, look around you, I mean this evening says it all, right? The movie was just like every other movie I have ever made, an exploration of the self and its boundaries, a pathetic, profligate waste of money, an orgy, a journey, a total clusterfuck."

"A what?" said Maria.

"Clusterfuck!" Hamilton repeated into the microphone, at which point the two handlers put their forearms into the small of his back and got his momentum going toward the theater door again.

"What a tool," Sara said. "Seriously, with the I'm-too-good-for-this routine. If you don't like being looked at, don't spend your whole life in front of cameras." Helen saw she was texting again.

"It's hard to be scrutinized all the time," Helen said softly. "And watch your language, please. Some actors find it hard just to be themselves. I don't think this is reflective of who he really is."

"How do you know who he really is?" Sara said. "And do not tell that story again. Can we go get some decent seats, please?"

The theater was already nearly full, though hardly anyone was seated. The lights were still all the way up. The aisles were crowded with people on their phones; Helen saw one woman who was clearly only pretending to talk to someone, then discreetly turning the phone every few seconds to take a picture. She looked around to see who was worth this small subterfuge, but in the front few rows of seats it was hard to recognize anyone, precisely because everyone had that look to them, that look of being someone whom you ought to recognize. "Keep going, keep going," Sara said to her bewildered mother. "I do not want to get stuck on the side." Helen pushed gently past five or six standing men, toward what looked like unclaimed space in the interior of one of the center rows. It was impossible to tell which seats were taken and which were not, because no one was willing to compromise his or her view of everyone else by sitting down.

"Can I *help* you?" a female voice asked incredulously. Helen looked down and saw a beautiful, dark-eyed, pint-size young woman with a headset and a tiny skirt, staring at Helen and her daughter as if they had just broken into her home. Her right arm was thoroughly, colorfully tattooed from the shoulder down to the forearm, at which point the design dwindled gracefully, like an unfinished chapel ceiling. Her red hair was stylishly, boyishly short, the sort of haircut models in fashion magazines sometimes fooled you into thinking you and your imperfect face could get away with. This woman got away with it completely, and it contributed to her air of almost biological disdain. Her question was of course rhetorical; as Helen was still smiling at her, prefatory to explaining how she could indeed help them, the tiny woman said, "This is the VIP seating and I am going to go ahead and guess you don't belong here."

"Probably not," Helen said affably. "Can you tell me where we do belong?"

"Staten Island?" the woman said. "I don't know. A word of advice, though. Next time you want to try crashing, don't bring a kid. That's just shameless."

Helen's smile dropped. "Listen," she said, feeling herself blush, "there's no call to get personal. I have just as much right to be here as you do. But if you can just tell me where it's okay for us to sit, we will go sit there."

"How is it my problem where you belong?" From the suddenly wild look in the woman's eyes, Helen could tell that someone very important was somewhere behind her. "All I can do for you is tell you where you don't belong. Do I not have enough to deal with? Do you even know how these events work? What, did you win your tickets in a contest or some shit?"

"Mom," Sara said urgently and put her hand on her mother's arm.

"You need to stop blocking this row immediately," the woman said.

"How can I even get out? You are blocking my only way out of this row."

"You need to clear this row or I will call security." She put her fingers to her tiny headset.

Helen's shoulders sagged.

"Mom!" Sara said.

"Excuse me," another voice said behind Helen, "they're with me." She turned, and there was Hamilton Barth, big as life, in a very elegant-looking dark suede jacket and jeans and cowboy boots. Their proximity to him did not seem quite real. He gave off a sharp smell. He flashed his weathered smile. "Are these my seats? Because these two are with me."

No sound came from the woman with the headset. Helen was looking right into Hamilton's face, and smiling expectantly, and he was smiling back at her, but in a reflexive way that made it clear to her he had no idea at all who she was. Not that he should have been expected to recognize her—someone he kissed at a party thirty years ago. Still, she was let down by the realization that as far as he was concerned he was just doing something impishly chivalrous for two unglamorous strangers.

"What's your name, dear?" he said to her.

"Helen," she said both pointedly and nervously.

He looked over her head to the young woman with the headset, whose expression was stony, as if determined to face disaster bravely. "Helen and her daughter are my guests. These are our seats, correct?"

The young woman nodded. It wasn't a lie; his saying it made it true.

"And your name?"

She swallowed. You could see her thinking that Hamilton Barth asking for her name was either the best or the worst thing that had ever happened to her. She wasn't some ordinary flack: she had bought into the ruthless values of her flackdom so completely that, just as she had not questioned Helen's inferiority to her, she stood before this famous person as she would have before a judge. "Bettina," she said clearly.

"Thank you for your help, Bettina," Hamilton said and sat down. He gestured grandly to Helen and dumbstruck Sara, and they sat as well, so that Helen was between the other two. She felt as if she had crossed into some new dimension. She could have made their forearms touch if she wanted to: he was handsome and rumpled and musky and tan and faun-like, but he seemed to radiate some ethereal quality above and apart from all that. From the corner of her eye she could see people surreptitiously shooting pictures of him, pictures in which she would reside forever and invisibly.

"I hope that's all right with you," Hamilton said. "I just can't stand watching these little martinet bitches treating people like that. A little bit of power, you know?"

"I do know. Thank you."

"And now she can spend the rest of the evening wondering if I'm going to have her fired."

"Are you?" Helen asked, idly curious, though it occurred to her that the young woman might even have been a Malloy employee.

"No," he laughed. "It's not her fault, really. She has a dark, dark heart." His eyes seemed to unfocus for a few seconds; then he turned to Helen again and grinned. "I'm Hamilton, by the way." He put out his hand, and she took it.

"Yes, of course I know who you are," she said. "But not for the reason you think I do."

Hamilton squinted. Nearly everyone was seated now, but she could still feel a thousand eyes on them. "Say again?" he said.

"He doesn't even remember you?" Sara said behind her, uncomfortably close to her ear. "That is priceless."

"Hello?" said an unfamiliar voice in the air around them; it was the film's director, who began a short introduction, which after two minutes gave no indication of winding up. Helen, impatient, shifted toward Hamilton and reflexively hunched lower in her seat. Hamilton did the same. "I hate these things," he whispered. "Always the same. Rituals about nothing. Why is it important that I be here? What does it have to do with me?"

"I can understand why a person would have a few drinks," Helen said incautiously.

"That gets exaggerated," Hamilton said, seeming unoffended, "because when I drink, I do stupid things. What did you say your name was again?"

She took a deep breath. "My name is Helen Armstead," she said. "It used to be Helen Roche. You and I were classmates at St. Catherine's in Malloy, New York, for eight years."

She watched his eyes try to resettle on her.

"We lived on Holcomb Street," she went on in a low voice. His mouth, like hers, was now below the level of the seat back. "My father was the pharmacist at the prison. I was friends with Erin White, whose sister you went out with, or at least that's what she said."

She felt terrified, as if she were divulging secrets. Hamilton was doing something with his eyes without even moving them. Sara was nudging her mother in the back to try to get her to sit up straight and stop risking the notice of strangers. There was a tepid rain of applause, and the lights in the theater went down.

"Keep talking," Hamilton whispered to her. "This is incredible."

As she did so, her eyes adjusted to the dark and his face came back into focus. "I was at your first communion," she whispered to him. "I was part of that group that got drunk behind the Little League field after your confirmation. Remember? I was there watching with you when Jerry Merrill flipped his boat on Sylvia Lake. I was there at Sue Coleman's graduation party when you fell asleep with a cigarette and burned a hole in their couch."

"Yes," Hamilton whispered in a tone of awe. "That was me."

"Sssh!" said someone in the row behind them.

"I sat behind you in Sister Edna's French class. I knew your mom from when I would help out my mom at the church flea markets on the last Saturday of every month. I knew your little brother who was in the first Gulf War. I can't remember his name, though."

"Gilbert," Hamilton said. "Gil. Oh my God. What else?"

"Would you shut up?" a woman said in the dark above their heads.

Helen didn't tell him that they had once made out. She didn't know why. The movie's opening credits were ending—there was scattered applause for each above-the-line name—and then she had the strange experience of sitting beside Hamilton as he watched himself act on screen. Gradually the sight of his magnified face seemed to bring him out of the trance into which her litany of childhood memories had lowered him. He fidgeted, and chewed at his thumb, until about a half hour into the film he leaned toward Helen and wrapped his fingers gently around her arm.

"I need to hit the bathroom," he said.

"I hope you don't feel ambushed," she whispered. "I didn't know if I'd get to talk to you at all."

"Of course not. Hey, I never asked you what you're even doing here. Do you work for the studio?"

"I work at a PR firm," she said. "Malloy Worldwide, it's called, if you can believe it. I think you work with them sometimes."

"Oh. Sure. Do you have a card or something?"

It was the polite thing you said to someone you knew you were never going to see again. Dispirited, feeling she had said the wrong thing somewhere, she fumbled in her bag for a business card and handed it to him.

"Okay," he said. "Well, listen." But then he couldn't seem to think what else to say. He leaned over and kissed Helen on the cheek, and then, remaining in his crouch, he discreetly exited at the other end of the row.

The movie was about a man who witnesses a killing and has to send his wife and children into hiding while he tries to figure out the murderer's identity before the murderer figures out his. By the time the lights went up, the on-screen Hamilton had muddied the real but absent one and Helen's exhilaration had given way to a peculiar, untraceable sadness. She wasn't particularly surprised that he'd never come back to his seat. She'd upset or offended him somehow. There was a Q and A after the closing credits, but so many people stood and left while it was still going on that Helen took advantage of the general rudeness to leave the theater as well. The street was choked with limos; they had to walk all the way to Madison to find a cab uptown.

Sara texted furiously in the seat beside her as they rode. Helen leaned her forehead against the cool window, staring into the empty boutiques, bright and unpopulated. "So," Sara said, without looking up. "There it was, right? Your big reunion. Did you reminisce about your great moment in the closet?"

"No," Helen said. "Nothing like that. I don't know what I thought would happen. He was a nice man, and I'm glad I talked to him, but in a way I'm sorry I told him who I was at all. People don't really want to go back to their past. They'd probably rather just get further away from it." But Sara's earphones were already back in, so this last thought was delivered to no one.

5

AFTER A PREMIERE there was always a party. Hamilton tried to remember where it was as he sat on the lid of the toilet in the Ziegfeld bathroom stall. The ordeal of watching his face on screen, like the window to a dead self, was hard to shake, and he was having trouble remembering even the most basic information about himself, much less something as arcane as the location of the party at which he would soon be expected to appear. If indeed he'd ever known it in the first place. That was the kind of thing other people knew for you. And then suddenly it hit him: he jumped up and burst out of the men's room and stood there on the thick carpet and, looking around to confirm it, realized that his two handlers, those corporate robots attached to him by the studio publicists for the movie, were not there. He'd shaken them when he got up and left in the middle of the show. What do you know, he said to himself with a reflexive pang of satisfaction, I guess they liked the movie.

He found a door marked Fire Exit and said a little prayer before pushing it open, a prayer that was heard, because no alarm went off. Just like that, he was outside the bubble, in the unritualized world of some foul-smelling alley on Fifty-fourth Street. He felt a constructive kind of fear. Industry parties were a Catch-22 because even though they were soul-scalding and hateful, at least you knew what would happen there; you knew everything every smarmy asshole was going to say before he opened his mouth and said it. If he could just remember where the party was, he could go there now and have a few drinks while it was still blissfully asshole-free.

But the party will not start until after the end of the movie, intoned a voice in his head, as conversationally as if it had been speaking all along. No one will be there. Plus it is the first place, maybe the only place, the handlers will think to look for you once they realize you are gone.

There will be drinks at the party.

But there are drinks everywhere. This is New York.

He checked to see if he was carrying any cash with him; then he cursed himself for openly thumbing through the contents of his wallet in some dark New York City alley. His greatest fear was that he was no longer suited for living—real living, without all the armature of fame that sprang up around you and brought you what you needed and tricked you into depending on it. He made his way out to the street and began scanning the signage for bars. He did not have a drinking problem per se, he felt; he just had so many other problems, so many other sensitivities, and they all eventually funneled toward alcohol as the only way, however temporary, of clearing the cache, of resetting himself. The first place he saw was full of young after-work types, but that would have been deadly for him: he'd be recognized on the spot. He could not stand to be *alone* alone when he felt this way; what he wanted was to be alone in a crowd, to have the same sort of border between him and strangers that those strangers had between one another. Beyond Sixth Avenue there was an ancient-looking, half-full, low-ceilinged dive called Cornerstone's, and he ducked in there like he was coming in out of a snowstorm.

He ordered a bourbon on the rocks. He saw a rare, expensive bottle of Pappy Van Winkle on the top shelf and wanted to ask for that, but he didn't dare call even that much attention to himself. The bartender, who was at least sixty, didn't so much as look at him. Excited, Hamilton tried not to power through that first bourbon too fast, but he still found his glass empty by the time the bartender completed a lap. "Again?" the bartender said. At first Hamilton misunderstood this entirely, but then he nodded and nudged his glass forward.

Somewhere behind him he was being watched—in the theater, by hundreds of people who stared at his ten-foot-tall face and had no idea what they were looking at, what he was doing, no apparatus for judging it at all. They corrupted it by looking at it. What was the point? Once he'd said in an interview that his dream was to make movies that were never shown to anybody; even people he considered friends had mocked him for that one. He wanted to give it all up, but it was too late, there was nothing else on earth he was equipped to do. His painting, his poetry, his publishing efforts, all these were ruined for him too by the corrosive quality of people's attention to them. And the ranch? Please. They were all laughing at him there, or they would have been if he weren't signing their paychecks. Not literally—someone else signed their actual paychecks, or so Hamilton assumed, never having seen one. He would have to make a note to change the way that was done.

When he watched himself on screen, he had one important thing in common with everyone else in every theater everywhere, and that was the understanding that, even though you were asked to pretend you were watching some fictional character with a made-up name, you knew at every moment that you were really watching a movie star named Hamilton Barth. That seemed like the greatest, most fundamental failing any actor could possibly admit to, and yet his whole life was based on it, it was perversely considered a mark of his success. Why should that seem so particularly humiliating tonight, though? He'd been through it many times before. There was always that strange confrontation between himself and his image on the screen—an image that should have seemed like a memory, since it was in one sense an actual record of something he'd actually done, but somehow it never felt that way to him, it just struck him as a vision of something that might have become of him if he'd led some other life—but tonight, he recalled, there was this third layer, that chick with the Chinese daughter who either had really grown up with him or else was the best-prepared tabloid reporter ever. Helen something, from Malloy. No, of course she was telling the truth, of course she had grown up in Malloy and remembered everything about him, things he had forgotten without even trying. Why didn't he remember her? Why didn't he remember anything truly specific or important about those years, the years that had supposedly made him who he was? Whatever the hell that meant. That was your only true, uncreated self, yet Hamilton knew eighty-year-old guys who remembered more of the arcana of their own grade school years than he did. Why? How had this happened? Why did this Helen look so old to him? Probably just because he so rarely came into contact with women his own age anymore. He had an urge to track her down again, recognize more of her thrillingly trivial memories; but what good would that do him, to research his own self the way he would research any other part? At his core he was nobody, and his nobodyness felt like something unforgivable.

He could sort of remember that cigarette-in-the-couch story. Or remember people talking about it. No, it was no use. He'd lost the capacity to look back. The past was too full of mistakes anyway, mistakes and crimes, your own and others'; if you kept your eyes forward, you didn't have to spend all that energy trying to resolve what couldn't be resolved. He would just continue moving forward, only forward, like an animal, though it did help a bit, he supposed, to know that there was someone out there who remembered him as he used to be, as he really was, someone in whom that memory still lived, so that he, Hamilton Barth of Malloy, New York, was not yet dead forever.

"On the house," said the bartender, smiling, and slid him another bourbon. Hamilton smiled back, gratified, until he realized that if the bartender was comping him without recognizing him, that meant this must have been his fourth drink, or his sixth, he forgot what the custom was. He looked at his watch. The movie must have ended about twenty minutes ago. There was no way to stop drinking now. He looked in his wallet again and counted about fifty dollars in there. Enough to pay for four bourbons, but maybe not for six. Where the hell was the afterparty? Somebody had told him at some point. It was fluttering on the outer edges of his memory. Saint something. St. Patrick's, St. Catherine's. He caught the bartender's eye and made a sickly scribbling motion in the air, and then he sweated out the thirty seconds or so before his tab arrived. Forty bucks. Thank God. He put all fifty on the bar and said, "What's the name of that guy, the old guy with the morning show on TV, shouts all the time, has a blond co-host?"

The bartender pulled his head back warily. Maybe the question was a little too out of nowhere, or maybe Hamilton, despite his best effort to act casual, had made it sound a little too urgent. "Regis?" he said icily.

The St. Regis. That was it. Hamilton had no idea where it was, and yet a short time later he found himself there anyway. Perhaps he had thought to ask someone; he didn't remember anything like that happening, though, and so he chose to believe the evening was starting to break his way. They were all in some sort of ballroom—he and two hundred other people—and now, instead of ignoring him because they didn't know who he was, as the good folks at Cornerstone's had done, they were ignoring him because they were trying to be cool about knowing precisely who he was. One young woman, obviously an actress, waved gaily to him from the other end of the bar. He thought she might have been in the movie with him, but that was the kind of boundary that was losing its sharpness now. Then he saw up close two faces he definitely recognized, the faces of his keepers from the premiere, Sturm and Drang. One looked relieved and the other looked pissed. They were like two halves of the same stupendously boring person.

"I'm glad you think it's funny," one of them said to Hamilton, who was straight-faced as far as he could feel. "We might not have jobs tomorrow. Where were you, in some bar?"

He nodded.

"Oh, great," said the angry one. "And I'm sure no one whipped out a phone and took your picture there. I'm sure you were totally incognito there. I'm sure that picture isn't on TMZ already."

"That's all correct, actually," Hamilton said. "Though weirdly expressed. Why, were you out looking for me?"

The two handlers' four eyes flashed toward each other, then back at Hamilton. "Seriously," said the relieved one, "I don't know whether to laugh or cry right now."

"Have a drink," Hamilton said, clapping them both on the shoulder, "and for God's sake, never, ever separate into two people. Because that is a slippery fucking slope." He made the journey from the bar at one end of the ballroom to the bar at the opposite end. People waved, and he waved back, and he hugged and kissed them lustily whenever they hugged and kissed him, but whenever they spoke to him it was as if they were a hundred feet away, and with no idea what they were saying he had to try to make the appropriate facial expressions until they stopped. Time passed and he had a vague sense of the ballroom being less crowded than it had been, unless it had somehow gotten bigger. He saw a young, red-haired woman in a very short black skirt—hot, but small, like some sort of curvaceous doll—sitting alone with her heavily tattooed arm across the back of her chair; at the far end of the arm was her hand with a martini glass in it; at the near end, her chin was sunk gloomily into her shoulder. With her legs crossed, she was more exposed to Hamilton and the rest of the room than she seemed to realize—

"Whoa!" Hamilton said. "Bettina!"

Bettina raised her eyes, the way a dog would do. "Well great," she said. "There goes my last shred of hope, which was that you'd forgotten what I looked like."

She was very drunk, which was exciting because it ran so afoul of his first impression of her. It was so boring to be right about people. "Bettina, don't worry, Bettina," he said, pulling up a chair in front of her; whoever had been at Bettina's table had abandoned her there. She had the look of someone who had already embarrassed herself, who was regretful but also past caring. "Are you afraid of me? There's no reason to be afraid of me."

She looked at him and smirked, as if offended to be considered stupid enough not to be afraid of him.

"Bettina, it is so important that we found each other," he said. "Let me go get you another martina. Martini."

The crowd had thinned out to the point where he didn't even have to wait in line at the bar. He held up the martini glass and then two fingers, as if it were very loud in the ballroom, which it no longer was. The chandeliers were so clean—whose job was that?—but he could not look up at them, he had to look down at the two precious martinis as he made his way across the floor, which seemed to have opened up to the size of a parking lot. Please let her still be there, Hamilton said to himself, please please please.

Not only was she there but she seemed to have perked up a bit. Her head was almost vertical. She accepted her martini with a look of deep cynicism. "What are you doing?" she said.

"I need," he said, "to get to know you."

She took a sip and closed her eyes. "You mean you think you're going to fuck me?" she asked him.

"It is not about that," he said. "I mean it is honestly only partly about that."

"I'm sure you're used to getting whatever you want."

"If only," he said. "I wish. As if." He tried to think of another phrase that meant the same thing.

"Can I ask you something? That old broad at the theater tonight, the one with the Asian daughter: you don't even know who she is, do you?"

"No," he said. "No idea."

She sat back and flipped her hands up in the air, satisfied and disgusted at the same time.

"I get treated like shit in my job," she said. "This is the part where I say: 'But I'm not a bad person.' But you know what? I am a bad person."

"No," Hamilton said soothingly.

She closed her eyes and nodded loosely. "This is the part where I say: 'Seriously. You don't know me.' But you know what? I think you do know me. You look at me and say, 'Oh, I know her,' and you're actually probably right."

"No, I do not know you," Hamilton said, his voice reverent now, a whisper. You are the one, he was thinking. Though he was unsure what he meant by that. *You are the one.* She was some kind of kindred spirit, that was for sure, some kind of sinner who understood what an unfairly hazardous world this was, at least when she was drunk, a state in which he determined to keep her. Himself too: usually these evenings shot up like a firework and ended in a blackout that was like a depressive rebirth, but with a partner like this at his side, a partner in crime, he had an interest in keeping things going, in postponing tomorrow morning for as long as humanly possible. He now found himself kneeling on the floor in front of her, in order to hear her better and also to worship her. Right alongside these feelings of worship, but somehow not corrupting them or affecting them in any way, were sexual imaginings of the most baroque, polluted kind, having to do with her smallness, her perfect scale, her miniature manipulability, various humiliating scenarios in which no part of her touched the floor, in which he dominated her as a giant might do.

"I mean I don't know why I should care," Bettina was saying, "about my stupid fucking job, whether I lose it, whether I keep it. Public relations—what the hell does that even mean?"

"I don't know anyone who knows," Hamilton said. He patted her hand with his. She didn't seem to notice, and in truth he couldn't really feel it either. He looked around for her martini and handed it to her.

"Don't you wish you could become someone else," she said, "just like that? Just say, 'This is the night I am absolved for every mistake,' and then just start again as this other person? Look who I'm talking to, though. Hamilton Motherfucking Barth. Like you'd be free to change who you are even if you wanted to."

"What do you mean?" he said. "I could do it."

She laughed at him. "No way José," she said. "You're fucked in that department. The world owns your ass."

He stood up. His anger only sharpened the sexual outline of his every thought. "Here's what we're going to do," he said, with no idea what his next sentence would be. But he needed to stay with her, and he needed to be somewhere that was not here. "Can you rent a car?"

"What?"

"I can't. I mean I can, but I know from experience that if they see it's me they'll drop a dime and five minutes later there'll be photographers up our ass like Princess Di. So can you rent it?"

"Don't need to rent any car. I own a car. I drove here. But where do you need to go?"

"We, Bettina. We. We need to go somewhere and be alone together." He lifted her gently to her feet. She was like a feather. "You have a coat somewhere, right? Where are you parked?"

"Is this really happening?" she said. They started toward the door. Already he felt reborn and invisible. "I need to tell you something," she said. "Back at the theater? I lied to you when I said my name was Bettina."

"That is the best news of all," Hamilton said.

SARA AND CUTTER did not have any classes together—not so unusual, in a school that size—and by third period on Wednesday she still hadn't seen him, though they'd been texting all morning, after texting well into the night before. They'd snarked on every camera-phone photo she'd sent him of that stupid ass-kissing zombie movie premiere, where everyone was so in love with themselves; still, she looked forward to doing it in person all over again. But when she got to the cafeteria, he wasn't there. She went to his French classroom before the start of next period, and he wasn't there either. Where had he been texting her from? She typed the question and received in return a photo of Cutter, grinning and wearing pajamas, in what she presumed was his own kitchen.

So he'd ditched. He did that more often lately. It wasn't as bad as the day he'd actually come to school but then skipped all his classes anyway, hiding in the library or the unlocked maintenance rooms or other little interstices he managed to know about—exercising a sort of pointless, arcane freedom, and waiting for pushback, which he never seemed to get.

Things with Cutter had progressed quickly, in ways good and bad. Sometimes there would be afternoons spent in each other's company— at some Starbucks, or on one of the benches in Carl Schurz Park watching the river traffic and the joggers and the checked out nannies pushing strollers toward the playground, or even just in Sara's apartment cracking each other up in front of daytime TV—that felt like love, or at any rate like ease. On the couch with their shoulders pressed into each other, they would laugh and eat leftover takeout and mock the clueless neediness of the Real Housewives or whatever other sad sacks were whoring out their dignity on reality TV, a genre of which they never tired. They made out a lot too. Which was great, but if she was honest with herself the major appeal of having him in her home with the TV on lay in the reduced risk of his acting out in some public way that might embarrass her, or endanger him, or both. She had already begun, for instance, finding excuses not to go into stores with him, because no matter what sort of store it was—a Duane Reade, a Starbucks, a Sephora—when they were back on the street he would pull out of his jacket something he had shoplifted for her. She started to understand why his other friends were always so careful to limit their exposure to him, to stay outside his bubble. She did not want him to get caught, of course, but she couldn't think of anything else that would stop him; and he never got caught.

What was worse was how bad he tried to make her feel for stressing. He mocked her for her fear of getting into trouble, but then, when she insisted she wasn't afraid of that—and she wasn't, not really—he critiqued her even more sarcastically, saying she was like someone whose jail cell door had been opened but she was too scared, too guilty to walk through it. Jail cell? As was often the case, she could follow what he was saying only so far, but no further. He'd always seemed older than she was, and one day he'd let slip that in fact he was almost sixteen. He'd been left back, despite being the single smartest person she had ever met.

His provocations could turn casually mean. But she forgave him everything. She could feel herself committing that cardinal feminine sin, the one you saw on reality TV shows all the time: she thought she could save him.

She answered the kitchen-photo message with a plea to return to school the next day. He promised that he would, but then on Thursday there was still no sign of him. She missed half of first-period chem standing in the hall outside his homeroom waiting to see if he would show up. Glumly she went back to her own schedule, and then, out of nowhere—at ten in the morning, in Spanish class, at a moment when she wasn't supposed to have her phone on but had forgotten to switch it off—she got a call. Mortified, she pulled the phone out of her bag and held it below the level of her desk, as if that would make any difference when it was blaring its ringtone; she started to shut it off, but then she recognized the phone number, even though she hadn't seen or used it in many months now. It was still programmed into her contacts, though; above the number on the tiny screen was the word *Home*.

"Señorita Armstead?" the teacher said testily.

When lunch period came Sara ran into the corridor and turned her phone back on, but by the time she had two bars she'd decided not to return the call anyway, whoever it was from. The whole thing was too creepy. Like a horror movie: *The call is coming from inside the house*. Whoever it was hadn't left a voice mail. She thought briefly, reflexively, about calling Cutter to get his take on it, but there was more than half a chance the call was from him in the first place—just using the time on his hands to prank her. They gave her only twenty-five minutes to eat anyway.

There were no missed calls when she checked her phone again outside school at the end of the afternoon. But then it rang while she still had it in her hand, almost as if someone was watching her. She was too freaked out to answer. She went home, did an acceptable percentage of her homework, and saw that Cutter had posted nine messages on her Facebook wall asking what she was doing; she called her mother at the office, ordered Mexican for dinner, and was sitting on the couch watching *16 and Pregnant* when her cellphone rang again.

"What the fuck?" was the way she answered it, having decided it was probably Cutter, who had hacked the number just to show her how far inside her head he could get.

"Is that Sara?"

She had a profound moment of unbalance, like tipping a chair back too far. She looked at the incoming number again. "Daddy?" she said.

"Hi, honey. I'm sorry I called you this morning. I was just so excited to call that I actually forgot—well, I didn't forget you went to school, obviously, but I guess I forgot what day it was."

"Dad, where are you calling from?"

He laughed, a sound she hadn't heard in a long time, though it wasn't enough by itself to calm the furious beating of her heart, or the anger that her fear provoked. "Caller ID, eh?" he said. "Okay, maybe it was kind of a gratuitous touch, but I called the phone company and they still had our old number available. I'm calling you from our house. Our old house. I bought it."

"What?" she said. "From who?"

"From your mother, technically."

"How did she not tell me that?"

"I don't think she knows. I kept it anonymous, because I figured she would never go for it otherwise. She told you the house was sold, though, right?"

"Yeah. She's all pumped to have the money."

"Well, good, that's kind of what I was hoping. Anyway, here I am. I don't know where our furniture is, but otherwise everything's the same. What do you think?"

What did she *think*? Even in moments of extreme weirdness like this, it was just easy to express herself to him. Much easier than talking to her mother.

"I think it sounds pretty messed up," she said.

"Well, granted."

"I mean, for one thing, I thought you were broke."

"I wasn't, it turned out. Though I kind of am now."

"And then—" She closed her eyes, not because she was upset but just to try to get her thoughts in order. "Why would you want to go back there," she asked him, "by yourself, when you made such a big display about wanting to get out when Mom and I were living there? You liked the house, it was just us you didn't like?"

A lengthy pause on his end. "Good for you," he said softly. "I'm not sure I know why, really. The short answer is, it's my home. And I don't necessarily mean that in a good way, because it's kind of a mess right now, but I made it, and I feel like I should live in it. And it gets you and Mom some of the money you should have gotten in the first place, and it keeps somebody else from moving in and just painting over, papering over, what happened here. I have to live here because it reminds me every day of who I am."

It was an event, this phone call, even apart from what was being discussed; she hadn't heard the sound of her father's voice in months. Texting had just seemed like the default way to communicate—it was the way she communicated with everyone, even Cutter—but she could see now that there was something else to it, some sort of insulation or remove, that maybe they'd both needed.

On the TV screen a baby's crying was muted. Framing the set was a view out the window of hundreds of apartments, hundreds of lives, all too small and too far away to be made out in any detail.

"So you're telling me all this why?" Sara said. "What do you expect me to do?"

"I don't expect you to do anything. It's not even important that you come back here ever if you don't want to. I just like the thought of you knowing that the place where you grew up is still here and that nobody else is living in it."

Her eyes began to sting. "This makes no sense to me at all," she said. "You had this huge meltdown, and you just got out of jail for it. Why go back? Why not just take your money and go somewhere else and try something new?"

"Turns out it's not so enticing," he said. "Turns out it's kind of frightening, being nobody. Anyway, telling yourself you're nobody doesn't make it true."

"It's better to be someone everybody's mad at?" Sara said.

He said nothing for a moment, then laughed softly. "You should see what happens when I go into town, to buy food and whatnot. Everyone who recognizes me hates my guts. Which is both a bad feeling and a good one. Good because it's bad. It's hard to describe."

Sara tried to imagine it. "Do any of them ever ask," she said, "whatever happened to me?"

"No," he said, "but that's only because nobody who knows you will speak to me at all."

"You said you're broke now. Do you have a job?"

"Yes. Of sorts."

"So you're just going to live there like nothing happened?"

"No," he said, "I am going to live here like everything happened."

She had a strange urge to tell him about Cutter—the stealing, the ditching, the self-destruction—and to ask for his advice, if only because she knew he wouldn't lose his shit over it the way her mother surely would. "So," she said instead, "what was jail like?" but then she heard the key turning in the front door lock behind her. "Gotta go, bye," she said to her father and hung up on him.

Helen came and collapsed on the couch beside her, coat still on. "I'm so sorry," she said. "It just never ends. Every day I look up and suddenly it's dark out. You poor thing." She kissed Sara on the forehead, looking at the TV. "What on earth are you watching?" she said.

She disapproved lately of all of Sara's habits, her likes and dislikes. As their circumstances bettered, her mother seemed determined to effect some corresponding improvement in Sara herself, some movement toward an ideal. This Sara resented intensely. Her mother wanted to change her wardrobe, to change the books she read, the TV she watched. She suggested that they join a gym together: "God knows I could use it," she'd say, as if that made the whole notion any less repellent, or less insulting. In this atmosphere there was absolutely no question of discussing, or even mentioning the existence of, her shoplifting, class-cutting, alcohol-consuming, iPod-mugging, disobedience-encouraging boyfriend. Helen would have heard only the bad parts about him and would have devoted herself full-time to scrubbing this ethically compromised boy out of her daughter's supposedly exemplary life. And this was why asking for advice on, or even mentioning, her sporadic contact with her father over the past several months would have been pointless as well. Her mother would have called the cops, and changed Sara's phone number, and for what? For the sake of some perfectly untroubled adolescence she was apparently supposed to have, some perfect life she was supposed to aspire to, like that of some saint, never mind if the life she had right now, with all its flaws and drama, was hers. A saint was exactly what she was not.

Take the question of private school. Her mother wouldn't let up about it lately. And it was true that the high school where she was enrolled next fall was overlarge and academically half-assed and socially fraught: but who imagined that Sara was too good for that? She herself was fraught in ways her mother was stubbornly unable to see. "It's just the two of us now," Helen loved to say. But it wasn't. Her father, the more she thought about him, constituted a kind of parallel universe, a splinter family, and Sara was starting to think that maybe that was the family to which she truly belonged. Just as he had—only more literally—she'd become aware as she grew older that she was not living the life she had been born to live. And the guilt generated by her escape from that life was something she, like her father, had no desire to run from. Why her, after all? She was not so special. She was not without her weaknesses, her faults. And her advantages—where did they come from? What made her more deserving of luck or grace than anybody else whose real parents didn't want them? It was important that she not pretend to be better than she was. Her father understood this kind of self-censure—more so than ever, in his current state. Her mother's heart was closed to it.

Two hours later Sara's phone went off again, this time a text from Cutter. *Hungry?* it read. Sara glanced up at her mother, six feet away on the couch in front of the TV, sound asleep. She texted back a single question mark, and a few moments later he had sent another grinning photo of himself, this time at a booth in a restaurant. It took her a few seconds to recognize it, from the menu he held in his hand, as the Hunan Garden just down the block from her apartment building. She felt her face grow hot.

Wtf are you doing?? she texted him.

Come on out. Free wine.

No way. Mom right here.

So I'll come up to your place, then?

"Whoo!" Helen said suddenly. "I just nodded right off there!"

Sara willed herself to be calm as her mother slowly made the move from the couch to her own bedroom and shut the door. She left a note on the kitchen table saying she had gone to the Duane Reade to buy a new highlighter—lame, but better than no note at all—and slipped out the front door and down the hall to the elevators as quietly as she could.

Cutter looked euphoric, fresh as a daisy. It was after ten o'clock, and the waiters were glaring at him. He beckoned her into the booth where he sat with a pot of Chinese tea and an untouched tofu stir-fry of some kind. "I can only stay a minute," she said. "You have to come back to school. Promise me you'll be there tomorrow."

"I was actually thinking about going out to the Island tomorrow," he said. "The weather's supposed to be nice. You should come with me. If we go tomorrow, we'll have the house to ourselves."

Her head drooped. If he didn't go to school, he would fail, and if he failed, the two of them would not be together next year. But she didn't want to make their relationship into the carrot. She was feeling a little locked in as it was. "So guess who called me tonight," she said. "My dad."

"No shit," Cutter said, his face splitting into a huge smile. "Is he back in the joint? Making his one phone call?"

She shook her head. "He's been out for a while. It was just a month, you know. Anyway, no, he actually called me from inside our old house upstate. He's back living there now. My mother thought she was selling it to some stranger but she was actually selling it to him. Isn't that insane?"

She was just hoping to amuse him and maybe garner some sympathy over the strangeness of her family; but he didn't look amused at all. His brow furrowed, and his chin even shook a little bit, as if he might cry. "So he wants you to move back up there?" he said finally.

"No, he doesn't. He said he doesn't. He said he's just doing it for himself. So he can go into town and have everybody hate him, or something like that. Crazy, right?"

Cutter shook his head. "Don't you see what this is really about?" he said. "Your parents feel guilty every time they look at you and so they try to get rid of their guilt by buying you things. You see that, right? The guilt?"

Though she didn't quite see it, Sara nodded soberly anyway, not wanting to agitate him any further. "Guilt over the divorce?" she said softly.

"No!" Cutter said. "Because you're Chinese!"

"What?" she said in a harsh whisper, conscious that they were now under the probationary stare of the old Chinese guy who worked the register.

"It's the American story in miniature," Cutter said. "They came into your home and took you away from who you were, from everything you knew, and then, in order to have it both ways, they spend your life trying to buy you off to get you to forgive them for what they've done. They've deracinated you, and they can't stand that you know that, and confront them with it, just by being. Just your face is a reminder of their crimes."

Sara hadn't heard the word "deracinated" before, but she got the picture. "I need to get back," she said. "My mother could wake up and then I'm screwed."

"Screwed how? What are you afraid of? What can they do to you they haven't already done? She'd probably just feel guilty. All parents feel guilty. Because they are."

She shrugged. He grabbed her wrist.

"You want to feel screwed," he said, "come out to the Island with me."

She shook him off and stood up. "Please go home," she said tearily. "I'm worried about you. I don't like being the only person who knows where you are."

He folded his arms. "Whatever," he said. "Go. I'm thinking about ordering dessert."

The next morning there was no sign of him, and Sara's chem teacher asked her to stay after class; her mind raced through all the different types of trouble she might be in, but it turned out that Ms. Markell wanted to nominate her for a scholarship to this summer chem-bio program at Columbia, a program designed to offer research opportunities to minority students. It was, she said, very prestigious, and down the road would put Sara on the radar of some very prestigious universities. "I guess I'll talk to my mother about it," Sara said, and Ms. Markell said of course, though she had already taken the liberty of emailing her mother with the great news. Sure enough, when Sara left school she had a text from her mom with three exclamation points and a suggestion that they meet at Hunan Garden for dinner.

"I hope you won't be mad," Helen said as Sara picked at some dumplings with her head down so that her hair concealed her face from the waiters, "but I called Nightingale and scheduled a tour for next Thursday. I know it's supposed to be hard to get in there after ninth grade, not a lot of spaces open up, but that doesn't mean it's impossible, especially not when you've got a credential like this in your pocket that very few other people have. Anyway, don't worry, a tour doesn't commit us to anything. It just seems worth a shot, especially now."

"Mom, there's something—"

"It's all girls at Nightingale, as you probably know, which may seem strange to you at this point, but all the studies say it's a good thing, at least in the classroom. Funny it isn't all that common anymore. Anyway, it's not like you'll never have the opportunity to, I don't know, date or whatever it is you—"

"Mom?" Sara said. "Shut up a second. I have to tell you about something."

Helen's BlackBerry made a whirring noise and started to squirm across the Formica, but she ignored it. "Okay," she said cautiously. "What is it?"

"I talked to Dad," Sara said. The whole restaurant seemed to fall silent. "I've been in touch with him almost all along. I even saw him once, back in Rensselaer Valley, before we moved. I want to go see him this weekend. I have a right to do that, and he has a right too."

"Do you even know where he is?" Helen said, the color draining from her face.

Try as she might, Sara couldn't completely suppress a smile. "Hold on to your hat," she said.

SHE HADN'T DRIVEN ANYWHERE in a while—another old-life routine she didn't miss a bit—but the next morning Helen walked to the Hertz three blocks from their apartment and returned behind the wheel of a clean, strange car. It wasn't even nine in the morning but there was nowhere to park on their block; her plan had been to go back upstairs, but instead she had to call Sara on her cell and let her know she'd be idling in the car outside. Sara, of course, reacted as if the inability to find a parking spot was purely a failure of intelligence. Helen hung up—she knew it would be a while now, that Sara would make a point of taking her time—adjusted the strange seat, which had a really disconcerting internal heating element she could not figure out how to control, turned the radio on and then off again, and then just sat there and grew furious.

She'd been made a fool of. What the hell could her ex-husband, the parolee, be trying to pull? Why buy back the house that was not only the scene of his disintegration but the reason for it as well, the house that had supposedly revealed itself to him over time as spiritually toxic and soul-snuffing and redolent of death? There had to be something. He did not play around where money was concerned. She tried to think what his angle was, but each idea made as little sense to her as the one before. Was it some sort of long con she was too dumb to understand? Though their divorce was technically final, they had agreed in principle to a future court date at which the judge would revisit questions of custody, alimony, etc., once Ben was done being sued and his financial picture was clearer. She had always assumed that the purpose of this hearing was to make sure she and Sara were sufficiently provided for, but why should she assume that? Was Ben somehow laying the groundwork to take all the money back from her, so that he would once again have everything? But that didn't explain why he was actually living there. Surely it was enough, for whatever cryptic legal purposes, just to own the house. He hadn't expressed anything but disgust toward it for as long as Helen could remember.

It crossed her mind, of course, while everything else was crossing it, that he wanted to reconcile with her. But even if such a thing was imaginable, this was a pretty antagonistic way to go about it. Their one phone conversation last night had been angry on her end and perversely calm on his. She'd threatened, with no sense of how realistic she was being, to have him arrested, for communicating with their daughter without her knowledge. His refusal to raise his own voice just made her crazier. He wanted to see his daughter again. That's all he said.

What really frustrated her, though, was that no matter how fearful and protective all this made her feel on behalf of Sara—this poor girl whose life had been flipped upside down by the father who had rejected and embarrassed her, and was now summoning her back to a parody of her old home as if none of that had happened—she couldn't find any pretext for expressing it because Sara herself was as happy as a clam. Every time Helen undertook some speech about how Sara didn't need to be scared or about how it was okay to be angry, her daughter would just laugh at her. Literally. Here she came now, waving charmingly to their weekend doorman, through the glass doors and practically skipping into the passenger seat.

"Look at you," Sara said in a tone of condescending gaiety. "Ten and two. What a good girl. Even when you're not moving."

"Did you lock the door?" Helen said, but Sara's earphones were in, which meant conversation, such as it was, would be one-way only.

Helen hated the angry network of New York City highways, even on a Saturday morning, when they would presumably be less choked, so despite the extra time it took, she crossed all the way over to the West Side; from there it was a straight shot to Rensselaer Valley. It was a beautiful morning, and a pleasant enough trip up the Saw Mill, and if Sara wasn't talking to her, at least that meant she wasn't mocking or insulting her. But somewhere around Chappaqua, when things outside the car began looking familiar to her, Helen started to feel so nauseous that she thought she might have to pull over. She hadn't expected to react so strongly. It wasn't as though she'd hated it while she lived there. They took the Rensselaer Valley exit, and Sara immediately perked up, like a dog, Helen thought uncharitably. There was the train station; there was the elementary school Sara had gone to, back when Helen was stupid enough to think that all was right in their world. That was it: she hated this place because she believed that some earlier, embarrassing version of herself still lived here. A kind of muscle memory took over once she passed the school, and in another moment, almost as if she were only a passenger in the car herself, they were at the top of the hill that led down to Meadow Close. There didn't appear to be any curtains or shades on any of the windows, but apart from that the house, from the outside, looked haughtily, insultingly unchanged, as if it could not have cared less what had gone on inside it. Helen turned in to the driveway and coasted to a stop.

"Are you coming in?" Sara asked.

"Absolutely not," Helen said. Sara shrugged and opened her door. Helen watched her walk up the flagstones and then push through the front door just as if she still lived there. Then there was nothing to see, nothing to hear. The wind came up and blew some of last fall's dry leaves around the brown, brittle, shameful yard.

Was she just going to sit there in the car for—she checked her watch—six hours, until the agreed time came for the end of Sara's visit? Maybe. There didn't seem anything particularly wrong with that plan right now. She certainly didn't feel like moving a muscle. But then it occurred to her that Sara and Ben might not plan to just sit and talk inside the house for six hours. They might want to go into town for some reason—to eat, for instance, since she doubted Ben had picked up any cooking skills in the joint—and if the garage door opened to expose Helen still sitting there in her rental car like a zombie, well, the looks on their faces would be a humiliation that didn't bear thinking about. Her face reddening as if they were already staring at her from behind the nonexistent curtains, she started up the car, backed out of the driveway, and headed into town.

There wasn't much to do in Rensselaer Valley on a Saturday, or any other day for that matter. There were two restaurants, three if you counted that little Polish bakery where no one ever went. Having had just a glass of cranberry juice for breakfast, she was tempted; but wherever she might go, the chances were too great that Ben and Sara would walk into the same establishment and find her sitting there alone. No version of what would ensue was acceptable to her. She thought about texting Sara to ask her to please stay out of the deli, but if a request like that sounded a little crazy to Helen's own ear, it would sound ten times as crazy to her daughter and she would never hear the end of it. At length she went to the newsstand across Main Street from the train station, bought a cup of foul coffee and a bag of peanut M&M's, and went back to the lot behind the storefronts to sit in the front seat of her car, which she still had trouble recognizing. The newsstand guy, a put-upon old Arab gentleman, was someone she had spoken to perhaps two hundred times before, but her face provoked not a glimmer of recognition in his. Good. She did not want to be recognized.

She hadn't brought any work with her—she hadn't given a thought, it seemed, to how she would spend this first-ever afternoon in which she had ceded custody of her daughter—but she was able at least to open up her email, and there was plenty there to keep her occupied. The board of supervisors in a town in California that was seeking bankruptcy protection apparently still had money in its budget to hire Malloy to burnish its image enough to get its members reelected. The head of a charity that had collected millions of dollars to build schools for girls in Pakistan and Afghanistan was combating news reports that the schools themselves did not actually exist. A corporate client in Poland, of all places, had been personally referred to Helen by the London office; the client was a natural-gas extraction outfit that had secretly released several tons of toxic chemicals into the Danube River, not just destroying livelihoods and threatening industries but actually killing people—eight or eleven, depending whose count you accepted. Strategy here was not the problem: the problem was the chairman of the company, who was a hoary veteran of the old Communist days and who magnificently resisted all efforts to squeeze out of him any sort of admission, public or private, of wrongdoing. The London team had grown so frustrated that they were trying to punt the case all the way across the Atlantic to Helen, just because they knew, or at any rate had been told about, her particular specialty. It was hard to tell whether they admired her or considered her a convenient sap.

She remembered her coffee, and took a sip, and just then a pair of gloved knuckles rapped softly on her driver's-side window and caused her to lose half the mouthful down her chin. The tapping startled her worse than a shout would have done. Holding the BlackBerry at arm's length to protect it, she turned to her left and saw Patty Crane, the mother of Sara's former best friend, Sophia, hunched over and staring at her through the glass as if Helen were Amelia Earhart. She made a ridiculous motion with her hand that Helen finally recognized as a plea to roll down her window. Sighing, she worked up a smile and obliged.

"Helen?" Patty said theatrically. She was one of those local women whom Helen had never really liked and yet with whom she had somehow spent, over the years, an awful lot of time. "I feel like I'm seeing things!"

"Nope," Helen said, laughing gamely, but not opening the door. "It's really me."

"Are you back in town? I drove by your house a week or so ago and saw lights on, but I just thought it had finally sold. It is so good to see you!"

No reference was going to be made to the past, to the source of her and her family's disgrace. More than that: it dawned on Helen that Patty knew exactly who was living in the old Armstead place, that every vicious gossip in town must have known about it within a day of Ben moving in there, but she was going to go on pretending that she didn't. Why? Why must it all be so ritualized? The mechanics of sparing Helen humiliation and actually humiliating her were so indistinguishable that surely even Patty didn't know which of the two she was doing, or why.

"I'm just here for the day," Helen said. "I'm waiting to pick up Sara." She waved the BlackBerry. "Doing a little work while I'm waiting."

"Oh, you're working? How exciting. What are you doing?"

"Public relations," Helen said. "Crisis management."

"How exciting," Patty said.

"How is Sophia doing?" Helen said, just to get the focus off of her; but then she failed to listen to the answer, which, unsurprisingly, went on for some time. She was thinking instead about Patty, with her bobbed hair and her down vest and the jeans stretched over her wide, field-hockey hips, and how if you took all that off her and put her in a bonnet and a gingham dress she might have been cheerfully handing out rocks with which to stone Helen and her whole family, or spitting on her in the stockade. Just then her BlackBerry buzzed; she glanced at it and saw an automated text from the IT department at work, informing her that the office servers would be down overnight, as if anyone would be sending business emails at 2:00 a.m. on a Sunday anyway.

"It's Sara," Helen lied shamelessly. "She's waiting. Gotta go. Patty, it was so great to see you, please give our love to Sophia and to"—she couldn't summon the husband's name—"to your whole family," and she started the car and backed away. In truth she still had almost four hours to kill. She couldn't return to Main Street now, though. She drove slowly through the familiar lanes. Across the train tracks, past the high school, and toward the fancier end of town there was a small pool club, to which the Armsteads had belonged when Sara was younger. Even on a Saturday, it seemed bound to be unpatronized this early in the season, and two minutes later Helen pulled into its empty parking lot and switched the car off again. Then, with the branches waving inaudibly in front of her windshield, she began to cry. She kept telling herself to stop. She didn't have a good enough excuse for it, she felt. Everything in her life, if you took a step away from it, was going pretty successfully.

STILL, SHE'D BARELY COLLECTED HERSELF by the time she picked up her daughter at the foot of their old driveway. "So how did it go?" she asked, expecting cruelty, in the form either of silence or of a diatribe about what a relief it was to have at least one parent who knew how to mind his own business, but what she got was even worse than that: six hours in her father's company had left Sara calm and expansive. "I'm sorry, Mom," she said. "I'm sure that was a bummer for you, being stuck all afternoon with nothing to do but worry. But there's nothing to worry about. He's great. I wouldn't say 'same old Dad,' exactly. He does seem a little different, but in a good way, to be honest. We just sat and talked. I think it would be good for me to spend more time with him. It didn't really seem that weird at all. The weirdest thing about it, actually, was being back in our old house. It shouldn't have seemed weird, but it did. It's like a cave. There is seriously almost no furniture in there."

Helen drove on, listening, more murderous than relieved. And she didn't feel much better even by Monday morning, when she arrived at work to find six messages already on her desk, left by the weekend switchboard: four were from London, but the other two had a U.S. area code, one she didn't recognize. No name, though, so she ignored them. She was supposed to get ready for a hastily scheduled meeting with someone who currently played in the NBA. Nobody seemed to know exactly when he was coming in. His name meant nothing to her, but she could tell he was a big deal from the way the male employees on her floor kept popping their heads in her office door, pretending to look for one another. It was something about a paternity suit filed by a teammate's wife, or maybe child support, but whatever it was apparently didn't constitute enough of an emergency to get him out of bed in time to meet before ten-thirty, so Helen went off to the morning meeting, where she hoped she wouldn't be expected to speak knowledgeably on the current state of mind of the dithering Polish executive.

At least she wasn't the only one feeling besieged. Arturo had new assignments for all of them—a rebranding in the wake of a mine collapse, a newspaper caught plagiarizing a blog—and affected to be unmoved by their complaints of being overworked already.

"I have to be able to service my existing clients," Ashok said hotly.

"Your clients might be just as happy to see a little less of you," said Arturo. "Everyone, these things go in spurts, as you know very well. So you have too much work and not enough time? It's a crisis. Manage it. See you tomorrow, unless you fuck something up between now and then."

Helen, having caught Shelley yawning three or four times, squeezed in next to her as they were filing out of the Fishtank. "You're buried too?" she said. "Anything I can help with?"

Shelley smiled and pantomimed embarrassment. "It's not work, actually," she said in a low voice. "Had a date last night. It went well, yada yada yada, I should maybe go down to the caf for a Red Bull. Want to come with me and hear the tabloid details?"

Helen begged off and walked back to her office alone. A date on a Sunday night? Well, why should that seem odd? There were ways to live other than the one she knew. She could be leading some other life herself. She could have gone out Saturday night: at one point on the drive up to Rensselaer Valley, Sara had taken her earphones out and asked about staying the night with Ben in their old house, and Helen had said no, but why? Why hadn't she just said yes? Then she could have driven alone back to the city—a single woman on a Saturday night in Manhattan, the most decadent place in America—and picked up some guy and brought him back home and screwed him and kicked him out and then picked up her daughter at the train the next day like a spy or a con artist, as if the two sides of herself didn't even care to know each other. But it was too late for that. Not just in terms of the weekend, but in terms of her ever becoming the kind of woman who knew how to do that kind of thing, without exposing herself as deluded or pathetic or ridiculous.

"You didn't bring any books. Don't you have homework?" Helen had asked instead.

Sara had closed her eyes. "Obviously," she'd said. "Obviously I have homework. It's the weekend, and I am not five years old. Did you seriously just ask me that?"

Her own office did not of course have glass walls, so Helen shrieked a little in surprise when she entered and saw a statuesque young woman, whom she had never seen before, standing calmly beside her desk.

"Helen?" the woman said. "I'm Angela. I work for Mr. Malloy. If you have a few minutes, he'd like to speak to you upstairs."

"Of course," Helen said, trying to recover. "I mean, it's very nice of you to come escort me, but the phone would have been fine too."

Angela smiled and held up a small silver key chain, with just one key dangling from it. "Special elevator," she said.

Though she knew full well that Mr. Malloy's office was only on six, somehow Helen had expected it to be higher, and the view to be better. When she entered, Malloy was looking out his broad picture window, through the rain, at the office building directly across the street. His hands were in his pockets, and he was smiling. Angela withdrew and pulled the door closed. He caught the reflection in the glass and turned around. "Ah!" he said. "The elusive one!"

"I'm sorry?"

"Never mind. I brought a visitor around to meet you earlier. I would have warned you, but I didn't receive any warning myself."

Helen sat down without waiting for an invitation, and crossed her legs and folded her arms. "The team meets every morning at ten-thirty," she said hoarsely.

"Yes, of course it does. Unfortunately I only remembered that when we got to your empty office, but I didn't want to go down the hall and scare everybody. So how are you doing, Helen? Of course I know you're doing very well, I hear good things, but I mean how do you like it here? Are you happy?"

If he'd left off that last bit, she could have given the reflexive answer one was supposed to give one's boss; instead, she just smiled and gamely nodded. She wondered what he had been hearing about her, and from whom.

"Good good good," Malloy said. "And your family?"

It was likely that he knew all about her family, just because he seemed to make it his business to know such things, but the question had a generic enough sound that she felt comfortable answering just by putting one thumb up in the air. "So you mentioned bringing someone to visit me," she said. "A client?"

His glasses rose a little higher on his cheeks as he refreshed his smile. "Yes, in fact. A man of the cloth. I have to say this is a new one in my experience. He works for the New York Archdiocese of the Catholic Church, if you please, and he comes here as the personal representative of the archbishop, who naturally can't be seen skulking around in places of ill repute like this one. They are in need of our services—specifically of the world's best crisis management advisers. I took the liberty of scheduling a meeting between the two of you tomorrow morning, at their place this time, and that meeting, my dear, you will not miss."

She struggled to think of something to say, but she was not fast enough to stop him from trying to interpret her silence.

"It's true that I have taken a special interest in you," he said. "Arturo and the rest of the merry band downstairs, they do a good job, but frankly I don't think they see it yet."

"See what, sir?"

"See you. See what you do."

"I'm starting to wonder," Helen said, "if I'm seeing it yet myself."

"Well, sure," Malloy said. "That doesn't surprise me. But I see it. What you're doing is the wave of the future. I think we're going to re-write the textbooks for crisis management before we're done."

"There's a problem of scale," said Helen. "The bigger it gets, the less real it seems to me."

"I think what you should be asking yourself," Malloy said kindly, "and what others will be asking themselves as they continue to watch you succeed, is not how real the process is, whatever that may mean, but what the results are."

His office was not as big as she'd imagined. He kept the blinds wide open. Her eyes refocused on a woman in the building across the street who was hitting a printer repeatedly with the heel of her hand, and then again on her boss, an old man with seemingly infinite patience, or maybe he just didn't have that much to do.

"You're telling me the archbishop wants to meet with me?" Helen said.

"Well, I can't guarantee you that His Eminence will be there in the room with you, but as near as dammit, as they say. They thought they were coming to talk to me, but I told them that you were my designated crisis management specialist around here."

"And what," she asked, "is the nature of their crisis?"

Malloy smiled crookedly. "Oh, come on," he said. "I assume you read the papers."

Angela knocked, and entered holding her key chain. A few minutes later Helen was downstairs in her office again. She felt sleepy. She felt like an instrument, but of what? She'd taken a job just to support her family, but now the job had grown to love her unabashedly and her family didn't seem to need or even want her anymore. She shut her door just to give herself a few extra seconds if the basketball player and his agent happened to show up. Her phone rang; the caller ID showed the same number left on the weekend messages. Above the number was the unhelpful semi-legend LKSD INN CLT VT. She picked up and absently said her name.

"Helen?" a man's voice said urgently. "Oh God, is this really you? Or an assistant?"

Helen's face twitched in surprise. "No, this is me," she said. "Who am I speaking to?"

"There's no one else on the line? Or in your office? Do these calls get recorded?"

The voice had a little catch in it, like a sob. "It's just me," Helen said, a little testily in spite of herself. "Who is this?"

"It's Hamilton," the voice said.

"Hamilton? Why are—how did you—is something the matter?"

"Yes," he said in a whisper.

"Where are you calling from?"

"A pay phone. I don't know."

"You don't know? You're not still in the city, though?"

"No, definitely not. I'm in some motel or something. I don't remember how I got here. There's a lake out the window. Champlain, maybe? I got on a binge after I saw you and I don't remember how I got here."

"Hamilton," Helen said, "that was five days ago."

"I remembered you said the name of your place was Malloy," he said, sounding more like he was crying now, "and I found your card, and I need help, and I can't call any of the people that I would normally call."

"Why not?"

"I think I may have done something bad," Hamilton said.

6

IN 1889, TWO CATHOLIC MISSIONARIES opened a home for way-ward girls in Malloy, New York—at the time a town of fewer than three hundred citizens, which would seem to indicate an unusual rate of local waywardness. The home later became an orphanage, and a convent was established to staff it, which led to an influx, after World War I, of young Catholic women on missions from all over the world, though a good ninety percent of them were from Ireland or England. For decades the nuns were actually the most worldly element of Malloy, a town otherwise composed mostly of farmers and, from the 1930s onward, workers at the maximum-security prison near Plattsburgh. Such was the church's civic influence that the convent went on to establish a school, called St. Catherine's, in 1939, open to Catholic children of either gender. Over the decades, the prison expanded, the town correspondingly thrived, but the congregation, somehow, inexorably shrank. The orphanage was closed in the sixties, the convent in the seventies. The school, though, stayed open, and was still thought of, at least by those who could afford it, as a worthy alternative to Malloy's one public elementary school, infamous for its dangerously low standards in all respects. St. Catherine's enrollment was now only slightly less than what it was when Helen attended. At least that had been true seventeen years ago, the last time Helen was there. It might be gone completely now. Helen, with no remaining connection to the place—no family, no friends she remained in touch with—had lost track.

This was the first time she'd driven that far north since then: in yet another rented car, along Route 7 through the western edge of Massachusetts, with a road map spread out awkwardly across the steering wheel. She should have asked for a car with one of those GPS systems included, even though the time that saved might well have been offset by the time it would have taken her to figure out how to operate the thing. She was useless with small gadgets, as her daughter seized every opportunity to remind her. Two hours after dropping Sara off in Rensselaer Valley, Helen still had the girl's remonstrations ringing in her ears: what the hell are you doing, it's a school day, are you kidnapping me or abandoning me, you've finally snapped, I knew it would happen one day, if you pick me up and then ditch me like this then don't expect me ever to come home again, I don't understand why the hell you won't even tell me where it is you have to go in such a hurry. At least now, as she crawled through the Berkshires, there was no voice but her own to reprimand Helen for not having figured out some faster, smarter way to go. At yet another stoplight she checked to make sure her silent phone was still getting a signal. No call from Sara, no call from work yet, no call from Ben, no call from Hamilton. She'd be lucky to get to Vermont by dark at this rate.

He'd never come right out and asked Helen to come rescue him, but there was no doubt that's what he wanted; and she understood that, even in his most unguarded moment, Hamilton expected people would try to anticipate his needs, because that's what he was used to. He would not say what was wrong, he would not tell her what he had done. Though technically not an actual client, purely in terms of visibility he was one of the biggest names on Malloy's books, and so Helen felt justified in canceling all her appointments, heading for home to pack two bags, and directing the switchboard to tell anyone who asked that she had been called away on an emergency. She told Hamilton not to leave his motel room. He said he was hungry, though. She called the motel's office, pretending to be a guest this while she was walking from her apartment to the Hertz outpost three blocks away—and got the number of a pizza restaurant in the nearest town. She called them, ordered a pizza to be left on the doorstep outside Cabin 3, and paid with her corporate credit card. Then she drove to Robert Livingston

Middle School and tried to explain to the security guard there that she was a parent who needed to take her child out of school immediately. In the end it took nearly twenty minutes just to get an assistant principal to come down the hall and talk to her.

Sara surely could have survived at home on her own for a day or two—fed herself, gotten herself to school on time, refrained from burning the apartment to the ground. She'd never been asked to do that before, though, and Helen knew what her reaction would be; she could hear the whole enraged listing of worst-case scenarios that would ensue. All in all, it just seemed simpler and less worrisome to dump her on her father for a few days. Helen wasn't unmindful of the bluff-calling element either. If they didn't like it, that was on them. Certainly more had been expected of Helen, in terms of self-sufficiency, when she was Sara's age. More had been expected of everyone else she knew.

Somewhere around Pittsfield the traffic eased up and she started making better time. At the stoplights, when she wasn't reconsulting the map, she kept trying to account for the fact that she was going to Vermont, of all places, or rather for the fact that Hamilton had gone there. Why Vermont? To make a movie? To hide? She'd read somewhere that even a cellphone with a dead battery could be used to track its owner's whereabouts, if it came to that. Cellphones had changed everything, in terms not just of communication but of privacy, secrecy, absence, alibis. All the minutes of her own adolescence spent frantically composing some plausible story, as you walked the last hundred yards home at ten or eleven at night, about where you'd been! All the desperate effort that went into looking as though you believed what you were saying! Once, just a month or two before they left Malloy, she spent a Friday night riding around in Charlie Lopinto's father's car with Charlie and his older brother and three other friends, and the cops pulled them over, not because they were drinking or speeding but because the brother had apparently had some massive fight with his folks earlier that evening and now they were reporting that the car had been stolen. Helen and her friend Libby cried so hard when they told the cop they hadn't known anything about it that he finally consented, snappishly, to let them go without escorting them home to their parents. They had to walk about three miles to get there, though, and it was late, and Helen could still remember Libby tenderly wiping all the ruined mascara off of Helen's face and making her rehearse their story one last time before she went in to lie to her mother and father about why she was getting home at that hour.

Maybe Hamilton was even there that night—not in the car, but somewhere along their route, among one of the groups of friends they stopped to talk to. He probably wasn't, but she could no longer remember every detail. She hated forgetting things like that, things she'd seen and done, even though it was only natural. Confession, when she was a kid, used to scare her for that very reason. Forgetting something wasn't the same as lying, really, but sin-wise there was not enough of a distinction.

All of a sudden she was almost there; she saw a sign for Exit 4, which meant, unless the numbers were going backwards and she'd missed it, that she had just one exit to go. The New England countryside, even along the highway, was so picturesque it was almost grating. The New York side, she knew, even though it was just across the lake, was far more grim and stubborn-looking. All she had been able to get out of Hamilton before leaving the office was that he was by himself, but his trouble seemed to involve some other person, and he kept saying that it was all over, without, it seemed, any consistent idea what he meant by "it." His career, she assumed. She had agreed to come find him because he was in need and had called her—it was as simple as that. As for his calling her of all people, just because he'd recently sat next to her and she'd foisted a card on him and because the name of her employer had reason to stick in his mind, you could look at it as random or you could say it was fate. She left the highway and spent the next twenty minutes traveling four miles on a two-lane strip of county road choked at what was evidently, even here in rural Vermont, rush hour. Then a turn toward the water, sporadically visible when she crested the hills, and then a flaked sign for the Lakeside Inn, a collection of weather-beaten, mildewed cabins on dirt lots that in the half-light of evening was one of the most sinister-looking places Helen had ever seen.

The lights were off, luckily, in the cabin with the Office sign; she rolled to a stop in front of Cabin 3. No lights were on in there either. Helen got out and knocked, but heard no movement inside, not even when she put her mouth next to the crack in the door and softly called Hamilton's name. She pulled out her phone and dialed his number, and only then did she notice a finger pulling back a corner of one of the old canvas snap shades at the window. It was rapidly getting too dark to see, though the lake still held some light. She heard the popping of an old hook-and-eye screen door latch, and then Hamilton was outside, next to her on the tiny porch, yanking the door shut behind him, his hand on her arm. She couldn't really see his face yet.

"Don't go inside," he said shakily but quietly. "Let's sit in your car."

She got a brief look at him under the dome light before he shut the door again, and honestly she had expected worse. He hadn't shaved in a few days, and he smelled awful, but he still looked like a movie star. He couldn't look unlike one. There were scratches, or what looked like scratches, on one side of his face, between the crow's feet at the corner of his eye and his ear. His eyes looked ill and afraid.

She waited for him to begin, but they just sat there in the growing dark. The surface of the lake still shone through the black trees. "Are you all right, Hamilton?" she said. "I mean, do you need any kind of medical attention or anything?"

"No," he said, just audibly.

"Okay. Well, before I know what the next step is, then, I guess I should ask what on earth you're doing here? In this place?"

"We were going to Malloy," he said. "At least I think we were. I wanted to show her where I grew up. Then on the Northway we saw the sign for the Vermont ferry and she said she really wanted to ride the ferry so we just got on it. And then this place was more or less here when we got off on the other side. That's all I really remember."

Malloy? Helen thought, but then snapped out of it. "Who's 'she'? You said 'she.'"

"Remember the premiere? Where we met?"

"Sure."

"She from there. Bettina. You remember her. That short, hot, bitchy one who tried to throw you out of your seat. Her. I picked her up at the party afterwards. Things got out of hand and we wound up taking off in her car."

"Last Wednesday," Helen said. "When did you get here, though?"

He shrugged, and made a coughing sound that might have been an effort to hold back a sob.

"Where is Bettina now?" Helen said.

He didn't answer.

"So you went on a bender, and now she's gone," Helen said soothingly. "She probably sobered up and left you here? Without any money or anything? Well, it's good you thought to call me—"

"Her car is still here. It's parked up by the office. But she's gone."

Helen tried to figure out what she was supposed to be putting together. It was true she had a hard time imagining that imperious girl walking in her heels five miles back to town. Especially when her car was here.

"I'm worried something might have happened," Hamilton said.

"Well, let's not panic," said Helen, which she knew immediately was the wrong thing to say. It was so dark now he had turned into a silhouette, and she couldn't tell if he was crying or just cold.

"Can we please go inside?" she said.

He sighed, and when he opened the passenger door again she saw that his jaw was now set. Everything he felt had to pass across his face in some outsize manner. She followed him, through the riot of bug and frog noise, back up the two steps to the cabin door. When they were both inside, he snapped the wall switch, and in the light of an unshaded ceiling bulb Helen saw a stripped bed, its thin mattress stained with what she had to concede was not a huge but still definitely a disconcerting amount of blood.

"I can't remember anything," Hamilton said right behind her, and in spite of herself she jumped. "What if I did something horrible?"

BEN'S ORIGINAL PLAN was to go into the office Monday at about three in the afternoon, to look over a brief for the zoning commission, the sort of menial help Bonifacio seemed to take particular, vindictive pleasure in paying him for. There was no reason he couldn't have gone in at nine—he was up at six these days, in part because the rags he'd found in the garage and draped over the curtain rods reached only about halfway down his bedroom window—but Bonifacio liked him to come in at an hour when they could have a drink while they worked without feeling too much like derelicts. It was the company, of course, more than the hour, that gave Bonifacio his cover. "So much for rehab, eh, old sport?" he liked to say. "What the hell, I bet this went on every day back in that white-shoe firm you used to work at." Which was far from true; anyone at his old job who required a drink during the day knew how to do it on the sly, in true alcoholic style. Ben's own rehab may have been for show, but he had learned a few things there.

So he'd been sitting in the kitchen trying to read the *Times* on his phone, an exercise in frustration he'd taken up to save some money, when his ex-wife, Helen, called from out of nowhere and said she was in a car on her way to Rensselaer Valley to drop Sara off with him for a while.

"Where are you going?" he asked.

"Not your business," she said.

"How long is a while?"

"Why? You have somewhere else on earth you need to be?"

"More out of curiosity," he said.

"I will let you know when I know. Listen: you wanted back into your child's life? Welcome to it. Not everything happens on your timetable. Sometimes your timetable just flies right out the damn window."

"Is she right next to you?" Ben said. "Can I speak to her?"

"We're on the Saw Mill," Helen said. "We'll be there in half an hour." She hung up. He put on some clothes and rinsed out his coffee cup, but there wasn't much preparation to be done apart from that: he was still living in the house virtually squatter-style, with a couple of canvas director's chairs he'd bought on sale at the hardware store, a TV with rabbit ears that sat unsteadily on top of the box it had been shipped in, a disconnected gas stove, their old fridge, and hardly any food. He heard the thin drone of a cheap engine growing louder down the hill, then one door opening and slamming, then the drone rising in pitch again and receding, and he pulled the front door open just before Sara got her fingers on the knob. She carried a duffel bag on her shoulder and looked furious.

"Hello, honey," he said cautiously. "Can you tell me what's going on?"

Sara dropped her bag to the floor, sank down next to it, and began rooting around inside. "Mom's finally cracked, is what's going on," she said coldly. "Déjà vu. First you and then her. Well, to be honest, I think it's probably better that I'm here anyway." She began pulling out t-shirts and bras. "She packed this bag for me," Sara said. "I do not have any frigging idea what's in here."

"You don't know where she's going?"

"She wouldn't tell me."

"You don't know how long she'll be gone?"

At that Sara stopped and looked right into his face. "No," she said. "Why do you ask?"

He found some leftover ten-ingredient fried rice in a take-out carton in the fridge. Sara accepted it and sat down wearily in front of the TV. Ben retreated to the bedroom to call Helen, but then decided against it; it felt like what she was daring him to do. For quite a while he just stood there. At two o'clock he changed his clothes and went back out to stand beside the television.

"I have to go to work," he said. "I'll just be a couple of hours and then I'll bring home some dinner. Will you be okay?"

"Is there any food in the house besides this?" Sara said.

He wasn't sure. But he could tell that her outrage was fading. "You have my number," he said. "Will you call me if you hear from Mom? And I'll do the same."

All through the car ride into town and through the two hours he spent trying to focus on the brief in Bonifacio's office, sitting in the folding chair by the window, he felt the touch of guilt, unfamiliar but somehow instinctive or natural-seeming, like the flare-up of symptoms from some seasonal allergy or chronic disease. He was at work, making money, and he hadn't even known Sara was coming until twenty-five minutes before her arrival. Still, knowing, for the first time in months, exactly where Sara was and what she was doing, and that he was responsible for her, stirred something in him, something he both welcomed and wished he could, just for the sake of his powers of concentration, dismiss. Rather than endure any questions from Bonifacio, any sarcasm or nosiness, he accepted his usual two fingers of Jameson and then, when Joe was on the phone with his wife, poured it into the dead plant.

He stopped at Price Chopper on the way home to pick up some food, all but paralyzed by the simple decisions involved. Of course it was never that simple a matter, going to Price Chopper. Women's eyes narrowed at the sight of him. Strangest of all were the ones who, even after carefully setting their jaws and shaking their heads to communicate their condemnation of him, would still want to talk to him invasively, as if he were some sort of disgraced celebrity. Head down, he pulled from the shelves by the deli counter a rotisserie chicken and a six-pack of Corona.

Would Sara be with him for two meals? Two days? What if she was not exaggerating and Helen really had gone off the deep end? It would have surprised him, certainly, but it wasn't as if he was in any position to judge her harshly. She had always been a little more tightly wound than she appeared to those who knew her only casually. He added ice cream, Cheetos, appeasements of all sorts to his cart. He felt a surge of panic as he opened his own front door, but Sara was still in the same canvas chair in front of the television, which, as she must long since have figured out, got only four channels. He put away the groceries, such as they were, put the chicken in the dead oven to stay warm, opened a beer, and stood against the windows behind the TV, facing her. Sara's expression was noncommittal.

"I bought a chicken," Ben said.

She glanced up for a moment as if she was going to get up and go find it—she must have been starving—but then she stayed in her chair. "Kudos," she said.

"No word from your mother?" Her immobility was his answer. He couldn't see what she was watching—*Entertainment Tonight* or some such, it sounded like—but then she muted it and fixed her father with a long, direct look.

"Can I have one of those?" she said. She nodded at his beer.

What was she, fourteen? He tried for a moment to recall himself at fourteen.

"Ever had one before?" he asked.

She made a derisive sound. "I'm not home-schooled," she said.

Well, he thought, if I'm in charge, then I'm in charge. It appeared neither of them was leaving home tonight. And she seemed to want something from him, he thought: not the beer, so much, but whatever the beer signified for her.

"I'll make you a deal," he said. "You can have one if you will turn off that god damn TV."

He thought about bringing the two director's chairs out to the screened back porch so they could drink their beers while gazing into the darkening woods behind the house, but there were holes in that screen he hadn't figured out how to fix yet—he'd always hated those smugly, competitively handy suburban homeowners, but there were certainly days you wished you were one of them—and every time he'd ventured out there himself since moving back in, some high-pitched bug wound up causing him to slap himself painfully on the ear. It was a decent night, though, with some breeze. He went back to the kitchen, popped the top off a second Corona and handed it to her; then he opened the front door and sat on the top step facing the empty street, and Sara docilely did the same. Lights were on in windows all up and down the street, at Parnell's and elsewhere. He thought it was probably too dark for the two of them to be seen; and then he thought, so what? What was left to fear there? None of them spoke to him anyway, and when he brought his garbage cans out to the curb they regarded him as if he was a madman. That was the point of living here now. Bring on their execration. "Cheers," he said and tapped his daughter's bottle.

He stared at her until she took a sip. Too dark to see what kind of face she made; that would have told him a lot. They were facing east, and all the color had gone out of the sky. They heard a distant police siren, maybe from as far away as the Saw Mill. Probably not coming for us, Ben thought.

"So no idea where your mother might have gone?" he said again.

Sara shook her head and had another sip.

"You know," Ben said, "we didn't really talk about anything last time, you and me."

"I don't want to talk about anything," she said. He nodded sympathetically and waited; as a parent, he still had some game. He wasn't sure, but he thought there used to be some kind of bird feeder hanging from the tree on their front lawn; he wondered what had happened to it.

"I don't like it the way it is now," Sara said. "I thought I would, but I don't. I mean living in New York, living with Mom, the whole thing. I think I belong here, with you. I just feel like you know me better. So," she said, gesturing vaguely behind her, "I guess this is what I wanted, actually. I just don't particularly appreciate the way it happened, Mom kidnapping me and all."

"What do you mean," Ben said, "you feel like I know you better? How would such a thing be possible? I've been a horrible father to you for the last year or so. I wasn't really interested in knowing anything about anybody other than myself."

"See? Like right there. When you're all humble, it seems real, but when Mom does it, it just seems over the top, like capital-H Humble. There's something fake about her."

"Fake, huh," he said. "Your mother's a lot of things, but personally I don't think fake is one of them. Of course, it's been a strange year."

"For instance, I knew you would be cool with this," said Sara, waggling her beer bottle. "One beer, at home. Safe environment and whatnot."

"And she would not be cool with that?"

"Perfect children don't drink beer," Sara said.

The house ticked behind them. It was fully dark now; the other homes on the street glowed like embers.

"I mean, it goes both ways," Sara said. "I understand you too. I get why you'd just wake up one day and say, Is this really my life? How did

I even get here? And if you can't answer that question, you might start to act a little crazy."

Ben sighed. He didn't want to discourage any point of connection she might feel to him, but at the same time, to allow his own failings to be employed as a parable of any sort was, in a way, to absolve them, and that he did not want.

"The important thing," he said, "is that none of it was about you. I mean it should have been much more about you, really, but I wasn't seeing things that way at the time. It was like I couldn't see past the walls of my own head. My life just seemed so questionable to me that I had to give it away. I'd already given it away in my mind, but that didn't actually change anything, so I guess I had to find some way to do it that everyone else would see too."

"And so now, you're, what, like trying to buy your old life back?"

"Now I have no life at all," Ben said. "But that's a start. In the meantime, it just feels right to be here, as strange and masochistic as I'm sure it looks to everybody else."

"So you're just basically waiting," Sara said.

"That's right."

"And you don't know for what."

"That's right too. Something, though. Just trying to stay open to it."

"Maybe it was this," Sara said.

She put her beer bottle down on the step and slapped a bug on her leg.

"I used to get drunk after school with the guy I was with," she said softly. "Almost every day. He's a little crazy. To tell the truth, I'm starting to get a little afraid of him."

"Why? What did he do to you? Or say he would do to you?"

"Wow," she said, laughing. "The lawyer in you comes out. No, he didn't really do or say anything. It's not that explicit or whatever. More like I can see there's something in him. And I think he knows I see it, which makes me feel like if it ever comes out, it'll come out in my direction, you know?"

She was pretty perceptive after half a beer, he thought. "Well, you're safe up here at least."

"True dat. Now nobody knows where the hell I am."

"Does Mom know about this guy?"

"Nope. It is not possible to talk to Mom about certain things, you know? Her world is pretty limited. It's like talking to a nun or whatever."

From somewhere on the dark block they heard the sound of a child crying, and then a window being slammed shut. For a moment, that silenced even the bugs.

"I'm not going back," Sara said.

They listened to somebody's dog barking, miles away probably.

"It's out of your hands," Ben said gently. "Mine too."

She shrugged.

"You should see me at Price Chopper, or at the Starbucks," he said, grinning. "It's pretty hilarious. All the local moms. Sometimes they actually get out of a line just because I'm in it."

"Well, you buy back your own house and then live in it with no furniture, like some hobo monk. You must know how pointless and creepy that looks."

"Yeah," he said, swigging forgetfully from the empty bottle. "I'm sure it does."

"So are you working again tomorrow?"

"Yep." She seemed disappointed, though he wasn't sure how he could tell, now that it was too dark out to see her face. "You want to see any of your old friends while you're here?"

She made a kind of hissing sound and tilted her bottle in the air. "If you don't mind a little advice," she said, "you need to purchase some chairs, and rugs, and forks and knives and such. It's a little ghetto in there."

"I don't really know how to buy furniture," he said, pulling out his phone. "You want to go online with me right now and order some stuff?"

She shrugged and nodded. "No offense," she said, "but it's not because you're broke, is it?"

"Not quite yet," he said. "Anyway, our credit is still good." He took her hand and helped her to her feet. "But listen, you don't happen to know, by any chance, where your mother stored all our old furniture?"

"No clue."

"Okay. Well, probably for the best, anyway."

"Can I have another one?" she said, holding up her empty bottle.

He ran his hand along the black hair at the back of her head, the silky spot that had always been there. "Nope," he said.

HELEN SPENT THE NIGHT in the car, sleeping fitfully, waking with her head tilted back to watch the moonlit clouds sliding over the tree line. Hamilton slept inside, on a chair he had dragged in from the porch, under a blanket made of threadbare towels, as he apparently had for the previous few nights. He would not go near the bed, or even look at it. At dawn she walked up to the cabin that served as an office; it was empty and unlocked. There was no guest registry either. Maybe the whole operation was illegal; in any case, whoever ran it seemed to have other things on his or her mind, which was, for Helen, the first good break. She left cash to cover four nights, plus an extra sixty dollars, which she stuck under a flyswatter that lay across the countertop; on a piece of paper she found in her bag, she wrote, "Cabin 3 — Sorry for the mess — Thanks!"

Then they were back on the road, pointed south again, but with no realistic destination in mind. Hamilton, who smelled repulsive, fell asleep almost instantly in the car, like a dog or a baby; he probably hadn't slept much, under those towels, for days. The first thing she determined to do was to stop in town and buy a new charger for his dead cellphone. She took the phone from him and went into a Best Buy in the largest of the endless mini-malls. He was too recognizable to risk getting out of the car. In fact she wasn't crazy about his exposure even in the car, so she parked behind the store, next to a dumpster. The Best Buy clerk, upon learning that Helen apparently didn't even know the make and model of her own phone, sold her with maddening condescension a charger that came with an adapter for the car — she hadn't even thought of that. They got back on the highway, waiting for the phone to wake up so Hamilton could check his voice mail. Finally he got enough of a charge and a signal to learn that his mailbox was full. It took almost twenty minutes for him to listen to the first few seconds of each message and delete it, tears forming in his eyes, until finally he repeated in terror the words the phone spoke robotically into his ear.

"That's the last message," he whispered, flipping the phone shut. "Nothing from her."

"But she wouldn't have your cell number anyway, would she?"

"No," he said, no less gloomily.

Helen's heart raced. "Anything from the police, though? Or any media?"

"No police. There's always some media, but they never say what they want. Mostly it's studio people, agency people, whatever, freaking out because they don't know where I am."

"So you've missed some appointments?" Helen asked.

"Probably," he said. "Definitely, going by their tone of voice." He stared out the window at the other cars, while Helen, her fingers tight on the wheel, tried to think of a way to ask him not to do that. "I'm hungry," he mumbled.

The problem was that they couldn't just walk into any restaurant anywhere, because someone would notice, probably within seconds, his face and his dissipated state. Outside of a small professional circle, he was probably not yet considered missing; those studio people were pretty good at keeping information private when they wanted to. But it didn't matter. Wherever he went, people would react as if they'd found him; they'd pull out their phones, they'd need to upload some record of their public proximity to him. Helen pulled off the highway just over the Massachusetts border and tooled around a likely looking small town until she found an actual drive-in restaurant, the kind with picnic tables in the back and a big steel garbage can capped by a cloud of bees. She wasn't about to risk even the picnic tables, though. She went to the window and a few minutes later brought back to the car an array of fried things on a red plastic tray. He tore into the food for the first few bites but then slowed down and grew morose again.

"I'm sorry," she said. "It must be difficult to feel like you can't show your face, even in a place like this where you're a total stranger, or should be. But it's only for a little while, until we get everything straightened out."

He frowned. "It's forever," he said. "You're always being watched by some unseen eye, everywhere you go, all the time, in your most intimate moment even. You're always being judged."

A car pulled into the space right next to them, on the driver's side mercifully, and a beleaguered looking mother got out and began unbuckling kids from car seats.

"And this is why," Hamilton said. "This is why they watch. Because they've been waiting for the mask to come off like this. They've been waiting for the real me to come out."

Helen picked at the hot dog bun and rolled bits of it between her fingers. "So look," she said, laboring to sound calm. "We've had a chance to get away from that place and take a deep breath and clear our heads a little bit. So let me ask you again, and you think about it again: what is the last thing you can remember?"

He shook his head. "I know you think things are going to come back to me, but they won't. Trust me, I have been through this before."

"Through what?"

"Well, through blackouts. But usually either I'm alone when it happens or there's someone else there when I come around who can fill in the blanks for me. Not this time."

"And so this time you're afraid you've done what, exactly?"

He scowled. "Well," he said after a long pause, "where is she, then?"

"You're not saying you think you *killed* her?"

"There's no other explanation," he said sullenly.

"There are a million other explanations! But look, you admitted you don't remember anything about it. So all you really have to go on is a feeling of dread or guilt—"

"And a missing person," Hamilton said irritably, "and a bunch of bloodstains—"

"That blood could be months old for all you know. You think they really care, at that place? The cabin didn't look like it had been cleaned in a year."

"You can put whatever spin on it you want — "

"And your clothes. There is no blood at all on any of your clothes."

"Maybe I wasn't wearing them at the time."

"And what do — " Helen said and stopped; she was going to ask him what he supposed he had done with the girl's body, but that aspect of things was probably not worth bringing up. There had been rowboats and canoes pulled up on shore near the cabins; and to tell the truth the lake itself had creeped her out from the moment she got out of the car. "The point is you don't know what happened," she said firmly. "You don't know. And it's ridiculous to just assume the worst, because frankly I know you're not capable of that — "

"You don't know me."

"I do," Helen said, feeling herself start to choke up a little bit. "I do know you, Hamilton. So the situation, as I see it as your adviser here, is that we need to stash you somewhere, just briefly, while I figure out where this woman is. This woman whose name you can't remember."

"It's not that I can't remember it. It's that she told me it wasn't her real name."

"But if I can produce this woman, then you will have to exonerate yourself, and then all we have to do is come up with some plausible story about where you've been the last few days, if anybody even asks. Right? We just can't let it go on for too long. So: it can't be a hotel."

"No way."

"It can't be anyplace with any sort of doorman or any employee like that." She could already feel where this line of reasoning was going, even as she thought it through, but she wasn't ready to get there yet. "We're too exposed, just sitting here," she said, starting the car again. "Did you get enough to eat for now?"

They were back on Route 7 a short while after that, headed south, but Helen wasn't frustrated by the pace of the traffic this time; she was in no hurry to get where she was going. This is crazy, she said to herself soothingly. We will figure out what happened. The girl is fine. She is somewhere telling the story of her weekend sex romp with a movie star. Hamilton is no judge of what's inside him.

"We were on the Northway," Hamilton said suddenly, softly, "and we saw the ferry sign. We were so high. It must have been me driving. 'We have to ride it,' she kept saying. 'We have to see what's on the other side.' It's the kind of thing that sounds really important when you're that high. We'd stopped in Beacon because she knew a dealer there, which should have been a red flag, obviously. She knows a dealer in Beacon? Anyway, I gave in and turned around, partly just because I knew I needed to stop driving for a while. And the ferry: you're in the car, and the car is moving, but you're not driving it, so that's pretty great. I remember she wouldn't stay in the car, though, once we were out on the water, even though it was freezing. She sat on the roof, over my head. I was so sure she was this once-in-a-lifetime woman. She was so fragile, so hurtful, so wounded and vicious, it just made you want to cry for her. She started yelling at the ferry pilot to cut the engine. Which he obviously wasn't going to do, but he did blow the horn for her. Why would she have been yelling at him to do that, though? She knew. She knew where we were going, that it would be horrible, but it felt so great getting there. Then she climbed down and got in the car again and I turned the heater up all the way and we smoked another rock, and I don't remember anything at all after that." He started crying. Helen kept her eyes on the road.

Half an hour later he was asleep again, but she had no such luxury. She hadn't done this much driving in one stretch since college. Her eyes ached in the sunlight. When they crossed the border into Connecticut, the dashboard clock said ten minutes to five, and that gave her an idea. She called the main switchboard at Malloy and asked to be put through to Shelley.

"Girl, where are you?" Shelley said excitedly. "Arturo has been in here three times asking if I've seen you today. He is ripshit about something. I told him your daughter is sick. I'm wrong, right?"

"Everyone's fine," Helen said and asked if Shelley knew anyone in Personnel, or in the promotions department, who would maybe be kind and patient enough to do her a favor. Shelley connected her to someone she knew from yoga named Courtney, who worked in their events division. "Courtney," Helen said, "I am so sorry to trouble you, but I need to contact someone who was working the *Code of Conduct* premiere last week, and here's the thing: I don't even know this person's name. I don't even know if she works for us."

"Shoot," Courtney said, "ask me something hard," and Helen wished she were powerful enough to do something astounding for this Courtney, to change her life.

"At least she was kind of striking-looking, if that makes it any easier," Helen said. "Short, like about five two, with short red hair and a short black skirt and just a beautiful face. And one of those arm tattoos, a sleeve or whatever they're called. She was working the VIP seating inside the Ziegfeld. Tiny, like a little doll, but superintimidating."

"Give me five minutes," Courtney said, and in five minutes she called back with the information that the woman whom Hamilton knew as Bettina was named Lauren Schmidt. She worked for a company Malloy sometimes used called Event Horizon. They were L.A.-based, but they had a New York office, to which Courtney was able to put Helen through. Even though this brought her abruptly closer to her goal, Helen felt a shiver of fright. Hamilton slept on, his forehead against the window.

"Hello?"

Helen's heart pounded; someone behind her honked as she inadvertently took her foot off the gas. "Lauren Schmidt?" she asked.

"No, this is Katie," the voice said. "Can I help you?"

"Is Lauren in today?"

"No, she isn't."

"Gone home for the day?"

"Lauren works as a temp for events. She doesn't have an office here. Can I help you with something?"

"Oh. Well, do you happen to know how to get ahold of her? This is a friend of hers."

"I can't give that information out," the voice said, losing interest now.

Asking more questions would probably only generate suspicion, Helen thought, so she said she would try back later and hung up. This was the problem with the situation they were in: it took an ever-increasing measure of belief to distinguish no news from bad news. She looked over at Hamilton, who was drooling slightly onto his collar. Please don't let anybody see him, she thought.

She'd known for at least a couple of hours what her only practical option was, but she'd been putting it off. Now, with time and space running out and with Hamilton sound asleep, she told herself the moment had come. She told herself the same thing four more times before she finally took out her phone again. She hated making calls while driving. Maybe someone would arrest her for it, she thought, and take this whole mess out of her hands.

"Are you all right?" Ben answered. "Where are you?"

"Not even a hello?"

"I saw the number, and we've been—"

"Yes, I'm fine," she said. It was a real effort not to hate him, now that she needed something from him. "Is Sara okay?"

"Of course she's okay. I have to warn you, she's a little pissed off at you."

"Really!" Helen said. "How unprecedented!"

"How are you, though?" Ben said. "I don't want to be nosy or anything, but is everything okay? I'm a little worried about you."

The hell you are, she thought. "Listen, I know you're probably really asking me how long you'll have to have Sara there—"

"Sara can stay here for as long—"

"But the news is I'm on my way there right now to get her. I'm in, I don't know, I think Cornwall right now, or whatever is south of Cornwall, so it'll be maybe another forty-five minutes. I don't want to get on 84, so it'll take me a little longer. But tell her to have her stuff packed—actually, I don't even know why I said that, she can just leave her stuff there if she wants. And there's something else you have to do for me, Ben."

"What are you doing in Cornwall? What's there?"

"Nothing. Just driving through it. Listen to me. I will be picking up Sara, but I will also be dropping somebody else off. A friend of mine is in trouble and needs a place to stay. It has to be a secret. I know that the house is now legally all yours or whatever, but it is still my home too,

Ben, in some sense, and on top of that it would be a huge, huge under-statement to say that you owe me one—"

"Okay," Ben said.

"Okay?"

"Okay. I do owe you one. It's fine. We're a little short on beds, though. Sara and I just ordered a new one today, obviously it won't get here in time—"

"Just give him yours," Helen said.

"Of course. I'll give him mine. That makes more sense. So who is this friend of yours who's in trouble, if I'm allowed to ask?"

Helen sighed. "Well, better I should tell you now, probably, than have you make a big deal when you see him. It's Hamilton Barth."

There was a silence. "The actor guy?"

"Yes."

"He's in trouble?"

"Well, probably not. I can't really go into the whole— It's not what you should be focusing on, anyway."

"I thought you said it was about a friend of yours."

Helen's jaw dropped. "You don't remember," she said, "that I went to St. Catherine's in Malloy with him? You don't remember me telling you that story about two hundred and fifty times?"

"Wait," he said. "Vaguely."

Give me strength, she thought. "Anyway, doesn't matter; he is here in the car with me, and he needs a safe place to stay where no one will look for him, just for a day or two probably, and we will be there in a while. I will pick up Sara and drop off Hamilton, and, Ben, I swear to God, you cannot let him be seen, you cannot let him out of the house, you cannot say one word to anyone except me about him being there."

"I can't let him out of the house?" Ben said. "So will there be pa-parazzi on our lawn and the whole bit?"

"The goal is precisely to avoid that."

Neither of them said anything for a few seconds. Helen was enter-ing a traffic circle, something she'd always hated. "So we're kind of like the Underground Railroad," Ben said. "But for celebrities."

"If that helps you," Helen said. "I have to go."

"Do you want to talk to Sara?"

There was a police car in the rotary. "No," Helen said and hung up.

Hamilton woke when she stopped for gas in Danbury, and she explained to him where she was taking him. "A safe house," he said, nodding. "Good." She told him that she would not be staying there with him but would go back to the city to find the woman he knew as Bettina so he could come out of hiding and admit that he was being ridiculous, that his world, and the world's esteem for him, were unchanged.

"What if you don't find her, though?" he said. "Or what if you do but—"

"The only thing you have to do," Helen said firmly, "is nothing. I know that will be hard for you. You can't go out. You can't contact anyone but me. You can't be seen by anyone, or talk to anyone, except my ex-husband, Ben, who will be there with you."

"Your ex-husband," Hamilton said. "You've got your ex-husband in a safe house too?"

Half an hour later, with the sun setting, Helen cut the headlights and rolled the rental car down the hill at the top of Meadow Close. She parked outside the garage, and she and Hamilton trudged up the steps and knocked softly on the door. Ben opened it almost before she'd lowered her hand again. It was the first time she'd seen him in nine months; he looked, much as the house looked, like some younger, scarily austere version of himself, but she had no time to dwell on such things now. He and Sara stood gaping on the threshold as if they couldn't quite credit what they were seeing, even though she had told them exactly what they would see.

"Let us in, please, before some neighbor looks over here?" Helen said.

They took two more steps backward than strictly necessary. Hamilton walked in, and Helen quickly shut the door behind him, standing stiffly three feet inside her own home for the first time since moving out of it. In the middle of the living room was a couch with various tags still attached; sitting on the couch was a giant pile of plastic wrap. The floors were bare except for a blanket with dirty paper plates and empty soda bottles still on it. Nothing hung on the walls or windows. The TV played silently.

"Who lives here?" Hamilton said.

Ben meekly raised a hand. "There's more furniture coming," he said. "Tomorrow, and then later in the week. Sara and I just ordered a bunch of stuff."

That's sweet, Helen thought venomously, but she said only "Remember that the delivery guys cannot see him."

Ben nodded. "Can I get your things out of the car?" he said to Hamilton, who replied by looking balefully at Helen.

"He has no things," she said. "You might get back online and order some clothes for him, actually. I'll reimburse you."

All this time Sara had been staring at Hamilton as if he could not see her—and indeed he didn't seem to—with an odd expression, her eyebrows down, that Helen finally recognized as the expression of someone who smells something terrible. And Hamilton did smell, it was true, though he still looked better than he had any right to, considering he had been wearing and sleeping in the same clothes for going on six days.

"You know," Helen said to no one in particular, "maybe for starters, just a shower?"

Hamilton's shoulders slumped with relief at the mention of it. "Follow me," Ben said.

"And we'll probably just get going, then," said Helen.

Everyone turned to look at her. "Are you sure?" Ben said carefully. "No offense, but you look exhausted. You really want to get right back in the car?"

"It'll be fine. Sara has to be back in school tomorrow, where she lives, and I have things to do. I'll call you first thing in the morning."

Something in the tightness of her voice made Ben resist questioning her further. He exchanged a look with Sara, and Helen saw him give her a quick, intimate, reassuring parental nod, to let her know everything would be okay. She wanted to punch him in the face.

He started down the hall after Hamilton. Helen could feel her daughter's burning stare but did not return it. "Or a bath," Hamilton was saying as they turned the corner toward the master bathroom. "Because I don't know how much longer I can stand up." Then Helen and Sara were left alone in the front hall, Helen never having advanced more than one step inside the door.

"This is a nightmare," Sara said. "You are my nightmare."

"Get your things, please," said Helen.

"No."

"How many beds are there in this house right now?"

"Two."

"Get your things, please," Helen said.

In the darkness of the underlit Saw Mill, she was soon crying from the effort to keep her eyes open. Sara's vengeful silence in the passenger seat, dramatic though it was, proved too difficult for her to maintain after the first five minutes. "How could you do that to me?" she began. "What is the matter with you? Is it menopause? Have you gone out of your mind? You yank me out of school in the middle of the day so you can go off and have some pathetic affair with some pseudo-celebrity who looks like a total hobo? Smells like a hobo too. You are too old to be acting like this. Who else knows about it? Did you lose your job or something? Or maybe you quit. Maybe you quit your job for one last sex romp with Hobo Joe, who you made out with a hundred years ago but you just couldn't bear to head into old age without going back and finding him to close the deal. God, it makes me want to vomit just thinking about it. Can't you just accept who you are? Can't you—"

Helen slammed on the brakes and jerked the car onto the shoulder, even though there was technically no shoulder there. Horns blared at them angrily, urgently, and headlights washed through their car. She turned in her seat to look at her daughter, who had pulled away so that the back of her head was up against the passenger side window. Sara was trying hard to maintain her edge, but Helen could see that her chin was quivering. Helen no longer wondered, as she usually did when her daughter teed off on her, what exactly she had done wrong; she just accepted now that she had done something wrong, or many things, even if it was not given to her to know what those things were. She leaned in a little closer, over the frantic rise and fall of the horns.

"I am begging you," Helen said.

THE NEXT MORNING Sara left for school without a word, and Helen rushed to get to Malloy fifteen or twenty minutes before everybody else. She knew she couldn't stay in her office for long. Malloy himself would be apoplectic about her having skipped the meeting at the archdiocese the day before. His surge-protector smile was probably threatening to crack open his whole head. Part of her was tempted to ask his advice on how to proceed with Hamilton Barth, a celebrity in hiding over something that had very likely not even happened; but even if Hamilton was, however tangentially or indirectly, a Malloy client, she felt that this was less a business issue than a personal one, and the idea of enlisting the boss felt like an evasion of responsibility.

It was all she could do not to call Ben again. She wasn't sure how often was too often to call, at what point Ben would resent it, which mattered to her only because his feeling fettered or mistrusted might be all it took to cause him to do something perverse and stupid. They were the two most unreliable men she knew, which made it hard to feel good about any plan that depended on how they acted when they were out of her sight. Still, there wasn't much trouble they could be getting into at 8:45 in the morning, so she turned to the other problem at hand, which was trying to locate this Lauren Schmidt.

But how do you find someone? How do you prove she exists? Helen had no skills in this area whatsoever. She Googled the girl, and found the usual sludge of five thousand random mentions of a woman with that name who may or may not have been Bettina. One had just finished first in the long jump at River Oaks High School in Winnetka, Illinois. So you could eliminate that one, but how many of the other hits might be referring to that one too? There was no way to know, or else the ways, Helen thought, were opaque to someone like her. She clicked on Images and, with a sharp gasp she was glad no one was around to overhear, recognized her, the horrid bitch from the screening a week ago. She'd been photographed by Patrick McMullan at some society benefit, smiling into the camera with her tattooed arm around some other austerely proportioned girl, both of them standing the way skinny women bred a certain way always stand. She looked utterly, aggressively self-conscious, like she was daring the camera to record her in any way other than the way she wanted to be seen. Beautiful, though. She and Hamilton must have made quite a couple, must have given off a concentrated glow in that moldy, colorless setting if, God forbid, anyone had seen them there.

There were all these professional directories, and all these services that promised to track down and collate vital information about anyone whose privacy you cared to invade. It was never more than two clicks before they started asking you for money, and Helen, using her personal credit card and address, subscribed to every one of them. She tried a phone number she found attached to Bettina's real name; it had been disconnected, though there was no knowing when. The only information she got of any substance, twenty minutes and about two hundred and sixty dollars later, was a street address, on Thirty-first Avenue in Astoria. By now she could hear other Malloy employees strolling past her closed door, and she knew she didn't have long.

Out in the street, head down in the rain lest anyone entering the building recognize her, Helen hailed a cab and rode all the way to Queens, repeating the street and apartment numbers to herself over and over, in keeping with her resolution not to write anything down. It was a narrow walk-up building next to a fish store. All the windows were dark. Shakily, Helen pressed Lauren Schmidt's buzzer, a total of three times, the last time backing quickly down the steps into the street to look up at the third-floor window for any sign of movement. No one was there; in fact no one other than Helen was on the sidewalk at all in the light rain in the middle of the morning, certainly not anyone who might live in one of the other apartments in Bettina's building and be able to answer a question about when she had last been seen.

But it could have meant anything Helen wanted it to mean. People with jobs, even temp jobs, were exceptionally unlikely to be at home during the day. Whatever emotion you felt as a result was just a matter of faith, really, and she took the opportunity to remind herself of her faith in the idea that Hamilton was simply incapable of doing what he was convinced he had done. Even with drugs involved, he was not some killer. It didn't matter that she had known him only as a child; her sense of what was and wasn't in him was stronger and more reliable, she believed, than was his own. That's why he had sought her out in the first place.

She couldn't find a cab in the rain to save her life, so she wound up walking west until she found a subway stop, on the Q line. She hadn't even known there was a Q line. She didn't get back to the office until about lunchtime, and when the elevator door opened she was face to face with Ashok, who looked as jolted to see her as if he had been told she was dead. "Mr. Malloy has been looking for you," he said in an unnecessary whisper. "He actually came downstairs to find you. He had somebody with him. He was not happy I didn't know where you were."

"I'm sorry," Helen said. She took off her ruined shoes, and put them back on again. "I'm sorry to put you in that position." Her own face was reddening. She struggled not to cry. "This guy he had with him," Helen said. "Did he— It wasn't by any chance like a cop or anything?"

Ashok looked reassuringly confused. "A cop?" he said. "No, you're way off, actually. He was— He had the collar, like a priest or a minister or whatever."

Suddenly it seemed like the most obvious mistake to have come back to the office at all. Big as it was, Malloy Worldwide wasn't physically big enough to hide in. "Listen, Ashok," she said, "I need to ask you to do something for me. I need you to tell Arturo and whoever else asks that I left you a voice mail saying I am taking a personal day. I don't think I've been here long enough to be eligible for any personal days, but let's say I didn't realize that."

"And why are you taking this personal day?" Ashok said, looking almost comically attentive, as he always did when strategy was being discussed.

"Let's say"—she closed her eyes, and sighed—"let's say that my daughter is in trouble. I mean, don't use that phrase, but . . . okay, that she's very sick."

He nodded.

"It is a terrible thing to ask you to lie about," Helen said. She gave in to an urge to reach out and touch his round face. "Forgive me for asking."

"For you, Helen, anything," said Ashok.

AT FIRST BEN WAS AFRAID to let Hamilton Barth out of his sight for more than a few minutes, because he just assumed, from the oversolicitous way Helen treated him, that he was the kind of guy who'd be inclined to make a break for it, out the window or over the roof until somebody recognized him and gave him a lift to the nearest bar. As if Ben himself, and his home, were some form of rehab. He'd seen men like Hamilton at Stages—morose, narcissistic, making a big show of their passivity—and he'd seen how closely the counselors watched them. But a day passed—a day about half of which Hamilton spent sleeping in Ben's bed—and by the next afternoon Ben was hovering for a different reason, which was that he thought the guy was sunk so deep as to be at risk of suicide. He had no idea what signs to look for, or anything like that; it was just something he felt. And he didn't want his house to become a shrine where some tragic, martyred movie star had breathed his last.

He called Bonifacio to say that he wouldn't be in to the office that afternoon; he said he felt he might be coming down with something. "Huh," Bonifacio said with his usual light, teasing malice. "Sick day, eh? Well, this may come up at your performance review. Have some chicken soup and an Airborne and let me know what tomorrow's story is."

Ben hung up. Hamilton was back in the master bedroom again, not by choice but because Ben had stashed him there, as ordered, while two jumpsuited guys carried into the house a dining room table and four chairs. Once their truck had receded noisily up the hill, Ben expected Hamilton to come right out again, but the bedroom door remained shut. He knocked, and nudged the door open, cautiously, when there was no response. Hamilton was lying sideways across the bed, in one of Ben's polo shirts and a pair of his jeans, his hands between his knees, his eyes watery.

"You hungry?" Ben said boisterously. "You must be starving."

"Not really," Hamilton said.

Ben's concern was mixed with relief since there was hardly any food in the house. Everything he'd been told about this Hamilton Barth character, or had read somewhere about him—his pretension, his genius, his tortured-soul routine—was suddenly dwarfed by the need to make some kind of masculine connection with him, to keep him from sticking his head in Ben's oven or hanging himself with Ben's belt. "How about a drink, then?" he said.

Hamilton's head turned slowly in his direction. The windows were still covered by rags; new blinds had been purchased, but Ben was going to have to hire one of the hardware store owner's sons to come put them up.

"What time of day is it?" Hamilton asked.

It was around one-thirty, but Ben just shrugged. "Five o'clock somewhere," he said, an expression he'd always hated. "Come on, we can't get in any trouble as long as we stay in the house. Come out to the kitchen with me," he said as he might have said to a small child, "and let's see what we've got."

There was a bottle of rum, which he didn't remember buying. It might have been there in the cupboard above the fridge since before the house went on the market, for all he knew. Anyway, mixed with some orange and cranberry juice it tasted like something legitimate to drink in the middle of the day. They finished their first one in silence; Ben took the glass from Hamilton's fingers and poured another. He could see raindrops on the windowsill. So what, Ben thought, it's not like we were going to take a stroll around the neighborhood anyway.

He found it surprising that Hamilton, distracted and depressed as he may have been, didn't ask any more questions about where he was, neither about the place nor about Ben himself: How is it you are living in your own home without any furniture? Why don't you have a job to go to? That kind of thing. But the man was a celebrity, a movie star. Even at his lowest moment—especially at his lowest moment—he just took it for granted that people's curiosity would bend toward him.

"So you grew up in Malloy, huh?" Ben said, into the mouth of his glass. Hamilton's chin lifted slightly, and he nodded.

"I've never been there myself," Ben said, just to keep silence from reasserting itself. "I've been to Watertown once, after her mother died."

"Helen's mother died?" Hamilton said.

"Yeah," Ben said, trying not to sound unreasonably excited that he had gotten Hamilton to say anything at all. "In Florida, actually, but we had to go and close up the house and whatnot. She used to tell me that Watertown was like the big city compared to Malloy. But you'd know all about that."

Hamilton considered it. "Probably I remember that about it," he said. "I've forgotten a lot. Truthfully I don't feel like I'm from anywhere anymore. I'm just here in the now."

"Sure," said Ben, as convincingly as he could. "Naturally."

They heard a man's voice outside in the street. Trying to appear casual, like an actor carrying out some stage business in a play, Ben crossed the kitchen and stood between Hamilton and the uncovered window.

"But you two did know each other as kids," Ben said. "In a little town like that. So what was Helen like, as a kid? I used to wonder about that."

"Truthfully," Hamilton said, "I don't remember her at all, but it's seriously nothing personal, I forget everybody from then. It's more like time travel with Helen, like she was sent here from my past."

Ben nodded, credibly, he hoped. While he felt proud of himself for engaging Hamilton at all, in truth the guy was a little hard to talk to. Spontaneously, half out of desperation and awkwardness, he said, "So is it okay if I ask you something? It's completely within the walls of this house. I know you don't know me, but believe me, I wouldn't want to betray Helen's trust again." That last word just slipped out, but Hamilton didn't seem to notice. "Why are you here? What are we hiding you from?"

The muscles in Hamilton's face worked a little bit, almost randomly, as if the rum were beginning to wake him up. "I think I had kind of a psychotic break," he said glumly. "I did something that— I was going to say 'that wasn't really like me,' but that's just it, actually. I think it was the real me. And the rest of the time—like right now—I just have this face that I put on. I did something that showed me who I am. Now I can't unsee it."

That made even more sense to Ben than Hamilton might have expected, and he didn't say anything in reply. He held his glass to his mouth until the ice cubes slid and clacked against his teeth. "You know what?" he said, taking Hamilton's glass from him again. "I take it back. It's your business. I know what I need to know."

Just then he felt his phone vibrate in his pocket: another text from Helen. "She's asking if you're okay," he said. "Are you okay?"

"So she hasn't found Bettina?"

Ben didn't know what that meant, or what an answer one way or the other might do to Hamilton's mood. So he just shrugged noncommittally, and then he texted back to Helen, *Napping*. "So how long have you been a client of Helen's?" he said. "I have to admit, I'm not sure what kind of work she does exactly."

"I'm not a client of hers."

"No? Oh. I guess I misunderstood—I thought this was a work-related thing."

"Not so much," Hamilton said.

"Did you meet professionally?"

"No," Hamilton said. "I mean I wouldn't call it that."

"And you didn't stay in touch over the years, or anything like that?" Hamilton shook his head.

"Why did you call her of all people when you were in trouble, then?" Ben asked. "Just out of curiosity."

For once, Hamilton met his eyes. "That is a really interesting question, man," he said. "When I met her again, it reminded me right away of the nuns, right, at our old school? I mean nothing personal, I'm not calling her a nun, I know she used to be your wife. But I got that nun hit off her, where you kind of wanted to laugh them off because they seemed so out of touch, but then when you got scared or in trouble you caught yourself thinking about them. Hey, I guess I do remember some of that Malloy stuff after all."

Ben stood up and began mixing them two more drinks, even though the orange juice was now gone.

"She is a trip," Hamilton said. "I totally get why you couldn't stay married to her. Hey, can I ask you something? That Chinese girl that was here—that's Helen's daughter, so I guess she would be your daughter too?"

"That's right," Ben said. "Sara."

"Is she from *China* China?" Ben nodded. "So you went over there to the orphanage and all that?"

"We went over there," Ben said, "but not to the orphanage. They didn't want us to see it."

"So has it been awkward, ever?"

"Has what been awkward?"

"Having a child who's a different race than you," Hamilton said. "I always wondered that about adoption. I mean I guess I've always assumed that it was basically vanity that made people reproduce in the first place, and adopting a kid who looks nothing like you—it doesn't seem like it would satisfy that. Am I wrong?"

Ben's phone vibrated again. That Hamilton plainly had no sense of this question as rude or invasive said a lot, Ben felt, about the kind of life such people led. "The whole adoption almost fell through, actually, at a couple of stages," he said, "and at the time, I was ready to live without it. It was Helen whose heart would have been broken. I don't think out of vanity. Do you? Anyway, it's got fuck-all to do with what they look like. You give them a life, and then they grow up and start calling you on your shit. You could maybe use one yourself." Out the kitchen window he saw a Sears truck inching along Meadow Close from house to house, looking, he was sure, for his street number. It was either the rugs or the bookshelves, but in any case, Hamilton was going to have to be shut back in the bedroom for a while. Ben sat down in one of the kitchen chairs, also new, so new it still felt stiff underneath him. "You know what?" he said. "We're going a little crazy locked up in here. Maybe later if we get in the car and drive out toward, say, Saugerties, get you like a baseball cap or something, I bet we can stay under the radar. I'll do all the driving. We'll find someplace to eat dinner and just sit and not say anything."

Hamilton smiled and shook his head sadly. "Doesn't work like that, man," he said. "There is always an eye on you. I feel a little like there's somebody watching me right now."

7

THE OBVIOUS COURSE—"obvious" in the sense that her only frame of reference in this situation was television—was to hire some sort of private investigator. There was no one to advise her on how to tell a good one from a bad one, though, so in the end, humiliatingly, she went with the one who had the most serious-looking website. His name was Charles Cudahy, and he was a retired New York City detective. Or maybe neither of those things was true. Conscious of the need to insulate Hamilton by exposing Cudahy to as little information as possible—just enough to get the job done—she called him from a pay phone, all the way over by Carl Schurz Park. Working pay phones were not easy to find anymore. She told him she needed to locate a young woman with an ordinary name.

"What else do you know about her?" Cudahy said, patiently enough. He had a much higher voice than she had been expecting.

"Her most recent place of employment," Helen said, "though it seems like she was only a temp there. A recent home address. A phone number that's I don't know how old."

"Let's have them," he said.

"Really? Right now? Don't—shouldn't we meet first, or at least talk about payment or something? I mean this is just an exploratory—"

"This is the age of the Internet," Cudahy said, "and for people in my line of work, you would be surprised how many cases can be solved in the first thirty seconds, without my ass ever leaving the chair. Not very Humphrey Bogart, but there it is. So how about this: if I can find this person in the next two minutes, while we're on the phone, you will owe me five hundred dollars. If not, if it's more interesting than that, then we will discuss a more traditional fee structure. Sound good?"

She rattled off what little she knew, and then she listened to the sound of him typing. The pay phone was near the East River, not far from the mayor's house; across the street was a posh new apartment building whose doorman rocked back and forth on his heels like an old Keystone Kop, while staring directly at her.

"Nope," Cudahy said abruptly. "This is a fun one. I'll have to put on my pants to solve this one. Just kidding, that's a joke, I promise you I am wearing pants right now. I work on a twenty-five-hundred-dollar retainer. Cash only. I see you're calling from a pay phone in Manhattan, so I assume you don't know how to get to Bayside?"

She wound up messengering a cashier's check—her own money—and then she waited. Her whole life felt like a pose now, a smokescreen, an alias. She was in backchannel communication with her own ex-husband, on whom, stupidly and perversely, everything now depended. She wouldn't have minded some sort of webcam setup where she could watch him, unseen, 24/7, both because she didn't trust him and because she knew that demonstrating that mistrust by texting him compulsively every hour was probably the best way to set him off. As for work, it was one thing to play hooky for a day, but she understood she couldn't hide out indefinitely—it would put too much of a spotlight on her. So she returned to the office after a two-and-a-half-day absence, telling everyone who asked only that Sara was fine, not sick, back in school, all of which was true but still upped the stakes on the initial lie by making it sound as if whatever happened was so bad she preferred not to talk about it. She wanted to go up to Mr. Malloy's office to apologize personally, but there was no way to access or even to buzz for his private elevator. So she settled for an interoffice email full of profuse and deceitful apologies. Two hours later, flowers were delivered to her office. She stared at them miserably.

And so that afternoon she finally, distractedly, went to work on what she still had trouble calling the Catholic Church account. They didn't want to risk a meeting where anyone might see her; she took the subway to an unmarked office building down by City Hall. The New

York archdiocese had been contacted by a *Post* reporter who led them to believe that a major story was in the works about a secret list of priests accused of sexual misconduct, priests who had not simply been reassigned to different parishes but who actually had their names changed.

"Does such a list exist?" Helen asked Father Clement, who was the archbishop's PR liaison.

"Isn't it easier for you to do your job," Father Clement said, "if you assume that the answer is no?"

Helen blinked a few times while trying to think what to say next. "If it helps you," she said, "think of me as your lawyer. I need to know the truth in order to do my job. While of course the notion of confidentiality is technically not legally binding around here, we do, actually, consider it" — she lost steam as she neared the end of this speech she had delivered to clients a hundred times before — "sacred."

Father Clement just smiled. "I understand," he said. "In that case, just between us: yes, while it does not preclude the likelihood that this reporter may be bluffing or exaggerating or making things up, a list of that sort exists."

"Well, then, Father," she said, aware that she was speaking with a touch less patience than she might have if there were fewer other things on her mind, "my crisis management advice is very simple — simpler in this case than in most, because presumably I don't have to explain the concept to you."

He smiled at her interrogatively.

"Confess," she said.

His smile broadened until she saw the condescension in it. "To whom?" he said. "To you? To the *New York Post*? I am gratified that you're looking out for our spiritual well-being. But we are pretty well taken care of on that plane. We come to you precisely because we are also living and operating in your realm, and, like any other institution, we need to keep moving forward." They spoke like that for another twenty minutes, and then Helen, nettled and distracted and checking her phone, got on the Brooklyn-bound subway by mistake. She didn't realize it until she felt her ears pop when the train was under the East River. By then it was too late to get back to the office by close of business anyway, so she consulted a subway map on the platform to figure out the simplest route home.

Her relationship with her daughter was now so cordial and businesslike that Sara had a vague sense of having broken something. Her mother hadn't so much as asked her a question in days. She worked longer hours than usual, or maybe something else was going on, for when Sara called her at Malloy at four in the afternoon to ask about dinner, she was told that Ms. Armstead had already left for the day. When Helen finally did get home, around six, she seemed immensely distracted, but not in a good way. Maybe that Hamilton Barth dude had broken her heart. Exceedingly hard to imagine, but that was how all the signs read.

And then, after two days in which Sara was relieved to hear nothing, Cutter had started popping up on her Facebook wall again. She'd missed a day and a half of school, and now there were only three more perfunctory, movie-watching days left in the school year. She was ashamed to catch herself looking forward to having to deal with Cutter only on the phone or online. But when he wasn't in school Wednesday, and she didn't hear from him, Sara got up the nerve to ask her former friend Tracy if she'd seen him.

"Very funny," Tracy said; then, catching the look in Sara's eyes, her interest grew, vengefully. "You really don't know?" she said. She told the story from her own perspective, as if that mattered to anyone: on Tuesday morning she had been running down the hall, trying not to be late for homeroom even though it was the last week of school so who would care, only to find the doorway blocked by cops, real cops. Apparently Cutter had gotten into an argument with Mr. Hartford, his American History teacher—not for the first time, Sara knew—that had ended with Cutter punching Mr. Hartford in the eye. So Cutter was gone and not coming back, that much was obvious, but past that point it was all ignorant speculation, about jail and lawsuits and whatever else, in which Tracy indulged gleefully.

Sara felt the water closing over her head. She hated herself for wanting to be free of him, for her weak and desperate hope that he would not try to contact her. She thought she might be in the clear after checking Facebook one last time before bed that same Wednesday night. Then on Thursday morning she had twenty-seven new posts on her wall, and they were all from him. The final one was a photo of her, taken on the sidewalk outside her building, in which she was wearing the clothes she wore yesterday.

She took down the posts and blocked him. He's only trying to scare you, she said to herself; but guess what, it was working. She went to the front door, and a good thing too—her mother had forgotten to lock it. It must be nice, Sara thought tearfully, just to live in your own little bubble, without it occurring to you that something bad might happen to you or to anyone else.

Helen, meanwhile, lost more and more confidence in the situation in Rensselaer Valley. The fact that she communicated with Ben mostly by text, since she still felt a surge of anger and embarrassment whenever she spoke to him, naturally contributed to the clipped and ominously terse quality of his status reports to her. Still, the situation could only be decaying. You just could not take two men of that nature, ask them to do nothing, go nowhere, talk to no one but each other, and expect that request to be honored indefinitely; but that's what she had done, that was her only plan. *What r we waiting 4?* was one of his last messages, followed a minute later by *Literally?* They were waiting for proof of Bettina's continued existence on this earth, proof that was turning out to be maddeningly, alarmingly, expensively elusive. That night Helen nervously floated with Sara the notion that she might take another quick trip up to Rensselaer Valley after work on Friday, just for an hour or two, to check on Hamilton. She made it clear that there was no need for Sara herself to come; but Sara insisted that she would.

Ben had taken the risk of leaving Hamilton by himself once or twice by then, just to go to Bonifacio's office for a couple of hours, and there hadn't been any incident. He wasn't a bad guy, Ben thought. A little self absorbed, maybe. In the evenings they watched TV and drank. On their fourth night together, a Friday, there was a good old-fashioned, window-shaking thunderstorm, and about ten minutes later the cable, installed earlier that day, went out.

"That's it," Ben said. "It's a sign. We have got to get out of here. I am trying so hard to do this for Helen, but it's too much, it's too open-ended. They are going to find us dead together in here and no one will ever know why."

"You know, that brings up an interesting point," Hamilton said. His eyes were glassy. "You two are divorced, right? I've never been divorced myself, but doesn't it sort of mean you don't have to do what she tells you anymore?"

Ben turned off the hissing TV. "It's complicated," he said. "I owe her something. I'm not sure even this is going to pay it off, actually."

"What did you do?" Hamilton asked somberly.

Ben had an idea. He swirled the ice cubes in his glass. "I'll tell you what I did," he said, "if you tell me what you did."

Hamilton considered it. "Okay, man," he said. "Only fair. But you may regret asking. It may raise the stakes for you a little bit."

"All right," Ben said. He was excited now; he figured Hamilton had maybe slept with some producer's girlfriend, like in *The Godfather*. "But not here. Seriously, we need a change of venue."

"No bars," Hamilton said warily. "I don't mind saying or doing something stupid in front of you, but if we are out I'll get recognized, and then we're both screwed."

Ben nodded. "Plus the nearest real bar is probably in New Castle, which is like ten miles from here, and if I get nicked for DWI again, it's back to jail for moi." Hamilton's eyebrows rose. "Okay, I have an idea. It's a little offbeat, but safe, at least. It doesn't matter where we go, you said, right?"

"I think you were the one who said that, but yeah, it doesn't matter to me."

"Anywhere but this house. Okay. Do me a favor and go grab the vodka."

Ben drove into town at about fifteen miles per hour and parked in the lot behind the hardware store. They stumbled up the steps and he opened the door with his key. "This is where I work," he whispered. "Don't worry, there's ice. I'm going to turn on the light, count to three, and then turn it off again, because it would not be cool if anyone were to see us up here. Ready?"

He flicked the switch, and together they took in the tiny office, which, like any office, looked unfamiliar and slightly malicious when empty: the cheap, pocked desk, the noisy filing cabinets, the chair pulled up to the window so he could rest his feet on the sill, the water-stained curtains, the potted plant. Realizing he'd forgotten to start counting, Ben slapped at the switch again and they returned to darkness, a degree or two darker than before. "Now I forget where the chair was," Hamilton said.

Ben's cellphone chimed again, and he jumped. Without looking at the incoming number—he knew it anyway—he turned the phone off.

Helen had been trying to reach him for more than an hour, ever since she got out of that day's meeting—another stalemate—with the Catholics; she'd dialed Hamilton's number as well, but he rarely answered his phone even under the best circumstances. Her next call was to the accursed Hertz outpost near her apartment. She had a premonition something was wrong. Her messages and texts left no room for misunderstanding in terms of the need to check in with her right away: if Ben didn't reply immediately, her last message had said, she was going to assume the worst and head up there. She picked up the car, called Sara to tell her to be ready in half an hour, and then drove to the pay phone outside Carl Schurz Park to make one more call that had been on her mind.

Not only had there been nothing in the papers or on the Internet about Hamilton Barth's disappearance but she had actually come across a *Hollywood Reporter* item that claimed he had been at a gallery opening three nights ago in Venice Beach. They were good, those people, but if they were already going to the trouble of planting items, they must have been in a full-blown panic. Hamilton's agent was someone named Kyle Stine—she'd looked it up—and with a prepaid phone card she'd bought at Duane Reade, she called his office from the lonely pay phone.

"No," she had to say to three different people, "I'm not calling for information about Hamilton Barth. I'm calling *with* information about Hamilton Barth. Please just give that message to Mr. Stine, and I'll hold." Hold she did, for almost ten minutes. She could see the doorman behind the glass wall of the building across the street, sitting at his desk, in the glow of the security-camera monitors.

"This is Kyle Stine," said a hostile voice.

Helen swallowed. "I'm a friend of Hamilton's," she said quickly, "and I know you probably haven't heard from him in a while, and I just wanted to let you know he's fine—"

"Where is he?" Stine said, in a tone whose attempt at calm could not have been more frightening.

"I can't tell you that," Helen said, "but I can tell you that he's okay, he's perfectly safe—"

"What the fuck do you mean, he's safe?" the voice thundered. "Who is this? Listen to me. You tell me where you have him right now."

"He's fine," Helen said. "He will be back in touch when he's ready."

"Do you have any notion of the interests you are fucking with? What, have you kidnapped him or something?"

"Oh God, no. I'm trying to help him."

But the voice formed its own judgment. "You are committing all kinds of crimes right now, you psychotic cunt, and if you think there is anything that I wouldn't do in order to track you down and eliminate every last trace of you, you are really fucking mistaken. Do you have any idea what's at stake here? What are you, some fan, you think he's got some kind of special connection with you? Some relationship? Do you have any idea how pathetic you are? There will not be enough left of you to form a fucking stain on my bootheel, if anything happens to him. Do you have any idea of the forces that are closing in on you right now?"

Red-faced, Helen hung up. The doorman was now standing and staring at her through the glass wall. She drove home and found Sara sitting in the lobby, staring at her cellphone, her purple duffel bag at her feet.

"What's that for?" Helen said. "We're not spending the night."

"I'm not coming back with you," Sara said. "I was going to take the train up tomorrow anyway, but this is better. I need to go home and be with Dad. I do not feel safe here. I do not feel safe with a totally checked-out mother who has no interest at all in her daughter's life."

"What about homework?" Helen said reflexively.

"I don't have any more homework. School ended today, thanks for noticing. Your job has turned you into some kind of zombie, apparently, but whatever, I choose to be with Dad now."

"It's not your choice," Helen said.

"Want to test me?" said Sara.

And, God help her, the thought flashed through Helen's mind that, if Sara were up there at the house with her father and Hamilton, it would be easier to keep them indoors, it would be harder for them to go out. Ten minutes later Sara had her earphones in and Helen drove in angry, agonized, private silence up the floodlit West Side Highway.

Ben still wasn't answering his phone, but now that bit of childishness on his part just made her laugh with anticipatory pleasure: oh, you wanted some warning that you were about to become a full-time parent again? Try checking your goddamn voice mail once in a while. When they got to the house on Meadow Close, every light in it was blazing, seeping around the closed shutters as if some sort of industrial hellfire was burning in there. Helen knocked on the door and then pushed it open, Sara two steps behind her. No one was home. She could not make the brazen fact of it sink in right away. Red-faced, she ran in and out of every room, each of which now looked like some half-assed warehouse full of unmatched new furniture.

"What's going on?" Sara said.

"I can't believe it," Helen said. "I literally cannot believe it. How stupid could I be?"

A mile and a half away, Ben and Hamilton sat with their eyes accustomed to the dark of Bonifacio's second-floor law office. Ben had stressed the need for quiet, which was why his phone was turned off. It was also true, of course, that he knew he was now much too drunk to pull off a non-alarming phone conversation with Helen anyway. The vodka was nearly gone, and they'd run out of ice half an hour ago.

"This is the first time I've been drunk since rehab, if you please," Ben said, in a voice just above a whisper. "I mean, don't worry, it was fake rehab. Real problems, fake rehab."

"I know lots of guys who have done that," Hamilton said.

"So look," Ben said, "can I ask you something? You're a fucking movie star. Men want to be you, women want to be with you, or however that expression goes. What the hell is that like? Is it just incredibly great? Because I have to say, when I hear people complain about it, like boo hoo I have no privacy or whatever, I just think, what pussies."

"Yeah?" said Hamilton idly. "You think you'd like that kind of life? Guys with cameras in your face everywhere you go, lies about you in the paper and on TV all the time? The true stuff is worse than the lies, actually."

"Yes," Ben said. "I think I might have liked it. I mean at least it's a big life. At least it's a consequential life. At least you're at the center of your own life, not on the periphery of it." He swirled the vodka in his glass and looked out the window at the streetlight. "Periphery," he pronounced slowly.

"See," Hamilton said, "you think that. People think that. But when you're in it, it's more like you're a character in a story. You try to be the one telling it, but you're not. And then you can try to get out of it, but when you do it's like the story was already one step ahead of you anyway. It's like Pirandello. Ever read Pirandello, man?"

"What?" Ben said. "No. What are you talking about? I mean look, let's get down to brass tacks, man-wise. These four days or whatever it is that you've been living under my roof, that's probably the longest you've ever gone without getting laid since like high school, right?"

Ben expected to bond over this bit of flattery and maybe to hear some good stories; but instead he seemed to have pushed a button. Hamilton put his drink down on the floor and placed his hands over his eyes. "I have this reputation as a very serious person," he said. "And I used to be. I mean even when I wasn't acting, in my downtime I painted, I wrote poetry. I actually published a couple of books. People liked to make fun of it because of who I was, but it was actually not that bad. But then I became less serious. Why is that? Older, and yet less serious. Why? Older, closer to death, less serious. It doesn't make any sense. Anyway, that's when I really started fucking a lot of chicks I didn't know. I'd say like over the last six, eight years. I mean it became really important to me. I never really knew what all that was about while I was doing it, what it was all pointing towards, but now I do know, man, now it's obviously clear, but too late."

"Right," Ben said. "Wait, what? What do you mean, now you know?"

"I told you all this," Hamilton said.

"You haven't told me shit!"

"I killed a girl," Hamilton said, and then that sentence hung there in the darkness for a while.

Ben felt the adrenaline cutting through his buzz. "What?" he said softly. "How?"

"I don't know. Funny that's your first question, though."

"Why?"

"I don't know that either, except that it apparently was in me, and something in her woke it up. All those years of getting away with murder. So to speak. It's emptied me out."

"Are the—" Ben stopped when he thought he heard something outside on the steps, but it must have been just his paranoia. "Are the cops looking for you, then? Helen is helping you to hide from the cops? That doesn't sound like—"

"I'm not hiding from anyone. Helen is making me stay here."

"Why?"

"Because she doesn't believe me. She doesn't believe I did it."

"Who does she think did it?"

Hamilton didn't answer.

"So the cops are not looking for you?"

"No. Nobody's looking for me, except my agent, Kyle, probably. No reason to."

"No *reason* to?"

"There has to be a body," Hamilton said sadly, "before anybody will believe there was a crime."

And there it was again—the creak from outside, but it was definitely not his imagination this time, there were feet on the steps that ran up the side of the building. What the hell is this turning into? Ben had time to think. He dumped the rest of the vodka into the plant and raised the empty bottle above his shoulder, without getting out of the desk chair. A face pressed up against the glass; then the knob turned and the lights went on and there, with as close to a look of disequilibrium as you were ever going to see on his face, was Bonifacio, wearing a Carhartt jacket over a pair of plaid pajamas, a set of keys in one hand and in the other, now dropped limply to his side, a gun.

"What the fuck is going on here?" he said. "I had three different people call and tell me someone had broken in. But it's what, an office party? In the dark? Motherfucker," he said, gesturing with the gun, "did anybody ever tell you you look just like Hamilton Barth?"

Ben stood and beckoned his boss into the desk chair. They had one more round, from Bonifacio's desk-drawer bottle of Jameson, while everybody calmed down, and then Bonifacio, though likely drunk himself, drove the two men home. When they crested the hill, Ben saw a strange car in the driveway, and he reached out and grabbed Hamilton's arm. "We're dead," he said. Bonifacio, tired and disgusted, made them get out at the top of the driveway. Trying gamely to sober up, they marched down the pavement toward the front door.

From the foyer Ben could see Helen sitting at the kitchen table and Sara stretched out on the new living room couch. He stood between them, paralyzed with fear, until Hamilton ungracefully squeezed past him, sat down across the table from Helen, and leaned toward her on his elbows.

"What have you found out?" he said.

"Where on earth," Helen said in a gratingly high voice, "have you two been?"

"It's not what you think," Ben said.

"Helen, please!" Hamilton said.

"We just needed to get out," Ben said. "But we didn't do anything too stupid. We just went to Bonifacio's office."

"Bonifacio's office?" Helen said incredulously. "At ten o'clock at night?"

"So we wouldn't be seen," Ben said.

"And did anybody see you?"

"Well," Ben said, "Bonifacio."

Helen put her head in her hands.

"Helen," Hamilton said again. "Have they found her?"

"Have they what? Oh. No, there's no word. We can't find her, but on the bright side, no one has reported her missing either. She doesn't really have a job to go to, and she has an apartment she hasn't slept in in a while, but that doesn't mean anything. Could just mean she found someone else to shack up with. Anyway," she said, softening as she saw the anguish on his face, "that's not why I drove up here, because I had news or anything. I just couldn't get ahold of you and I was worried. Oh, and also," she said to Ben, "apparently your daughter wants to live with you now. So there's that."

Hamilton sighed, got up, and wandered unsteadily toward the living room. He and Ben were clearly too drunk to keep up any kind of productive conversation for long; and Sara, scared and resentful and confused and tired, hadn't spoken for more than an hour.

For a long moment, Helen, thinking of the three of them, felt that she would like nothing more than to get away from there, away from a sense of her own accountability for any of it, much less all of it. But a powerful inertia kept her in that ugly new kitchen chair, and she realized that she too was far too exhausted right now to get back in the car and go anywhere. "Hold it," she said loudly, and everyone turned around. "Sara in her room. You two in the master bedroom. I'll stay out here and then leave in the morning."

The two men looked at each other. "I can sleep on the couch," Hamilton said, "if—"

"That's not happening," Helen said. With great effort she rose, walked to the living room, and, after a brief search for the TV remote, just pulled the plug out of the wall, which caused Sara to stand up without a word to anyone, go into her once and future bedroom, and close the door. The men went off dutifully to pass out on the bed together, closing the door behind them as well, and finally, for as long as she could manage to keep her eyes open at least, Helen was alone.

No point, she knew, in even looking anywhere for extra blankets or sheets. She lay down on the stiff, new-smelling couch and closed her eyes. As she drifted off, she recalled that there was a cedar chest full of very nice blankets at the self-storage place in New Castle. One of them had belonged to her mother. Her eyes fluttered open again and took in the ceiling above her living room, strangely shadowed without all her old lamps and sconces, but still startlingly, reproachfully familiar. There had to be some meaning in it all, she thought, some logic, because it so strongly resembled a joke: the moment at which everything about her life seemed lost, useless, outside of her control, was also the moment when they were all reunited under one roof—not just any roof either, but their home, the home it had once comforted her to think she would die in. Now it was both itself and a mean-spirited parody, both a freshly sold, newly furnished suburban house and a ruin. She wished she had never lived there, and at the same time she began to dream, with her arms folded across her chest and her coat thrown over her like a too-short blanket, that the house was on fire, and that Sara and Hamilton and Ben were all standing on the lawn screaming at her to run out, to abandon it, to save herself, and she wouldn't do it.

The next thing she knew, there was just enough light outside to let her see the overgrown back lawn painted in shadow, and Hamilton was kneeling patiently on the floor a few feet away, waiting for her to wake up. Her head jerked painfully.

"You were talking in your sleep," he said.

She looked at him, disoriented.

"This obviously can't go on," he said, as if they had already been talking. "It isn't viable, especially not now that you're all back here. I mean, I can't just live indefinitely in your basement or whatever. I have to just accept responsibility for what I've done and let you get on with your lives."

"Well, good," Helen said raspily, raising herself on one elbow. "I agree. I mean with the part about you getting on with your life."

"I charged my phone this morning, and no surprise, people are out looking for me. Plus my agent says he got a phone call from someone who said she kidnapped me. Anyway, I just have to get back to the world and face the consequences. I can't wait around for them to find me, because if they find me then they find you."

"There won't be any consequences, Hamilton, because you didn't do anything. But I agree, you have to just go back to your life. It's time.

So what do you want to do? How can I help? I mean, all you have to do is walk out the door, though you'll probably want a car to the airport or something—"

"I need you to forgive me," Hamilton said.

"For what?" She felt a slow surge of panic. "There's still no reason to think you did anything worth forgiving. People will just think you're insane."

"Yeah, I know. Exactly. The whole thing will never make any sense to anyone except you and me. So the only person who can help me with it is you. I know something happened. I know I did something. So I'll be going back to my old life waiting every second for the knock on the door, or for the hand on my shoulder. I can live with that. But I still need the other part. You know. The absolution."

"The what?" She struggled to sit up. Ben had now wandered into the living room as well. "Do you—I mean are you saying you want me to take you to church?"

"No. I haven't been inside a church in like thirty years."

"So?" she said.

Absurdly he inched forward on his knees. "I just need it from you," he said. "If you think about it, you're the one who knows the most about me. You know where I started, where I came from. And when I ask to be forgiven for what I did, even if you disagree with me, you're literally the only one in the world who knows what I'm even talking about in the first place." He glanced down at the floor, and when he looked up again he was crying. She stared at him to try to gauge how real it was. "I'm so sorry, Helen," he said. "I'm sorry for everything. I'm sorry for ruining your life like this, and for being who I am and not who you think I am. Will you forgive me?"

Oh, where is the girl? Helen thought. Where is the stupid, arrogant, thoughtless girl who can end all this? She looked at the agony contorting his face: the curse of being a good actor, she thought—no difference between the truth and its flawless simulation, not even for him anymore. His whole life was a Method performance, a dream within a dream, but whatever he wanted from her, however preposterous, she was not free to refuse him. She put her hands on his two cheeks, brought his wide-eyed face to hers, and in full view of her ex-husband, kissed him as long and as deeply as she remembered how. After a few moments he began reciprocating. She opened her eyes to make sure his were closed, and they were. It went on for a full minute, at which point she realized it might start to get out of hand. Not that she could do anything to stop it if it did. A door opened inside her; and then she realized that that was the sound of a real door, which could only be Sara's door down the hall, and she quickly but gently disengaged from him and stared, flushed and shaking, into his eyes.

He smiled at her, his movie-star smile, which she had not seen since the night they met at the premiere. "Thank you," he said. Then he turned to Ben, who hadn't moved an inch. "Brother," he said, "could I trouble you for a ride somewhere?"

BY THE TIME Ben got him to the airport in Newburgh, the agency had chartered a plane there to return him to Los Angeles; even though they surely could have paid someone from the charter service to record the license plate of the Hertz rental car in which Hamilton was transported back to his old life, such vengeance was apparently forsworn, and neither the police nor anyone else turned up asking questions. Once Ben had texted her that Hamilton was safely in the air and that he was on his way back to the house, Helen went into her old bathroom and took a shower, even though she had no choice but to put back on the same clothes she had slept in. She went into the kitchen and found a brand new coffeemaker; rooting around in the fridge, which was still their old fridge, she unearthed a bag of ground coffee but very little else in the way of something an adult human might eat for breakfast. Pulling open the empty crisper drawers, muttering incredulously, she became aware of the presence of someone else, and when she straightened and turned around, she saw Sara leaning in the doorway, wearing an old soccer jersey and a pair of pajama bottoms, chewing lightly on a cuticle, and watching her.

"Did you sleep all right?" Helen asked.

"Yeah. I've been up for a while, though," Sara said. She remained in the doorway. Helen pushed the fridge door shut with her foot and walked across the kitchen with her hands full. "This is a really high-end coffeemaker," she said, trying to keep any tension out of her voice. She still wasn't sure whether or not Sara had seen her kissing Hamilton on the couch, in front of her father. Good luck explaining that one. "Did you help him pick this out?"

"What are you making?" Sara said quietly.

Helen looked over what she'd put on the counter. "I guess I can do some sort of omelet," she said, "although it might have chicken in it."

She found a pan in the sink, rinsed it out, and turned the burner on. It was still her old stove. Well, what difference does it make if she saw? Helen thought. You have to start seeing your parents as real people at some point. She shredded some chicken with her fingers, dropped it into the pan, and looked at it skeptically. She looked at the spot on the countertop where the knife block and the spice rack used to be.

"It's so strange," Helen said, "to be back here and not know where anything is."

"What do you need?" Sara said.

Helen bit her lip to keep from crying. She turned to look out the window. Sara walked behind her and, opening and closing drawers and cabinets, produced two plastic plates, two forks, and a rubber spatula. She placed them noiselessly on the counter beside the stove. "Thank you," Helen said. Whatever it was she was making, when it seemed done the two of them sat at the small kitchen table and ate it.

"Are you all right, Mom?" Sara asked.

Helen put her fork down and sat back in her chair. "I'm all right," she said. "Are you all right?"

Sara nodded. She finished eating but did not get up from the table.

"I'm sorry for everything," Helen said. "I really am."

"I don't know why," Sara said. "You did the best you could. You feel too responsible for what everybody else does, is the problem."

"Oh," Helen said. "So then why are you so hard on me?"

"Somebody has to be," Sara said. She wasn't smiling. Their heads turned toward the sound of Ben's car in the driveway.

Helen drove back to the city on the pretext that the rental car had to be returned. Though it was Saturday, she went in to work, expecting the silence of the office to be more tolerable than the silence of her apartment. That night, and the next one, she went home to the East Side; but the solitude, and the worry over Sara, were too much for her, and she hardly slept. Without letting Ben know in advance of her plans, she took the train back to Rensselaer Valley after work on Monday, and on every weeknight thereafter.

She still slept on the couch, and the arrangement was not discussed. Since they had only one car now, Ben drove her to the train station in the morning; though cabs were available in the early evening, once he figured out what train she usually took, he thought he might as well go down to the station and wait for her then too. Something in her balked at the hassle of renting a truck to go to New Castle, where all their old furniture was still piled in the storage unit; and in any event deliverymen kept showing up at the house with previously ordered new stuff. Then one night toward the end of June, Helen looked into Sara's bedroom and saw a profusion of familiar items there—posters, stuffed animals, old yearbooks—so familiar, actually, that they might well have been there for a few days already without her noticing. When asked about it, Sara admitted that she and her father had driven into the city one morning, while Helen was at work, and collected a few things she said she didn't want to be without.

Helen might have been angry with them—in particular about this new flair they seemed to have developed for deciding things together without telling her—and she resolved to have a strong word with Ben about it, but by the next day her edge was dulled, and she never did get around to it. Later that summer it occurred to her to wonder, since no one had mentioned it to her, whether perhaps Ben had enrolled Sara in school for the fall. Again, something made her disinclined to ask. She rationalized it by recalling that she had spent the last decade or more in charge of these sorts of dull domestic necessities, and that it would not have occurred to her back then to bother her spouse with them either.

One sweltering evening in August, safe in the maxed-out air-conditioning of the northbound commuter train, Helen saw her phone light up inside her bag on the seat next to her. She pulled it out in case the call was from Sara or Ben—anyone else and she would let it go to voice mail; she did not want to be one of those people shouting into their cellphones over the noise of the train—and saw that the name on the caller ID was Charles Cudahy. When she got off the train in Rensselaer Valley twenty minutes later, she held up one finger toward Ben, whom she could see waiting in the car beside the platform, and called back.

"How did you get this number?" she said.

"I know, right?" Cudahy said cheerily. "It's like I'm a detective or something!"

"Do you know my name?" Helen said, trying not to grow frantic. Even at seven o'clock it was so hot she was already sweating again.

"Course I know your name," Cudahy said. "Your check had the name of your bank on it, and I have friends here and there, and like this and like that. Anyway, no need to freak out, I only bothered to track you down because I have news for you."

Helen said nothing. She looked at Ben, who smiled back patiently. Patience was itself one of those new things that threatened to make him unrecognizable to her sometimes.

"Lauren Schmidt," Cudahy said. "I found her."

Helen's eyes closed. "She's alive?" she said.

"What? Yes, of course she's alive," Cudahy said, his tone a little less friendly all of a sudden. "I didn't even know that was the issue. She was in some fancy rehab center in Vermont, but here's what made it so tough: she checked herself in under a fake name. They don't care what you call yourself at those places. She didn't want her family to know, was the issue, I guess. And so maybe that's you? You're family?"

"How did she get there?" Helen asked. "Her— I know she wasn't driving her car."

"Well, that was the key to the whole thing, actually. She got sprung from rehab and went looking for her car, which had been towed to some small-town police station and was just sitting there with grass growing around it. She came and showed her license to prove it was hers, and they run the registration online, and bam, she's back on the grid again."

"So you know where she is?" Helen said. "You've spoken to her?"

"Not really my business to speak to her, but yeah, I know where she is. She's back with her parents in Laguna Beach, California. I've got an address, an email, a phone number, the whole schmear. You want it?"

She couldn't imagine anything good coming of it. It was enough to know. She asked him if she owed him any more money and he said no, he'd technically made the crucial phone calls on his own time, just because unsolved cases raised his blood pressure. She hung up, walked across the parking lot, and motioned to Ben to roll down the window.

"One more call," she said. "I don't want to make it from home. Sorry to make you wait."

He shrugged. "You don't want to make it in the car? Nice and cool in here," he said. He was wearing jeans and a polo shirt. She turned away. At rush hour trains into Rensselaer Valley ran only about twenty-five minutes apart; cars were already starting to flow into the lot again. She didn't have much time. She dialed Hamilton's cellphone number and listened to a recording informing her that it had been disconnected.

She'd Googled him idly once or twice over the summer, and found a fully restored flow of gossip items and trade-journal mentions linking him to this or that actress, or to this or that unproduced script. *Variety* had him shooting a new movie this summer in Copenhagen, playing the part of Paul Gauguin. There was no way of knowing how unmanufactured these various sightings were, but they sounded right to her.

She remembered the agent's name, Kyle Stine, and got that number through information, dreading the call but feeling she had no choice. An assistant halfheartedly offered to take a message; "Tell him it's the woman who knew where Hamilton Barth was," Helen said. She felt the eyes on her as she waited—the only person out on the steaming pavement—the stares of all her neighbors inside their idling cars. Nothing new there: she and Ben were stared at everywhere they went now. "What can I do for you?" Kyle Stine said. "Holding another one of my clients hostage, maybe?"

"I need to speak to Hamilton right away," Helen said, seeing even as she said it how this conversation was going to go. "I have some information that could save his life."

"You don't say," answered the agent. "Listen, um—hold on a second—Helen Armstead, who works at Malloy Worldwide in New York, this phone call has actually made my day. And not just because it's so funny. Because you seem not to know who I am. If you knew who I am, you would know how badly you have just fucked up by calling me on your own phone. Tomorrow, when you go to work? There'll be someone else's name on the door, because you won't have a job anymore. I can make that happen and more."

"Please," Helen said. "It doesn't matter. I just need to speak to Hamilton. Will you at least ask him to call me?"

"Not in this lifetime," Kyle Stine said and hung up.

The next train's headlight was on her, and she hurried down from the platform rather than be swallowed in the next discharge of passengers. She got into the passenger seat of the Audi, and Ben pulled out of the lot without a word. She knew every quizzical face they passed in the parking lot; she knew he did too. They had lived here forever. But they had only each other now, and she was surprised to feel a pang of something like contentment when it occurred to her that Ben was the one person in the world who could listen to the story of what had just happened to her and understand what the hell she was talking about. As for Hamilton, the more she thought about him on the ride home, the more she imagined that he was probably leading a better life now anyway, on some set somewhere waiting for his own personal judgment day, feeling, with equal parts humility and arrogance, that it was inevitable. There would be no such judgment, in the end, but knowing that felt like a burden, and thus she was happy to keep it to herself.

"Are you picking up Sara?" she said to Ben as the car crested the hill. Sara had a summer job at the multiplex in town, taking tickets. She had to wear a red vest and complained of the toxic effects of prolonged exposure to morons.

"She says she has a ride," Ben said. "Some boy."

Helen turned to stare at him as he made a right into the driveway. "Some boy," she repeated skeptically. "Driving a car. At eleven o'clock at night."

Ben sighed. "I think we can trust her to make good decisions when it comes to that stuff," he said. "But I can go pick her up if you want."

Good decisions! She was fourteen. Still, the theater was barely a mile from home. And Ben had a fair point about their daughter: it didn't pay to underestimate her. Consciously or not, the girl had achieved the impossible dream of every child of divorce ever; if she could pull that off, it was hard to think of any other life situation she couldn't manipulate. Helen laid her hand on Ben's arm, feeling sorry already for this overmatched boy. Sara was probably inventing her own field sobriety test for him right now.

"Her I trust," she said gently, "but this anonymous boy, not so much. Boys and cars—you never know. I'd feel better if you went and got her."

Ben shrugged. "At your service," he said. They pulled up in front of the garage door; he got out and stood with his hands in his pockets, gazing at the sunlight sieved by the tree line, until Helen had made her way around the car and started up the path ahead of him. "The yard still looks like hell," she said distractedly as they walked up the steps.

"Sorry," Ben said. "Tomorrow." He held the door for her and then let it swing shut behind them.

A THOUSAND PARDONS

Jonathan Dee

A READER'S GUIDE

A Conversation with
Jonathan Dee and Dana Spiotta

DANA SPIOTTA is the author of three novels: *Lightning Field*; *Eat the Document*, which was a finalist for the 2006 National Book Award and a recipient of the Rosenthal Family Foundation Award from the American Academy of Arts and Letters; and *Stone Arabia*, which was a finalist for the 2011 National Book Critics Circle Award. Spiotta has won a Guggenheim Fellowship, a New York Foundation for the Arts Fellowship, and the Rome Prize in Literature. She is an assistant professor in the Syracuse University Creative Writing Program.

DANA SPIOTTA: Helen's apology wrangling is described as a gift, a vocation, and an accidental specialty. It is mysterious to her exactly why, yet her idea of "total submission" works. This process strikes me as almost religious.

JONATHAN DEE: I'm not interested in current events per se, but I am interested in how certain aspects of social or public life that might seem ultra-contemporary actually take their place in a long American continuum. If you look at the practice of "crisis management," and maybe squint at it a little, you can make out in the corners of your vision the ghosts or the vestiges of a much older, but still thoroughly American, form of public life, one centered not on public opinion but on religion. The theater of press conferences, Oprah sit-downs, et cetera is like an old, sacred vessel into which all this contemporary, profane content gets poured. To me, *A Thousand Pardons* is a book not about spin or scandal or PR or even forgiveness, but about religious heritage. But I wanted the story itself to have a smooth surface, and to wear its ideas lightly.

DS: A *Thousand Pardons* has a breakneck pace. Events propel the characters forward, and as soon as they react to one event, another event happens. It's hard to resist the momentum, and then the reader wants to go back and read it all again, more slowly. Tell me why pace was so important in this book?

JD: It would be going way too far to say I wanted the novel to be a parable, but I wanted it to have some of the formal aspects of a parable or a religious tale. Parables are short and sweet; they move only forward, from event to event, as you say; they don't contain flashbacks or other devices for re-ordering time; and there's no pause in them for reflection or commentary or explorations of meaning. Those things exist outside the story, to be provoked by it.

DS: Helen believes abjection and confession are transformative. But why doesn't Ben's abject apology toward the beginning of the book work on Helen? Does he need to atone as well as apologize?

JD: She's too angry, at that point, to accept it. And she stays angry with him for a long time; she's been wronged and humiliated by him, so she can't bring to his case the same sort of objectivity she brings to the dilemmas of her clients. As for Ben, being a lawyer I think he understands too well the negotiability of words; he knows that the road back for him will be about repenting not in speech but in service. He just has to hang around long enough to learn what that service will be.

DS: Public relations has cynicism built into it. It is brilliant and slightly perverse to posit such a sincere person as a public relations savant. Where did the idea come from?

JD: In order to describe a particular subculture, you might want to portray people who are typical or representative of that subculture; but to dramatize it, to make it an interesting setting for a story, you want to bring someone anomalous into that setting, to see how she conforms to it, and it to her.

DS: Did you read a lot of tabloids when you decided to write about crisis management? Public scandal is now so performed and mediated—

did the machinations behind these events fascinate you? How do you know so much about it?

JD: What I read, mostly, were memoirs, first-person accounts written by veterans of the crisis-management industry. That's always the most productive research—research into tone, into voice. Facts are nice too, but facts are more raw material than creative inspiration.

DS: Why are the stories of powerful people brought low so compelling? Has the ritual of public apology become a way for the culture to remind itself of how we define "good" behavior? Or is it just an opportunity for hypocrisy and schadenfreude?

JD: You've said the magic word, which is "ritual." The culture is periodically made to yield up these figures who are first exalted, then rejected, then given the opportunity to return to grace by performing certain highly ritualized acts of public contrition. So I don't think of it as hypocritical. It serves a genuine need. It brings the congregation together.

DS: In A *Thousand Pardons*, some of the characters want a break from the past and the accountability that comes with contemplating the past. But Helen remembers everything, and certainly confessing and apologizing are acts of remembering. Do you see a connection between memory and morality? In your previous novel, *The Privileges*, the Moreys refuse to contemplate the past and their refusal deforms them. Is this an American problem, a kind of willful amnesia?

JD: The opportunity to remake yourself by cutting yourself off from your own past, and the spiritual difficulties thereof: this has always been one of the classic American literary themes. I don't think it will ever be exhausted. We want to moralize about it—to say that it's impossible, that you can only run from who you are for so long—but the Moreys are really good at it, and being so good at it is ultimately what makes them so rich. Helen would not have had much use for the Moreys (in fact, just imagining her sitting across from Cynthia is pretty amusing). To her, the only way forward is to acknowledge your sinful past.

DS: Helen's gift reaches its limit with the Catholic Church. Has she finally lost interest in absolving powerful men?

JD: What Helen sadly discovers is that when it comes to leading sinners to contrition, there is, as she says at one point, a problem of scale. She is happy and successful in the exercise of her spiritual power when her clients are individuals. When her clients are corporations or institutions, it's a lot harder to know the difference between the genuine and the feigned, the real and the merely strategic. And if you can't tell the difference, does the difference still exist?

DS: You leave the ending of the novel somewhat open, and, like the rest of the book, it happens quickly. Did you want the reader to imagine what happens next to Helen, Ben, and Sara?

JD: The reason for the abruptness of the ending goes back to the idea of the religious tale. No drawn-out endings, no reflection or interpretation or summary, no flashing forward to let us know how everything ramified. Just the characters closing the door behind them. And then you're left to decide what it meant.

DS: You resist the impulse to have the narrator indicate the judgment the reader should have about the characters. A lot of the tension in your recent novels comes from a feeling of being very intimate with and yet slightly pulled back from the characters. Why is this narrative restraint so important to you?

JD: To me, any apparent moral judgment of one's own characters—whether positive or negative—is always a mistake. That's the reader's job. I think what you describe as "pulling back" is maybe just a sort of matter-of-factness on my part about the characters, because I am trying not to judge them but to inhabit them, to see the world inside the book as they see it. Let's not forget that I am creating these figures: the notion that I would then praise or condemn them for some attribute I gave them in the first place seems way too easy to me.

DS: Ben says he is "almost comfortable" in his disgrace, he likes the "sad, clear vision" he has. There have been some great recent books about disgraced men. Philip Roth and J. M. 'Coetzee come to mind. Did you think about these books when you were writing yours?

JD: Not consciously, though I am a huge Coetzee fan. If I had a model in mind, it was not a novel but a short story: "Life Is Better than Death," by Bernard Malamud, a story about a widower who meets a young widow in the cemetery where their spouses are buried, then seduces and abandons her. That story has just the tone—the unbroken momentum, the apparent simplicity, the refusal to interpret itself—that I wanted A *Thousand Pardons* to have.

DS: At various points after the scandal, Sara, Ben, and Helen lurk around their Westchester town trying not to be recognized. Yet in the end they return to their house there. Why can't they leave and start over somewhere else?

JD: I liked the idea that the house itself—not some gorgeous, Howards End–like manor that's been in the family for generations, but just a regular, somewhat unlovely suburban house through which many families have passed—exerts its own unexpected pull. All the Armsteads, in their different ways, want to leave it behind, but in the end, one at a time, it draws them back.

DS: Although there are many serious moments in the book, there is also a lot of dry wit, sly humor, and many moments of sharp irony. There are even some elements of screwball comedy. Is it wrong to call it a funny book?

JD: I sure hope it's funny to others, because parts of it seem funny to me. It's a comic novel in the sense that everybody winds up reunited, sort of happily, possibly forever after.

DS: Ben's journey takes him from a despised life of upper class security to abjection to something close to integrity. His storyline does not go the way the reader expects, partly because he refuses to let himself off the hook for what he did. Has he redeemed himself by the end?

JD: Ben's sufferings are of course totally self-inflicted; but he needs to manufacture this sort of midlife purgatory in order to remake his relationship to himself, to his labor, and to the people he loves. He commits the sin in order to feel the guilt, because repenting for that guilt will give him a sense of purpose, which he lacks. It's a pretty narcissistic journey, but at the end of the novel it seems like it might be working out the way he hoped.

DS: The collection of clients needing the help of Helen and particularly Malloy Worldwide is a pretty nasty group. Why does she not hesitate to help bad guys? Does she think everyone is redeemable? Are her nonjudgment and her sympathy part of what makes her special?

JD: Not to put too fine a point on it, in the scheme of the book, Helen is a priest. Not only would she never withhold her offices from a sinner, her obligation increases in proportion to the depth of the sin. She's scared to be alone with that assemblyman, as she should be, but refusing his request for help is out of the question.

DS: Both lawyers and PR people use storytelling to create an effect. Yet Helen sees her own gift as a rebuke to lawyers and other PR reps. Helen feels inspired by Harvey's claim that we all use stories to understand ourselves. Does Helen reclaim storytelling from lawyers and public relations firms?

JD: Stories are redemptive; they teach us to be humble by coercing us into seeing the world from other points of view. You could really get crazy theoretical and say that any story, properly told, is an admission of guilt. But I think what Helen is trying to reclaim is not storytelling per se, but confession. She's trying to rescue the private from its dilution in the public. Confessions, as she remembers from her Catholic school days, require abjectness and purity of heart if they are to gain you anything at all. She doesn't see why this should be any less true in the secular realm than it was in the religious, and for a while, it seems like she's right.

Questions and Topics for Discussion

1. Scandals seem to be perennially topical. Did you see any parallels in the novel with real-life events?

2. Jonathan Dee's novels are often described as social critiques. Do you think *A Thousand Pardons* should be interpreted that way? If so, what is the author criticizing?

3. Helen has a special gift for making powerful men apologize. Why do people respond the way they do to these apologies?

4. Why is Sara drawn to Cutter? Does it have anything to do with why Helen was drawn to Hamilton?

5. Hamilton asks Helen for forgiveness but she thinks, "His whole life was a Method performance, a dream within a dream, but whatever he wanted from her, however preposterous, she was not free to refuse him." What transaction is being completed when she kisses him?

6. How did Sara's relationships with each of her parents change throughout the course of the book? Did you find Sara to be sympathetic?

7. Do you think Hamilton will ever find out the truth about what happened to Bettina? Why does Helen hope that he never will?

8. By end of the book, Ben and Helen find themselves back where they started, at the house on Meadow Close. Have they come full circle? How have they grown or changed over the course of the novel?

9. Do you think Sara orchestrated her parents' reunion? If not, what brought Ben and Helen back together?

10. Do the characters in the novel deserve to be forgiven for their various transgressions?

11. Was the ending satisfying? What do you think will happen next?

12. Is there anyone in your life who should issue a public apology? Or to whom you'd like to apologize?

PHOTO © ULF ANDERSON

JONATHAN DEE is the author of five novels, most recently *The Privileges*, which was a finalist for the 2010 Pulitzer Prize. He is a contributing writer for *The New York Times Magazine*, a frequent literary critic for *Harper's*, and a former senior editor of *The Paris Review*. He teaches in the graduate writing programs at Columbia University and the New School. He is the recipient of fellowships from Yaddo, the MacDowell Colony, the National Endowment for the Arts, and the Guggenheim Foundation.

BOOKS BY
JONATHAN DEE

A THOUSAND PARDONS

In this sharply observed tale of self-invention and public
scandal, Dee raises a trenchant question: What do we really
want when we ask for forgiveness?

THE PRIVILEGES

The story of a charmed Manhattan couple's relentless rise to
the top, guided above all else by their epic love for each other.

PALLADIO

An unforgettable portrait of a man haunted by memories of
the woman who got away, only to be lured into a creative
vortex of art, memory, and the very woman who left him
devastated so many years before.

ST. FAMOUS

An aspiring writer abducted by a young African American in
the middle of a riot becomes a reluctant hero at the center of
a racial maelstrom.

DOUBLEDAY   RANDOM HOUSE   VINTAGE

RANDOM HOUSE, INC

Available wherever books are sold